Colorado Moon

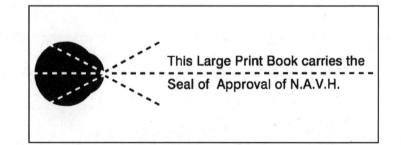

This Large Print Book carries the
Seal of Approval of N.A.V.H.

A JARED DELANEY WESTERN

COLORADO MOON

JIM JONES

WHEELER PUBLISHING
A part of Gale, Cengage Learning

GALE
CENGAGE Learning®

Farmington Hills, Mich • San Francisco • New York • Waterville, Maine
Meriden, Conn • Mason, Ohio • Chicago

GALE
CENGAGE Learning®

LIBRARY OF CONGRESS CATALOGING-IN-PUBLICATION DATA

Jones, Jim, 1950–
    Colorado moon : a Jared Delaney western / by Jim Jones. — Large print edition.
       pages cm. — (Wheeler Publishing large print western)
      ISBN 978-1-4104-8167-2 (softcover) — ISBN 1-4104-8167-0 (softcover)
      1. Outlaws—Fiction. 2. Frontier and pioneer life—Fiction. 3. Large type books. I. Title.
PS3610.O62572C65 2015
813'.6—dc23   2015020822

Published in 2015 by arrangement with Cherry Weiner Literary Agency

Printed in the United States of America
1 2 3 4 5 6 7 19 18 17 16 15

FOREWORD

The story continues and as always, I try not to let the facts get too much in the way. I do believe, however, that it is important to be as accurate as I can be with period details and I have done my best to do so. To the extent that I have been successful, much credit goes to the following folks: Ramblin' Ralph Estes, Martha Burk, Kerry Grombacher and Bonnie Rutherford for their able editorial assistance. Randy Huston for his cowboy expertise which helped me get the cow lingo down pat and the wrecks right.

I would like to express my great appreciation to the loyal readers who lovingly nagged me about finishing the second book in the series. I can only hope that when you've finished it, you will nag me to get the third and final book done.

CHAPTER 1

Poised on the crest of the ridge, the bay mare's ears stand at alert, twisting this way and that as she listens for sounds that signal danger. Her eyes scan the horizon and she tentatively paws the ground. Sensing no threats, she relaxes. In the saddle, Jared Delaney relaxes as well as he looks out over the herd and smiles. The cows have some weight on them and the grass is beginning to get green and high as far as he can see to the east. He looks to the south and can see the stark granite towers marking the entrance to Cimarron Canyon in the distance. Without looking back over his shoulder at the foothills, he knows the clouds are surging in from the west for an afternoon shower. His experience tells him this is the case, and so does the dull ache in his shoulder. As he thinks about his shoulder, he grimaces. Whether the ache is from the soreness in the joint or the painful emotional residue isn't clear, even to Jared. His shoulder rarely hurts unless the weather is changing and he seldom thinks about the troubles that led to the injury. His life has been relatively calm and happy for quite a while now. He has little reason to reflect on the dark events from the past . . . except when his shoulder aches.

Three years ago, though at times it seems longer, he had ridden into the town of Cimarron in Colfax County up in the northern New Mexico foothills. With an arsenal of cowboy skills and a past shrouded in mystery, he was only looking for work on a ranch. Instead, he found himself ensnared in a raging range war between the owners of the smaller ranches and the clannish O'Bannon family, led by the oldest brother, Morgan. Confused and unsettled by the trauma of losing his parents in a raid by marauding outlaws when he was just a child, Jared went to great lengths to avoid getting too attached to anything or anybody. However, his growing friendships with Sheriff Nathan Averill, rancher Ned Kilpatrick and his wife Lizbeth, and the beautiful schoolteacher Eleanor Coulter, had finally broken through his wall of mistrust and before he knew it, he found himself smack dab in the middle of the fray.

He discovered that when you let yourself care, there are times when you have to make hard choices and stand your ground in the face of danger, just because it's the right thing to do. This realization led him to a life and death showdown with an evil man under the dim light of the quarter moon, the one they call the rustler's moon. When the dust finally settled, Morgan O'Bannon and his two brothers were dead and Colfax County was free from their tyrannical reign.

Sadly, he lost his best friend, Ned Kilpatrick, who was gunned down by Morgan. But Ned's wife, Lizbeth, offered him a partnership in the ranch, and after some serious thought, he accepted. He shakes his head as he remembers how complicated his life had been for a while as he split his time between working the ranch and courting the lovely Eleanor. He figures he had been busy enough for three cowboys with all the coming and going. Still, he can't complain about how it has turned out. Two years ago, Eleanor agreed to become his wife and since that time, he has known happiness and security beyond anything he could recall in his life. He laid his life on the line for these people and if push came to shove, he would do so again in a heartbeat.

"Things still get a might tricky," he said

to his horse, who was an excellent listener, "what with Eleanor livin' at the ranch but still keepin' a hand in at the school." His wife had taken former "soiled dove" Christy Quick under her wing and trained her to take over as the school marm. Christy, who now went by her given name of Christine Johnson, is doing an excellent job, but she still needs to bend Eleanor's ear on occasion and hit her up for advice. Jared hopes that before too long, Christy will feel confident enough to make a go of it on her own and not require Eleanor's guidance. He is eager to have his wife join him full-time on the ranch, and secretly he is thinking that maybe they should start a family. "A couple of sons and daughters to help out with chores and fence-mendin' wouldn't hurt none at all," he says to his horse, who nods.

The distant rumble of thunder shakes Jared out of his reverie and reminds him that a storm is brewing. After eyeballing the herd once more to make sure everything is as it should be, he heads his horse down the rise in a southwesterly direction toward the ranch house. No need to get caught in a mountain rain shower, especially since Eleanor is due back from town sometime this afternoon.

Jared misses her with an ache that is out of proportion to her two-day absence. It really has more to do with his almost losing her three years ago when Morgan O'Bannon had the drop on him. If not for the courage and cunning of Sheriff Nathan Averill, he would not have survived to wed the love of his life. Now, he counts every day as a blessing. He is also busting with excitement to share an idea with her and Lizbeth. He has already discussed it at length with Juan Suazo, the hired hand who plays an integral part in the working of the ranch. Jared sets out at a steady lope and expects to reach the ranch house in about half an hour.

CHAPTER 2

The horse pulled the buckboard along at a pretty good clip. With part of her mind, Eleanor Delaney paid attention to the trail, looking for any new and unexpected chug holes to avoid. With another part of her mind, she mulled over the situation with Christy at school. Since coming on as Eleanor's assistant three years ago, her progress had been amazing. She was very bright and had a knack for getting the best out of the students who were sometimes less than enthusiastic about their studies. This was related in part to the fact that Christy was polishing her own skills by studying many of the same subjects as her students and the passion she had for learning seemed to be contagious.

Prior to taking on the job of school teacher, Christy had lived a dead-end life as a lady of the evening at the wild Colfax Tavern. Now, she saw her new profession as not only an opportunity for an honorable career but also a chance for redemption. Ironically, the skills in getting overzealous cowboys to toe the line, which she had learned during her time at the tavern, were also useful in alternately cajoling and browbeating students into doing the repetitious class work necessary to learn the material. Smiling, Eleanor thought to herself that it might be best not to share that observation with the parents of any of their students. There had been some initial resistance to Christy's taking the job because of her shady past, but with strong support from Reverend Richardson and Father Antonio Baca, the resistance dwindled to mild grumbling from a few parents.

Eleanor's dilemma was that, as well as Christy was doing, she still lacked confidence and preferred to have Eleanor with her in the classroom much of the time. Eleanor loved teaching but her heart was really out at the ranch where she now longed to be full-time. Jared needed her help in managing the daily chores as well as with duties such as bookkeeping, something he found tedious and often neglected. She, on the other hand, was good with numbers and seemed to have a head for business. Unlike some men she knew, her husband was not threatened by her competence and welcomed her input as a partner in the ranch.

She chuckled to herself as she thought about the situation. It was a good thing Jared was not threatened by strong women since he had a wife and another woman for a partner to boot. When her husband, Ned, had been gunned down by the vicious Morgan O'Bannon a few years ago, Lizbeth Kilpatrick could have given up and sold out the ranch she had helped run. Lizbeth, however, didn't have an ounce of quit in her and had decided that the best way to honor her late husband's memory was to offer an even partnership to Jared. He owned half and managed the day to day operation of the ranch while she continued to provide the support that kept things running smoothly such as cooking for the cowboys and doing all the vital chores that they sometimes felt were "beneath them." Lizbeth sometimes joked that if she could figure out a way that a person could cook and clean while in the saddle, the cowboys might be more willing to help out.

It occurred to Eleanor that if she were successful in getting Christy to take over the teaching job without requiring her support and assistance, she would then be faced with the challenge of increasing her responsibilities at the ranch without stepping on Lizbeth's toes. Since her marriage to Jared two years ago, she and Lizbeth had found a comfortable balance in sharing their duties, but Eleanor had always spent a considerable amount of time in town attending to the school. Once she was at the ranch full-time, things were bound to change. She had known Lizbeth since she was a young girl and had a great deal of respect and admiration for her. Still, she could imagine that there might be some rough spots in the transition.

Images of the hard times they had faced together in the past ran through her mind and reminded Eleanor that they had come through much worse. All things considered, she imagined they could figure out simple things like who was going to cook and who was going to do the dishes. She knew that like all the cattle ranchers in the New Mexico Territory, they faced some major changes in how they operated their ranch. With the increase in the number of railroads connecting the markets in Pueblo and Denver, the days of the big cattle drives were coming to an end. Before long, they would have to figure out how to sell their cattle locally in sufficient numbers to make a living, and she suspected that they would have to make other adjustments as well if they were to survive.

One of Eleanor's ideas was to put in a more extensive vegetable garden and sell what they didn't consume to the folks in the town of Cimarron. She knew Jared, a cowboy all his life, would be skeptical if not downright scornful of the notion of becoming a "farmer" and she suspected that Lizbeth might have her doubts as well, having spent her adult years as a ranch wife. Eleanor had her own stubborn streak, however, and she was confident that when she presented the details of her plan, Jared and Lizbeth would see its wisdom.

The horse strained to get the buckboard to the top of the rise and she looked down in the valley at the ranch house which had become her home two years ago. It was a combination of adobe and unfinished lumber and, while it was rough looking, it was sturdy enough to withstand the harsh northers that blew across the land during the Colfax County winters. The adobe walls kept them warm in the winter and cool in the summer, and a person couldn't ask for a great deal more than that.

As she guided the buckboard down the path towards the gate, she was happy to see her husband's bay mare tied to the fence of the corral. She had noticed the clouds gathering to the west and suspected that he might come in early in order to avoid an unnecessary soaking. Sure enough, as she pulled up to the stable, Jared came out on the front porch and headed her direction with a big smile on his face.

"Eleanor my love, I reckon you'll be wantin' me to unhitch that horse and take care of him for you?"

Since their marriage, Jared had taken to calling her "Eleanor my love." She thought of herself as a practical person but she had to admit that the romantic side of her cowboy husband wasn't that hard to take. Still, she couldn't resist the urge to tease him. "You might as well," she said, "since you don't seem to be doing anything else productive right now. It's a good thing you have Lizbeth and Juan to carry the load around here."

Jared laughed heartily and said, "Sounds like you've been payin' too much attention to Juan. He's always sayin' he carries me. I just hope he didn't hear you or he'll never shut up."

Jared helped his wife down from the buckboard, swinging her around and giving her a kiss before setting her down. He then went about unhitching the horse and leading him over to the stable where he began to brush him down. Eleanor could see the horse responding to his firm but gentle touch and again marveled at how skilled her husband was at all the tasks associated with the cowboy life. He rode like the wind, he knew the ways of cattle and he was a leader when it came to dealing with hands. He expected a great deal from his cowboys but no more than he expected of himself. The aforementioned Juan Suazo continually joshed with Jared but would take a bullet for him if necessary, which he had proven beyond the shadow of a doubt in the past.

"I'll go help Lizbeth get the evening meal started," Eleanor said. "When you get through out here, come in and keep me company. I've got some ideas I want to tell you about. I think you'll like them."

"If by keepin' you company, you mean settin' the table, I can't hardly wait. I swear, between you and Lizbeth, I sometimes think y'all are tryin' to turn me into a ranch wife," Jared said with a grin. He paused a beat, then said, "I got an idea I want to discuss with you, too. I think I've come up with a way to make some money and get this ranch on solid ground."

Eleanor was curious about what new

scheme her husband had come up with but he had turned his attention back to caring for the horse. She decided not to press him and went inside. As she expected, Lizbeth was already starting to prepare a meal for the three of them. Juan Suazo and his wife, Maria, lived in a smaller bunkhouse about a quarter mile from the main ranch house and usually dined there, although it was not uncommon on a Sunday for them to come over for a small feast. "Let me help you with those potatoes, Lizbeth," Eleanor said as she walked over to the table.

"Why thank you, Eleanor, I can use the help. Your husband's a fine cowboy but he ain't much help when it comes to preparin' meals. I expect if it weren't for the two of us, he might starve."

One of the primary forms of entertainment around the ranch was giving Jared a hard time. They generally took turns and Jared handled it pretty well unless they ganged up on him. Then, he might bow his back a little but they were usually able to coax him back into good spirits without much difficulty. All in all, they got along quite well and, including Juan and Maria, considered themselves to be family. Eleanor looked out the window at her husband and thought to herself, *the only thing missing is some young'uns running around getting into things. I wonder if Maria or I will be the first to add to the family?*

"How are things in town?" Lizbeth asked.

"Things are going well. Christy is gaining confidence every day at school." Tentatively, she said, "Before long, I think she may be ready to take over completely without my help." Eleanor watched Lizbeth carefully to gauge her reaction to this news.

Lizbeth was quiet for a moment as she continued peeling potatoes. Then she smiled and said, "Eleanor, I know you been wantin' to be out here full time and you been worryin' about what I'd think. I hope you know me well enough to know that we can work out the rough spots." She chuckled. "Lord knows there's more than enough work for two women."

Eleanor sighed. "I can't tell you how relieved I am to hear you say that, Lizbeth. I want to be here with Jared, and you as well. I certainly don't want it to cause problems."

"I expect it'll more likely cause a little consternation for your husband cause he'll worry that between the two of us, we'll really get him henpecked. He may be spendin' even more time with the cattle once you're here day and night."

Eleanor had to laugh at that. "You may be right. He went all those years without a family and all of a sudden, he's got more family than he knows what to do with."

"Speakin' of which," Lizbeth said with a sly grin, "maybe it's time to add some little Delaneys to the family."

Eleanor blushed. "We'll get to that in good time, Lizbeth. Right now, we've got to decide what to do about the changing cattle market so that we don't all starve to death out here."

Lizbeth was about to respond when Jared walked in and announced he was there to keep them company. They looked at each other, shook their heads in mock disgust and immediately put him to work setting the table. Jared complained briefly but seemed resigned to his fate and got to work. As he was gathering plates, he asked Eleanor, "Did you see Nathan while you were in town?"

"I did," she replied. "We had a cup of coffee at Miguel's place." To a casual observer, Miguel Mares appeared to be a peace-loving café owner, but Eleanor remembered how he and his two sons had stood with Jared and Nathan Averill to face Morgan O'Bannon and his henchmen. *Funny,* she thought to herself, *sometimes, the folks that seem least likely to be heroes are the ones who step up when danger threatens.* Miguel Mares was that kind of man.

"How's Nathan gettin' along?" Jared asked. "Last time I saw him, it seemed like he'd aged about five years. I know his shoulder still pains him quite a bit."

Nathan Averill, the Sheriff in Cimarron, had been wounded in a shootout with Morgan O'Bannon's two brothers, Pete and Jake, three years earlier. He had killed Jake in the battle and later saved Jared from a certain death when Morgan got the drop on him. He was also the first person in Cimarron to look beneath Jared's outward appearance as a wandering cowboy and recognize the strength and basic decency that resided at his core. Jared felt that he not only owed his life to Nathan but also his promising future. Nathan thought it was a bunch of hooey and refused to discuss it.

Eleanor frowned. "He does seem older all of a sudden and he's moving slower, too. You know he would never complain but he rubs his hands quite a bit, like they're hurting him."

Lizbeth joined in the conversation. "I don't know how much longer Nathan's gonna be able to handle bein' sheriff. It's a job for a younger man and that's God's truth."

"In a pinch, old Nathan's worth about three younger fellas," Jared scoffed. "I wouldn't go puttin' him out to pasture quite yet. He may be a bit stove up but he'd still be a wildcat in a fight."

"Well, hopefully, there won't be as much need for fighting as there was in the past," Eleanor said. "Since Governor Wallace took office, things have calmed down. It seems like that no-good Santa Fe Ring bunch has crawled back under their rock."

"Maybe so," Lizbeth said, "but I ain't sure those fellas'll give up that easy. It wouldn't surprise me if they made another try to grab some land around here. I just hope Nathan's up to stoppin'em one more time."

Jared had finished setting the table and was clearly eager to share his new idea with Eleanor and Lizbeth. "Y'all know that Nathan would have a fit if he knew we were talkin' about him like this. I think we should change the topic."

Eleanor recognized her husband's desire to discuss his new scheme, whatever it was. She said, "Let's get the food on the table and then maybe you can tell us about your new plan to put the ranch on solid financial ground."

Lizbeth's ears perked up and she said, "I'd sure like to hear about that myself!"

Jared grinned and said, "Let's eat, then I'll talk."

The women served the food and for a time, the only sound was the clanking of plates and utensils. Like most cowboys, Jared had quite an appetite, yet he remained rail thin due to the hard labor in which he engaged daily. Finally, he sat up in his chair and said, "That's another fine meal to thank you ladies for. Do we have any coffee to polish it off?"

Lizbeth stood up and as she walked over toward the stove, she said, "Of course we do and we have some fresh apple cobbler as you well know, since you been sniffin' the air like an old hound dog ever since you came inside."

Jared laughed and said, "You caught me. At least I didn't try to sneak any when you weren't watchin'."

"I expect you know better," Lizbeth sniffed. "I know how to deal with a cobbler rustler. I whack'em on the hand with one of my big spoons and they learn their lesson mighty quick!"

They shared a chuckle as Lizbeth served up the sweet delight, then Jared turned serious. "We all know that with the trains comin' to Pueblo and Denver, the days of the long cattle drives are about done. If we don't find a solid market for our cattle, this ranch will go under. That's the long and the short of it."

He paused to let the weight of what he'd said sink in. Eleanor and Lizbeth waited expectantly. "I think I've hit upon an idea. The mining business is startin' to boom up around Pueblo and they're hirin' folks hand over fist. Those folks all got to eat and they got families to feed, too."

"I hear a lot of those people are from Europe," Eleanor said. "The mining business is growing so fast that they haven't been able to fill all the jobs with local people. You could be right about this being an opportunity. What are you thinking?"

Jared looked smug and said, "Eleanor my love, I'm not just thinkin', I'm actin'!"

Eleanor and Lizbeth both looked curious and Lizbeth said, "You look like the cat that ate the canary, Jared. What mischief have you been up to?"

"I contacted a man at the Colorado Coal and Steel Works Company. Nathan knows the sheriff in Pueblo and he helped me find out who to send a telegram to. He's offered me above-market price to deliver a small herd of 300 cattle. The catch is, he needs'em in four weeks."

Lizbeth looked concerned. "Jared, four weeks ain't a lot of time to pull off a cattle drive. You could sure do it if you didn't hit any snags but what are the chances of that happenin'?"

"Lizbeth, this fella is givin' me a chance, kind of a trial run, I guess you could say. If I can get it done, it could be the difference in whether we make it or break it. I say it's worth takin' the chance. Besides, it's just a hop, skip and a jump up the Goodnight-Loving Trail." Jared paused, then said, "Course, we're partners and you got just as much say in this as I do." He turned to Eleanor and said, "We're partners, too, and I wouldn't do this if you weren't behind the idea. I sure hope you'll both give it some thought. It could set us up proper if we do it right."

Lizbeth and Eleanor looked at each other and didn't speak for a moment. Then, Lizbeth said, "I reckon you wouldn't have told us about your idea without makin' some plans for how you could make it happen. Am I right?"

Jared grinned and said, "Well, I might've talked the idea over a bit with Juan, just to see what he thought."

Lizbeth smirked and Eleanor just shook her head. "Well, let's hear it," Lizbeth said.

Jared leaned forward in his chair and began to talk in an excited manner. "Here's how we'd do it. Me and Juan would go, of course, and Miguel would run the wagon."

Eleanor looked startled and said, "Wait a minute, Miguel is in on this, too? Who would run the café?"

Jared looked a little sheepish and said, "Well, yeah, I talked with Miguel a little bit about it, too. He thinks it's a fine idea and figures Anita, Estevan, and his sister can manage the café for a while. We'd take Tomas with us." Anita was Miguel's stalwart wife who had given him two fine sons, Tomas and Estevan, along with a beautiful daughter, Esperanza.

Lizbeth looked at Eleanor and said, "Do you get the feelin' that we're the last ones to know about this scheme?"

Eleanor said nothing although she looked annoyed, which made Jared nervous. Not wanting to give her too much of an opening to take him to task for leaving her out of the discussion, he quickly continued on with his tale. "It'll take more than the three of us to handle a herd of three hundred cows, though Juan's as good a hand as you could find anywhere. We'll need to hire some other cowboys to help out. I figure we can make do with four more, though it'd be a stretch."

"Where are you gonna find four good hands at the drop of a hat?" Lizbeth asked.

"I thought that out, too," Jared said quickly. "Brandin's done on all the ranches and I know Bill Merritt is havin' to let a couple of boys go." He laughed and said, "Well, he told'em he could use'em to mend fence and help out with chores around the ranch house . . . which amounts to lettin'em go." Jared, like most cowboys, was disdainful of any work that wasn't done from the back of a horse.

"That makes two, maybe three more hands if you're lucky," Lizbeth said. "Where you gonna get the other one or two?"

"Same place you found me," Jared said proudly. "Nathan told me he'd talked with two brothers who just rode into town last week lookin' to hire on with an outfit. Said they seemed like a decent sort and told him they'd worked cattle before."

At that, Eleanor exploded. "Jared, you've talked with almost every one you know except the two people you should have discussed this with first! How could you think so little of me and Lizbeth?"

Jared looked crestfallen and stammered, "Uh, I didn't think about it like that, Eleanor my love. I thought you two would be pleased if I gave you the whole plan tied up in a nice package with a ribbon on it."

Eleanor looked at Lizbeth, then threw up her hands. "The plan sounds fine to me but I would like to have had the chance to take part in making it. You could be gone as long as five, maybe even six weeks if something goes wrong. We've got to be prepared to handle the ranch without you and Juan. Did you think about that when you were doing your planning?"

"Well, sure, I did, Eleanor," Jared said defensively. "School will be out directly and between you, Lizbeth and Maria, you can cover what chores need to be done." He tried to make light of the situation, saying, "Heck, without me and Juan around stuffin' down all your cookin', that'll cut your work in half." When neither woman responded to his lame attempt at humor, he continued quickly. "I figure Estevan can come out some to help and Nathan can look in on you from time to time."

Eleanor got up and walked over toward the stove, clasping her hands behind her back as she thought about what her husband was proposing. What he said made sense, although she shared Lizbeth's concern about the four-week deadline to get the cattle to Pueblo. Jared could do it if they hit no snags but the basic rule of a cattle drive was that "whatever can go wrong, will." In addition, she was hurt that he hadn't included her in the planning. She didn't doubt that Jared loved her, but sometimes she wondered if he respected her intelligence and competence. She had always been strong-willed and independent, and she felt like she had worthwhile ideas that she could have contributed to the discussion. On the other hand, she realized that there was little time to get bogged down in hurt feelings. A decision needed to be made and her feelings aside, Jared's plan made sense.

Eleanor turned and walked back to the table where Jared and Lizbeth sat. She sighed deeply. "As I said, I don't like being left out of the planning. But I think it's a good idea and I believe you're right that it could lead to more business for us. I don't think it will be too long before the mining companies come down into the New Mexico territory, and if we've got a good reputation established, it would stand us in good stead."

Jared smiled at his wife. "Eleanor my love, I'm glad you approve." He looked down at the table, then looked her in the eyes. "I'm awful sorry I didn't think to talk to you and Lizbeth before hand. I really was hopin' to surprise you both but I guess I wasn't thinkin' right."

Lizbeth chuckled and said to Eleanor, "Don't worry, hon, it took me a few years to get Ned trained, too. These cowboys ain't used to listenin' to their women folk. Heck, most of'em don't spend any time around women with a lick of sense; they just take a few moments pleasure with some desperate lady of the night and go about their business."

Jared was uncomfortable with the direction of the conversation. Before Eleanor could respond to Lizbeth's comments, he quickly said, "Lizbeth, you haven't said what you think about the plan."

Lizbeth put her elbows on the table and cradled her chin in her hands. After a moment, she said, "Funny that I brought up Ned's name just now. When I have to decide somethin', I generally try to think about what he would say."

Jared nodded. "He was a top hand and he knew the business, too. What do you think Ned would do?"

"Jared," Lizbeth said, "Ned would have done everything you did, prob'ly right down to the part about leavin' us out of the

31

conversation at first. It just makes sense and I think we should do it."

Jared smiled and said, "I don't know that Ned would have left you out of the plannin', but I think you're right about the rest of it. He knew that things were changin' and that we'd have to change, too, if we're gonna survive."

"He did, that's a fact," Lizbeth responded. "I have to tell you though, I'm still worried about you tryin' to make it in four weeks. I'm afraid you'll be cuttin' it mighty thin. Can you get'em to extend the time?"

"I might be able to squeeze an extra week out of'em," Jared said, "but I don't wanta push it any further than that. They're lookin' for someone they can count on to work fast. If we can't do that, they'll just look somewhere else."

"Reckon you're right," Lizbeth said, "but I'm sure gonna fret about the time until you get them steers there safe and sound."

"We'll all be frettin', you can count on it." Jared turned to Eleanor. "You told me outside that you had some ideas you wanted to talk about. What were you thinkin'?"

Eleanor was still miffed at Jared's thoughtlessness in leaving her out of the planning for the cattle drive, and she figured that planting a vegetable garden paled in comparison to Jared's grand scheme to get the ranch on solid financial footing. The last thing she needed right now was for her husband to make fun of her plan or turn up his nose at the idea of farming. "It wasn't anything big," she said. "I'll tell you about it some other time."

CHAPTER 3

Young Nathan saw the mama cow split off from the gather and light out over the rise. He spurred his horse and flew after her, galloping over the sandhills of Nebraska with the wind roaring in his ears. He was gaining on her and forming a loop when out of the blue, he felt a sharp burning pain in his right hand as if someone had stabbed him with a knife. Confused, he slowed up to figure out what was happening and noticed that it was getting dark. He closed his eyes momentarily and when he opened them, he found himself on his cot in the back room at the sheriff's office in Cimarron, New Mexico, no longer a young man. His hands still ached sharply. "Damned arthritis," he muttered.

Nathan Averill had still been a relatively young man when he took on the job of sheriff in Cimarron nearly twenty years ago. He'd done his best to keep the peace, and he had lived through what some folks called the Colfax County War . . . a bloody battle with the domineering O'Bannon clan who were backed by a shady outfit in the territorial capital known as the Santa Fe Ring. This group had bought and sold land grants that didn't belong to them and done everything within their considerable power to take advantage of the poor folks who had lived for centuries in Northern New Mexico.

The territory now had a new governor, Lew Wallace, who, in Nathan's opinion, seemed to be more honest than his predecessor, Governor Axtell. As a result, things had calmed down considerably in the past couple of years. Most folks thought the Santa Fe Ring had lost its clout and sure enough, things seemed to be running smoothly. Nathan wasn't so sure, though. Maybe he'd been doing the job so long that he'd become cynical, but he suspected that some of the members of the ring were lying in the bushes, so to speak, waiting for a new opportunity. He'd heard about one fella in particular by the name of William Chapman who seemed to be looking for ways to get a toehold in Colfax County again. The land was prime for cattle ranching and there was talk that the big mining companies could be moving in within the next few years. Where there was money to be made, Nathan knew that there would be greedy, lawless men who would try to profit at the expense of the less powerful. Cynical or not, he figured that's the way it was. It was his job to try to stop them.

Nathan eased out of bed and stiffly made his way over to the stove to get a fire going and make some coffee. He longed for the days when he could leap up from his bedroll and saddle up for a day's ride free from aches and pains. *Reckon those days're long gone,* he thought ruefully.

He waited for the water to boil and thought about the day's tasks in front of him. There were fewer pressing law enforcement issues these days now that the O'Bannons had been defeated and lay still in the cold red clay. He had plenty of time to wander over to the Mares Café for a nice big meal of steak and eggs accompanied by a lively discussion with Miguel Mares, or perhaps with the Reverend Richardson and Father Antonio Baca, who started most mornings with a spirited and spiritual debate. Nathan was more concerned with the present than the hereafter but he got a kick out of listening to the two men of God argue. The fact that they were the best of friends didn't stop them from challenging each other in religious matters. Whenever things started to settle between them, Nathan or Miguel would make some comment to stir the pot and get them going again, much to the delight of the patrons of the Mares Café. *You take your fun where you can find it,* Nathan thought and smiled to himself.

His smile faded as he thought about information he had received from friends over in Taos. Rumor had it that there was a fella with the look of a gunslinger who'd been hanging around town. His name was Curt Barwick, but folks referred to him as "the gentleman" because of his soft-spoken, polite manner, which according to some, he never dropped, even in the midst of a pitched gun battle. It was said that he'd spent time over in Arizona and up in Colorado, building a reputation in both places as a man who was good with a six-shooter, ruthless and more than willing to hire out his talents to the highest bidder. What concerned Nathan was that Barwick had been seen several times in the company of William Chapman and Tom Catron. Both men were charter members of the Santa Fe Ring and Nathan figured that those scoundrels were up to no good. *Reckon I'd better keep my ear to the ground on this one,* he thought.

As he thought about the possibility of more trouble stirring, Nathan felt a heaviness in his limbs. He sighed. He knew he was getting a bit long in the tooth and was concerned that he might not be able to handle trouble like he had in his younger years. There was a time when he'd been quick as a snake with a six-gun and pretty handy with his fists, too. Age takes its toll, though, and he knew his eyesight had dimmed a bit and his reflexes had slowed. He'd been lucky to survive the big dust up with the O'Bannons and wasn't sure how much longer Lady Luck would smile on him. Still, it was the job he'd signed up for and he knew that risk came with the territory.

Guess I'll keep at it until someone younger comes along who's willin' to do what needs to be done. He'd hoped that Jared Delaney would stay on as his deputy after the O'Bannon trouble, but Jared had had his heart set on cattle ranching and settling down with Eleanor Coulter. He wondered if perhaps Miguel Mares' older son, Tomas, might be interested in the job in a few years. The lad was steady and had proven himself brave in the past, standing beside his father when the bullets were flying. Nathan realized that there was no immediate solution to the problem of who might succeed him as sheriff so he finished his coffee, pulled on his boots and sauntered out to do a walk-through of Cimarron before heading over to Miguel's place for his breakfast.

CHAPTER 4

"I talked it over with Eleanor and Lizbeth," Jared said as he rode along with Juan Suazo. The two were headed out to look for strays as they began gathering cattle in the south pasture in preparation for the upcoming cattle drive. "They asked some of the same questions you did but when it came down to it, they thought it was a good idea."

"Senora Lizbeth knows the cattle business," Juan replied. "I figured she'd think hard about this before she said yes. I knew she'd say yes, though. It makes good sense to do this thing." He grinned. "Let me guess . . . they weren't happy that you had planned things before you talked with them?"

Jared didn't say anything for a moment, then spoke a little stiffly. "Yeah, you were right about that but don't let it swell your head." He shook his own head and said with chagrin, "I really thought they'd be pleased to hear how much we'd already planned out. Heck, it saved'em a lot of grief."

Juan, who was two years older than Jared, said with a smirk, "Amigo, you still have a whole lot to learn about women, especially those two. You don't have to protect them from making decisions. They enjoy doing it and they take it as an insult if you don't include them."

Jared nodded vigorously. "That's exactly how they took it. You'd of thought I'd questioned their virtue or somethin' from the way they acted." He shook his head again in consternation. "The funny thing is that I know they both got real good sense and I ask their opinions on one thing or another most every day. Guess they forgot about that."

"Like I said, amigo, you still got a lot to learn about women." Juan laughed. "But you got years to work on that and right now, we got a cattle drive to plan. Tell me again how we gonna get these steers to Colorado in four weeks time?"

Eager to talk about something other than his lack of understanding of women, Jared spoke enthusiastically. "Juan, we got most of them cattle gathered already and you know it. I already spoke to Bill Merritt about his boys and he was willin' to let'em go along. He figured it'd be good experience for'em."

Juan looked concerned. "Those fellas are green as a couple of gourds. I expect Bill wouldn't mind them getting their feet wet on somebody else's drive."

Jared laughed. "I see your point but think of it this way. They got no room to complain about ridin' drag."

Juan chuckled along with Jared. "So amigo, what about those other two hombres Senor Nathan told you about . . . the brothers. Will we have to wet nurse them, too?"

"Nathan tells me they've been up the trail more'n once," Jared said.

"Si, but was it for real or just tall tales they spin?" Juan asked.

Jared frowned. "Juan, you know it ain't easy to sell Nathan Averill a bill of goods. He talked with'em for quite a spell and told me he was impressed with'em. They've ridden with a couple of different outfits that're top notch and Nathan said they seemed to know what they were talkin' about."

Juan shrugged. "So we got you and me, Miguel and Tomas, and four more hands."

"That's about the size of it. It's closin' in on the end of May now. I figure we can shoot for leavin' a week from today which gives us three full weeks to make it to

Pueblo. Mr. Wheeler with Colorado Coal and Steel wants the cattle by June 25. If we make twelve miles a day, we'll get there by June 21 and that gives us four extra days for delays, which we know are bound to happen here and there. I don't see a problem at all."

"Me neither, amigo," Juan said with a smirk. "Except for bad weather, stampedes, maybe a little Indian trouble and outlaws. Other than that, I think everything will be muy bueno."

Jared snorted in exasperation. "There you go, thinkin' negative. I ain't worried about Indians. We might see some Ute but they ain't generally hostile like the Comanche. We might need to give'em a steer or two but that'll likely satisfy'em."

"Maybe so," Juan replied, "but what about outlaws, stampedes and the weather?"

"I figure you, me, Miguel and Tomas all earned our spurs a few years back. I don't reckon there's any outlaws we'll run into that'll be tougher than them O'Bannon boys and if you'll recall, that turned out all right."

"Maybe so," Juan said, "but we were pretty lucky back then, too. I wouldn't want to do it over again. And remember, we had Senor Nathan on our side then and he's not going on this drive."

43

"No, he's not," Jared said, "but I'm not gonna worry about how we'll handle that kinda trouble, if we even run into any. I've been on drives before and there's not rustlers waitin' around every bend lookin' to steal your cattle, for Pete's sake. Yeah, it could happen but that don't mean it will." Jared swatted at a fly that was buzzing around his face. "To tell you the truth, what's got me most worried is how them greenhorns'll handle it if the cattle do get spooked."

Juan nodded. "We'll have to spend some time with those boys talkin' about how to turn the leaders and get them milling."

"Yeah, we can talk to'em about that," Jared chortled. "You been in stampedes before, Juan. Was it anything like they told you it'd be?"

Juan smiled ruefully. "I guess not. But that doesn't mean we shouldn't talk to them, amigo. If they have some idea of what they're supposed to do, there's less chance that they'll panic."

"Reckon you're right," Jared said. "We'd best get'em as prepared as we can and hope for the best. We're goin' up before the heavy rains are due to hit, so maybe we'll draw some luck and not have one of those thunder boomers that gets'em spooked."

44

"Could be," Juan said doubtfully.

Changing the subject, Jared asked playfully, "So what does Maria think about you goin' off and leavin' her for six weeks?"

Juan looked uncomfortable and mumbled something under his breath. Jared said, "I didn't catch that, amigo. What did you say?"

Juan cleared his throat and said, "I said that I haven't told her yet." Jared burst out laughing and Juan said defensively, "I was waiting for the right time!"

When Jared could slow down his laughter sufficiently, he said, "I think the 'right time' will be when I'm about ten miles away from your bunkhouse, pard." He laughed some more, then took a deep breath to get himself under control. "What were you tellin' me before about understandin' women? I think I missed somethin'."

CHAPTER 5

As the day of departure approached, Eleanor found herself becoming more anxious. On top of her concerns about the many things that might go wrong on the trail, she had an uneasy feeling about what might happen at home while Jared was gone. Although she couldn't put her finger on a specific fear, she just had this sense that trouble was stirring. *Woman's intuition,* she thought to herself.

Beyond these worries, she had found herself nauseated the past several mornings. Initially puzzled by this, it suddenly dawned on her that it might mean there would be an addition to the family in the months to come. She debated with herself about telling Jared but decided against it. She figured he had too much to think about already with getting prepared for the cattle drive and anyway, she wasn't certain yet. Too many things could go wrong at this stage and she didn't want Jared getting his hopes up only to have them dashed. Still, it was hard to keep the news secret and she was tempted to tell Lizbeth what she suspected.

She laughed wickedly to herself, thinking it would serve Jared right for Lizbeth to find out first after his failure to include her in the planning for the cattle drive. In her heart, though, she knew this was different, and she found herself eager to share the joy with him. He had lost his parents at a young age and he'd made it clear to her that he wanted to be a strong and loving father for their children. *I expect he'll be back home toward the end of June,* she thought. *I should be pretty sure by then.*

She was putting the wildflowers she'd picked in vases around the ranch house when Jared came swooping in, tossed his hat on the table, took her in his arms and swung her around.

"Eleanor my love, we're just about ready," he blurted out enthusiastically. "Juan and the boys have got the herd gathered up by the big spring and we ought to be able to head out at first light in the morning."

Eleanor felt a tightening in the pit of her stomach but tried not to let her concern show. "That's wonderful, Jared. I guess Maria has finally forgiven Juan for not telling her about the drive."

Jared laughed merrily. "Not until she broke a few clay pots. He's just lucky she didn't break'em over his head."

Nathan was sitting at his desk looking over some "Wanted" posters that had just come his way but his mind kept wandering back to some disturbing news he'd recently heard from Taos. Not long ago, a young attorney had filed a civil suit against Catron, Chapman and their bunch, charging them with defrauding one of the old Spanish land grant families out of their acreage. Before the case could make it to court, the attorney vanished and the family in question withdrew their claim. Several days later, the attorney's bullet-riddled body was found on the high road north of Taos. Gentleman Curt Barwick had been quite visible around town prior to this event but suddenly he was nowhere to be seen. The alcalde was talking to folks, trying to find a witness or someone who had heard something, but no one seemed to know anything pertinent to his investigation. Some of the citizens of Taos were outraged and demanded that Barwick be arrested but the alcalde really had no witnesses or evidence against him and anyway, he couldn't find him.

There's times I'd rather be wrong, Nathan mused, reflecting back on his thought just the other day that the Santa Fe Ring hadn't gone away. He figured it didn't bode well for the people of Colfax County if Tom Catron, Bill Chapman and their crew were back to their old tricks. More immediately, he was concerned about the whereabouts of a certain gentleman gunslinger. There was no telling where Barwick was hiding out, but Nathan knew that there were quite a few places to hide out in Cimarron Canyon just west of town. He thought about taking a little ride out that way but then reconsidered. When he thought about how many blind alleys he could go up and still draw a blank or worse yet, find himself the victim of an ambush, he figured it wasn't a good investment of his time. *Reckon I'll just wait and see if he comes to me,* Nathan thought.

As he contemplated the possibility of once again having to confront a stone cold killer in this little community that he was sworn to defend, he couldn't help thinking that it was a bad time for Jared Delaney to be heading out on a cattle drive . . . and taking with him most of the able-bodied and battle-tested men he could usually count on. He knew this was a vital job for Jared and that it would go a long way towards

49

securing the future of his and Lizbeth Kilpatrick's ranch, but the timing was terrible.

At first light, Jared and Eleanor stood on the porch of the ranch house, holding hands. Eleanor had promised herself she wouldn't cry, but she could feel the tears welling up anyway. She found herself annoyed with her husband because in his excitement about the cattle drive, he didn't seem the least bit bothered by the fact that they would be apart for the first time since they'd gotten married two years ago.

"I don't want to keep you," she said tentatively. "I know you're eager to hit the trail."

Jared looked carefully at Eleanor's face in the dim gray light of the dawn and recognized what she was trying to hide. "Eleanor, my love, I'm sure 'nuff eager to get this cattle drive movin' cause the sooner we leave, the sooner I can come back to you. There won't be a minute's time I won't be thinkin' about you."

A tear trickled down her cheek but she smiled. "You know I don't like it when you lie to me, Jared. I know you can't wait to get back on the trail but I do appreciate your trying to make me feel better." She brushed away the tear. "We'll both be so busy the time will fly by. You just be sure to send me a telegram when you make it to Pueblo so I'll know you're safe."

Jared smiled at his wife and pulled her close in a loving embrace. He kissed her long and passionately, then held her at arm's length. "You know there ain't nothin' will come along I can't handle. I'll get back to you before you know it."

They embraced again, clinging to one another with a ferocity that communicated more than a thousand words could. Finally, Jared pulled away and with a bittersweet smile said, "I can't get there if I don't start and this ain't gettin' any easier. I love you with all my heart."

He tipped his hat, turned, took two strides and mounted his bay mare. With a wave, he rode off. Eleanor stood on the porch for several minutes as his figure faded into the distance in the early morning light. She had a sinking feeling in her midsection that she couldn't quite figure out. She knew she would miss her husband, but she had confidence in his skills and didn't expect any real problems on the short drive. No, this was something more. She puzzled about it for another minute but couldn't pinpoint what was troubling her. She turned and went inside.

As Jared eased his pony into a jog, he felt a pang of loneliness that rocked him in his saddle. Despite his bravado, he was well aware that things could go wrong on a cattle drive and for a fleeting instant, he considered calling off the whole enterprise. That thought and the pang of loneliness passed quickly, however, and he felt his excitement increase as his natural optimism took over. He knew this was a great opportunity for them and he had no intention of failing.

The sun peeked shyly over the mountains but it was full daylight by the time Jared got to the north pasture where Juan had the herd gathered. There was a slight chill in the air but Jared knew it would warm up soon. Miguel had his sturdy mules hitched up to the wagon and had built a fire to make some Arbuckle coffee for the hands while they waited. Tomas, who would serve as the wrangler on this drive, was several hundred yards away looking after the remuda. Jared had managed to scrape together a herd of thirty horses, though some were not up to the standards he was used to in his days riding for Charley Goodnight's JA brand. He figured beggars couldn't be choosers, though, and they weren't traveling as far as he'd been accustomed to in his time with Goodnight. *Heck, it's only about a hundred and sixty miles,* he thought to himself. *We ought to make it with no problem.*

Miguel hailed him as he rode up to the wagon and the other hands, who had been loosely holding the herd, trotted over. As they dismounted, he surveyed his outfit. He'd been pleased to discover that Bill Merritt had three young cowboys who were looking to go on a cattle drive. Two were pretty green but the third had been up the trail before and seemed to know what he was doing, if he could be taken at his word. The two first-timers were Tom Stallings and Joe Hargrove, both no more than boys in their late teens. Jared hoped they were of an even disposition, since they would most likely wind up riding drag for most of the trip. That's the way it worked on cattle drives . . . the youngest and least experienced hands got that duty. Most cowboys understood that and didn't complain too much. The third hand from the Merritt ranch was Felipe Munoz, a handsome young man of Spanish lineage whom Juan Suazo knew in passing. Juan had spoken up for Felipe when Jared asked him about the cowboy, saying that he was a good hand who could rope and keep a clear head in a pinch. He'd worked on Frank and Charlie Springer's CS ranch, and when Jared inquired about him to the foreman, he'd gotten a good report. Given the options available for cowboys, Jared was pleased to have hired an experienced hand.

The two hands that Nathan had sent his way were brothers, Patrick and Sean O'Reilly, who'd come over from Ireland five years ago. They landed in New York and immediately headed west, having taken the notion that they were meant to be cowboys. Both were in their early twenties and were jolly sorts, teasing each other without mercy. They told Nathan they had worked on several different ranches in Texas and when he checked with a fella he knew who had lived in those parts, he'd confirmed their story. Jared figured they could ride the flanks. That would leave Juan to ride point, which made the most sense, as he was a top hand. It would also leave Jared free to scout ahead and keep an eye on things.

When the outfit had assembled, he looked them over. "You boys ready to ride to Colorado?" They all nodded and the younger ones had big smiles on their faces. Jared figured the smiles might fade after a couple of days on the trail, once it settled in that their big adventure was mighty hard work after all. Still, he couldn't begrudge them their excitement. He remembered his first cattle drive, and how he could hardly sleep the night before he left. He also remembered how he'd wished he had gotten those few extra hours of shut-eye after he'd spent two straight sleepless days as he and his pards had kept watch over the herd during a long storm. Truth be told, though, he, too, was excited and could barely suppress a grin.

"I told each of you this when I hired you but I want to say it now in front of y'all together so there's no misunderstandin's. Your wages are forty and found. All of you have a saddle, a bedroll and the horse you rode up on. You each get to pick three horses from the remuda. Top hand goes first . . . that'd be Juan . . . and then we go in order of your experience. Same is true of where you ride herd." Jared watched the two young hands, Stallings and Hargrove, to gauge their reactions. "You youngsters are gonna be eatin' some dust on this drive. I hope you brought bandanas." Jared noted that young Hargrove grinned real big when he heard this news, while Tom Stallings frowned. He didn't want to read too much into it but figured he'd keep an eye on Stallings to see if he might be a malcontent. The last thing any cattle drive needs is a cowboy who's always grousing about his duties.

"I'll be your trail boss and that means what I say goes. If I ain't around, Juan's in charge and what he says goes." Jared surveyed the hands and said, "Any questions about that? If you got'em, now's the time to speak up. If we run into trouble on the trail, we won't have time to sit down and parley."

When no one spoke, he continued. "Now, I don't expect any trouble, mind you. We're just takin' a little over three hundred head on this drive and we're only goin' a hop, skip and a jump up the trail." Jared smiled. "Thing is, though, if them steers stampede and run you over, it won't matter to you whether it's three hundred or three thousand, you'll be stomped to a bloody pulp." There were a few nervous chuckles from the younger hands.

Jared waited for a moment to let the laughter pass. He wanted to establish Juan's authority with the outfit as well as his own, so he turned to him and said, "I'm gonna let Juan Suazo here tell you about the plans."

Juan stepped forward and looked around at the group. "We work together and this drive'll be like a ride into town on a Sunday afternoon. We're gonna take it slow, maybe

56

make ten to twelve miles a day." Juan saw the surprised looks on the faces of the cowboys and said, "Hey, I know, we could make better time but we want them beeves to fatten up on the way up the trail." He grinned and said, "We get paid by the pound, boys. That means we don't like skinny cattle."

Joe Hargrove cleared his throat and then tentatively raised his hand. Juan said, "What is it, boy? This is not the school house, just speak on up."

The young hand tentatively asked, "If we was to have a stampede, sir, just what exactly would you want us to do?"

Juan looked at Jared who nodded for him to respond. "Well, son, I would say the thing for you young hands to do is to stay back out of harm's way as best you can. You want to stay close so that once we get them milling, you can help out and round up any strays that high tail it for the brush."

Jared spoke up. "Juan's right, we don't want none of you gettin' stomped. Dependin' on how much open land we got for'em to run, we might let'em go a ways to tire'em out. Sooner or later, we got to turn the leaders in so they start millin' around, which breaks their speed. We got some experienced hands who can handle that chore but you might find yourself caught up in the stampede, and if so, that's what you need to do. Ride for the lead." Jared shook his head and continued. "Boys, there's just no predictin' what'll spook'em and whether or not they'll run. Lightnin' will do it, sometimes a wolf or mountain lion lurkin' about and sometimes you got no idea what caused it. Once they go, it don't matter why."

Patrick O'Reilly spoke up in his Irish brogue, saying, "We could just let Sean ride ahead and start singin'. Sure and once those steers hear his voice, they'll want to go the other direction fast, I can promise you." Everyone laughed at that and Sean leaned over and gave his brother a playful poke to the shoulder.

Juan waited to see if there were any more questions, then he continued. "We'll cross a few streams pretty quick but we won't cross any rivers until we get to Colorado. We shouldn't get much rain this early in the season but we'll have to deal with the snow runoff. That'll swell them rivers up wide and fast, which'll make our job pretty rough. We'll talk more about that when the time is closer."

Jared stepped forward and took over. "Boys, we ain't in a big hurry, as Juan told you, but we do have a deadline and you never know what might slow you down. If we had more time, we'd trail further east and head up through Tinchera Pass. But I reckon we're gonna have to take'em through Raton Pass and pay Uncle Dick Wootton his toll. We might run into some snow, but this late in the spring, blizzards ain't all that likely." He laughed and said, "Course, just cause it ain't likely don't mean it won't happen. You can catch a snow storm in the middle of summer up there in those mountains."

The younger cowboys laughed nervously as their bosses went down the list of what all could go wrong. Jared could see they were getting antsy and figured they'd have plenty of time to school the lads as they rode up the trail. He said, "I got just one more piece of advice and this is the most important part." After the litany of hazards he had mentioned, the hands looked at him with wide eyes. "Miguel Mares is your cook and you'd best treat him with the utmost respect. You do any complainin' about the food and you're likely to find the portions in your next meal considerably smaller and grittier. You boys 'sabe' that?" The hands looked over at Miguel and saw him looking stern. They couldn't decide if Jared was joshing them until Miguel broke into a grin.

Sean O'Reilly spoke up. "Faith and be-gorra, me and Patrick's been eatin' spuds all our lives. Anything Mr. Miguel cooks has got to be better than that!"

Everyone chuckled, then Jared asked, "Any of you got any more questions right now?" No one said anything. He continued. "Well, we're gonna take it easy these first few days so we'll have some time if you think of anything. Like I said before, if you got somethin' to say or ask, I'd prefer you do it when things are calm than when we're in a tight spot."

With no further questions, Jared sent the hands over to Tomas to choose their horses from the remuda. He and Juan had already picked their mounts, so he instructed the outfit that they would pick in the order of Felipe, Patrick, Sean, Joe Hargrove and last, Tom Stallings. He put Stallings last just to see his reaction and wasn't too surprised to see the boy complaining to Tomas about the quality of his mounts. Once again, he thought the young hand might become a problem on the trail and figured he would bear watching.

Once they'd drawn their mounts, Jared instructed Juan to take the point and told all the other hands to assume their assigned positions. Jared had picked out their lead steer several days ago and had decided to name him "Old Ned" in honor of his friend and former boss, Ned Kilpatrick. *I reckon he'll get a chuckle out of that,* Jared thought to himself. Juan urged Old Ned forward. With a whoop and a holler, they were on their way to Colorado.

CHAPTER 6

Eleanor was pretty certain she was expecting a child and was having regrets that she hadn't told Jared before he left for Colorado. She was unaccustomed to self-doubt and found her second thoughts distracting as she went about tidying up the ranch house. As she dusted the mantle, she found herself thinking, *what if something happens to him and he never knows that he's going to be a father?*

Thus preoccupied, she didn't give it a minute's notice when she heard hoof beats approaching the house. She assumed it was Estevan Mares who had agreed to help out with chores after lunch, and when she heard boot heels on the wooden porch, she went to the door and opened it. She was shocked to find a man, whom she did not know, standing quite close to her. In an instant, she registered that he was tall, handsome and carrying a double-rig holster with two

Colt .45s. She caught her breath and took a step back. Her mouth was suddenly dry but she managed to inquire, "May I help you, sir?"

The man on the porch took off his hat and made a sweeping bow. When he straightened up, he was smiling but Eleanor noticed that the smile did not seem to extend to his eyes. He had the eyes of a predatory bird, glancing around and taking in everything at once. She shivered involuntarily. "Howdy, m'am. Gentleman Curt Barwick at your service. I'd like to speak to your husband about purchasing this fine ranch. I wonder if he is available."

Flustered, Eleanor responded, "No, he's not available and this ranch is not for sale anyway."

The man smiled again and said, "M'am, everything's for sale. Where might your husband be?"

"I don't see how that's any of your business, sir," Eleanor said with an edge in her voice. "Nor do I appreciate your not accepting my word that this ranch is not for sale. We have no further business to conduct and I'd appreciate it if you would be on your way."

"Not so fast, little lady," the man said, showing no inclination to leave. He was still smiling, but there was something ominous in his demeanor that gave Eleanor a queasy feeling in the pit of her stomach. "You don't know who I represent. When you find that information out, it will likely change your opinion of whether or not the ranch is for sale."

Eleanor assessed her situation and was not reassured. This man was clearly a gunslinger and while he hadn't directly threatened her, she believed that it would not take much provocation for him to do her bodily harm. Lizbeth had taken the buckboard into town for supplies and she wasn't sure where Maria Suazo was. Although Estevan was coming out from town, he wasn't due until after lunch and it was only now late morning. Besides, she had a sense that Estevan would be no match for this seasoned shootist. There was something about the man that made her skin crawl. Eleanor had faced danger before during the conflict with the O'Bannon clan but this time, it felt different. She realized that she not only had her own life to look out for but also that of her unborn child. As she thought about that life growing inside her, she felt a wave of panic sweep over her that she knew she would have to control.

With a quaver in her voice that she had

never heard before, she said, "Sir, it doesn't matter whose interests you represent, I repeat . . . this ranch is not for sale." Struggling mightily to contain her fear, she drew herself up and said, "Now, sir, I would appreciate it if you would get on your horse and ride away."

The man smirked and glanced around. His predatory gaze returned to her, a look that resembled that of a hawk sizing up a field mouse. "I don't think so, my pretty miss. I don't feel like leaving just yet and it doesn't appear to me that you can make me go." He took a menacing step forward as if to come in the door. "Maybe after I sweet-talk you a bit, you'll change your tune."

Eleanor experienced a terror that she had never known before. In her entire life, she had never once begged another human being for anything, but the stakes were higher now than they'd ever been before. She had to protect the precious being that she carried in her womb at all costs. "Sir, I implore you, go about your business. I promise that as soon as my husband returns, I'll tell him of your interest and encourage him to listen to your offer." The pleading tone in her voice sickened her. She was alarmed to see that, rather than convincing the man to leave, it seemed to amuse and titillate him.

The smile was gone now. "I like it when they beg," he said, almost as if to himself. "Lady, I'm going to have a little fun now and if you want to live through it, you'd better act like you're enjoying yourself, too."

As he stepped forward through the door, Eleanor heard two clicks . . . the unmistakable sound of a double barrel shotgun being cocked. Maria Suazo stepped up on the porch directly behind the man and said, "Senor, stop right where you are or I'll blow you in two."

The man appeared to calculate his chances of grabbing Eleanor and using her as a shield but Eleanor had instinctively stepped back when the man started forward, and fortunately she was out of his reach. Maria spoke again in a louder, more urgent tone. "Raise your hands, now, senor, or I will shoot. I mean it."

Seconds passed as they stood there as if frozen in time. Then the man raised his hands and stepped back from the door. In a most reasonable tone, he said, "If I turn slowly, you won't shoot me, now, will you?"

Guessing that the man was looking for an opportunity to go for his guns, Maria responded, "Si, senor, I will. You don't want to try me, I promise you." As the man moved slowly to the right of the door with

66

his back still toward her, Maria circled to her left on the porch. "You keep your back to me and walk very slowly to your horse. I'll be close enough that I can't miss if you try anything."

The man looked Eleanor in the eyes and in a cold voice that only she could hear, said, "Don't think this is over, missy. I'll be back and you'll pay for this." All pretense of courtliness was gone. She could see the monster just beneath the surface. With his back to Maria, he continued to move slowly toward the steps of the porch. In a voice that sounded oddly polite, given the circumstances, he said, "I'm doing what you asked, m'am. Don't let that trigger finger of yours get itchy."

"You just keep moving slow, senor, and you'll be fine," Maria said. "When you get to your horse, you mount up and head on out of here pronto."

Barwick and Maria moved in a circle, as if they were dancing a quadrille to music only they could hear. When he got to his horse, Barwick swung up into the saddle, turned and nodded politely to both women as if he'd just paid a social call. "I'll see both of you again, I promise." With a smile and a wave, he turned and rode off.

Eleanor and Maria stood like statues until

Barwick rode over the rise to the southwest. Once he was out of sight, Maria lowered her shotgun and ran over to where Eleanor still stood in the doorway. "Are you all right, senora?"

Eleanor was deathly pale and trembling. She tried to speak but couldn't find her voice or catch her breath. She shook her head and tried to slow her breathing as she turned to go into the kitchen where she collapsed into a chair. Only then was she able to speak. "Oh, God, Maria, I've never been so frightened in my life! I didn't know what to do or say." She doubled over as she sat, almost as if she were in physical agony. "I was such a coward, I can't believe I behaved in that fashion. I'm so ashamed of myself."

"The man was dangerous, senora, there is no shame in recognizing that fact."

Eleanor continued to rock in her seat. "I don't know what he would have done if you hadn't come along," she said, although in her heart, she knew and was terrified. She stopped her rocking and looked at Maria. "How did you happen to show up here armed anyway?"

Maria said, "I was coming over to see if you needed any help. I've seen several rattlers lately and I wanted to be ready in case there was trouble." She smiled. "I just wasn't expecting a snake with two legs."

Eleanor burst into tears. She covered her face with her hands and for several moments sat sobbing uncontrollably. Finally, she calmed down enough to speak. "I've never been in a spot where I felt completely out of control before. I never would have thought I would act the way I did."

Maria came and sat next to Eleanor, putting her hand on her arm. "Senora Eleanor, you are being too hard on yourself. You reacted as any mother would who had two lives to be concerned about."

Eleanor's head whipped around as she looked at Maria in shock. "You know?"

"Si," Maria said with a smile. "Senora Lizbeth and I both know. Maybe you can keep this a secret from the men but the women, we know."

"All I could think was 'Please, God, don't let him hurt my baby.' I would have done anything he asked to keep him safe."

Maria noticed that Eleanor referred to the baby as "he" and thought that it would be fitting that she and Jared have a little boy for their first-born. "A mother will do what she must to protect her child."

"I've never begged anyone for anything before," Eleanor said in a tone full of self-loathing. "I'm just disgusted with myself."

She slammed her open hand down on the table. "I don't know who that man is but I hate him!"

Maria glanced nervously at the door and said, "I don't know who he is either but I know he's a killer. We'd better keep a close watch right now in case he doubles back." She stood and walked to the door, holding her shotgun in the crook of her arm.

"Estevan is coming out this afternoon to help with chores," Eleanor said. "As soon as he gets here, I'm telling him to turn right around and head back to town so he can let Nathan know what happened." A look of fear crossed her face. "He said something about representing the interests of some other men. I don't know who or what he was talking about, but maybe Nathan will know. Why would he think the ranch was for sale?"

Maria shook her head slowly. "I don't know, senora . . . but I know that our husbands picked a bad time to go on a cattle drive."

CHAPTER 7

The scent of pine in the fresh morning air filled Jared's nostrils as he rode out to scout what lay ahead. He cast his eyes over the broad, rolling plains in front of him and marveled at the majestic Rockies that lay in the distance to the north. The sun was just making an appearance over the horizon and the mountains had a dark purple hue. It was a beginning that inspired optimism.

It was the start of the third day and so far, the drive had gone off without a hitch. They'd only made about seven miles the first day, as Jared wanted both the herd and the hands to get the feel of the trail. The second day, though, they'd made a solid eleven miles with no untoward incidents. They'd crossed one shallow stream with ease after watering the herd and found a suitable campsite both nights. Night herding had gone well, too. Contrary to what his brother had said, Sean O'Reilly had a beautiful Irish tenor voice that transformed "Annie Laurie" into a gentle night wind that had an almost magically calming effect on the cattle. The only problem was that as he had feared, Tom Stallings seemed to be a malcontent. He'd complained about riding drag even though he was clearly one of the two least experienced hands and he'd also groused about taking the second shift at night. This presented Jared a quandary, as he needed every hand he had but didn't need the grief that a dissatisfied cowboy could cause. Still, he reckoned if this was the worst problem he encountered, he'd count his blessings and deal with it with a smile.

Reluctantly, he tore himself away from the awe-inspiring vision of the Rockies. Riding back to camp, he saw Miguel buttoning down the chuckwagon and the hands saddling up to get in position. The day was clear and Jared thought they might make twelve miles before nightfall if they were lucky. At that rate, they could make Raton in two more days, which would put them ahead of schedule. He figured he could give the boys a night on the town in Raton before they started the difficult trek up through the pass. He chuckled to himself. *To think I have to pay old Uncle Dick Wootton a toll for the privilege of enduring that hardship.* Although they would be navigating the pass in June, it was not uncommon for cattle drives to encounter snowstorms at the summit. That was a challenge he'd be happy to avoid.

Jared rode up to the chuckwagon where Juan and Felipe Munoz were finishing up their last cups of Joe. "Juan, I think you got this drive under control. I may ride ahead and find a shady place to take a nap this mornin'," Jared said.

Juan accepted the veiled compliment and said, "I figured that's what you'd been doing these last two days. Still, you're getting old, you need your rest."

Jared laughed and turned to Felipe. "Pard, you're a mighty fine hand. I appreciate a cowboy that don't make it look too hard, just shows up in the right place at the right time without a lot of fuss. Maybe some of these youngsters will learn a thing or two from you."

Felipe acknowledged the praise with a nod. "Si, senor, I think most of the boys you hired will catch on pronto."

Jared had the sense that something was being left un-said. He cocked his head quizzically. "You said 'most' . . . does that mean you think we got somebody who don't take kindly to being taught?"

Felipe shrugged. "It's early in the drive, boss. Maybe things will get better once everyone is used to the trail."

Recognizing that Felipe wasn't going to say any more right now, Jared nodded and said, "I hope you're right. Sometimes it works out that way. Let's get the herd movin'." As he rode up to the point, he thought to himself, . . . *and sometimes it don't.*

As the sun rose higher, the chill faded and the cowboys started to work up a sweat. Ol' Ned was proving to be a fine lead steer and moved along at a slow, steady clip. Every now and then, a steer showed signs of wanting to wander too far afield, and Juan or Felipe would shade him back toward the flow of the herd. The O'Reilly brothers watched all this with interest and had been discussing the topic with the top hands the night before around the campfire. Juan explained that there was no need to keep the herd tightly packed during the course of the day. They could spread out over as much as a half a mile as long as they all kept moving in the right direction. The trick was to gently nudge them along without worrying them a great deal.

By late-morning, Jared was satisfied that

Juan had a handle on things and decided to ride ahead to scout out the next stream. There hadn't been any rain since they left Cimarron, so he didn't anticipate any problems, but he reckoned it was better to be safe now than sorry later. He thought he'd be able to make it back in time to have a bite of jerky for a mid-day meal as they grazed the herd. Once they got the herd across the next stream, he planned to scout ahead for a place to bed down for the night.

Riding back to let Juan know of his plans, Jared noticed a bank of clouds far off in the southwest. June was a tricky month . . . sometimes it was dry as a bone and sometimes those storm clouds would come rolling in from Mexico every afternoon the way they typically did later in the summer. There wasn't anything he could do about it other than be prepared. He filled Juan in and then headed northeast at an easy lope. As he rode along, the sights and smells of the range flooded his senses. The thought crossed his mind that if there was a better life than being a cowboy, he couldn't imagine what it might be. He knew there were men who possessed fortunes but stayed holed up in an office building from morning to nightfall. He figured there was more than one way to be rich and being out on the rolling plains driving a herd north was sure one of them.

Jared experienced a wave of contentment as he rode along, but at the same time, he felt a sense that something was lacking. He smiled as he thought about what was missing . . . his lovely wife and the first true home and family he could remember knowing. He felt a pang of longing for Eleanor and wondered what she was doing right at this moment that he was thinking of her. She could be watering her flower garden, milking the old cow or maybe even heading into town for a talk with Christy about the students at the school. Although he had no reason to think anything bad was happening back in Cimarron, he had a vague sense of uneasiness and felt a flash of guilt for being so far away. He knew that Eleanor was tough and self-sufficient and she had Lizbeth, Maria, Estevan and especially, Nathan Averill to help out if trouble arose. Somehow, knowing that didn't seem to help. He was still worried.

I reckon that's the price you pay when you love someone, he thought. *You never want anything bad to happen to'em and you spend most of your time thinkin' about what they're up to.* Still, the love, affection, and honesty he received from his wife more than made up for any uneasiness he experienced.

With his mind thus occupied, it seemed only a matter of minutes before he reached the stream, although in reality it was a couple of hours. Jared found the water flowing gently, much like the previous stream they had crossed. The herd could drink their fill and there was an abundance of grass for the cattle to graze on before they resumed their journey. Once he had assessed the situation, he headed back to rejoin the cowboys and grab a bite to eat. As he rode along, he saw that the cloud bank he had seen earlier seemed to have remained stationary.

When Jared got back to the herd, the sun was directly overhead. He rode up to Juan, who was riding point, and asked, "Any trouble while I was gone, amigo?"

Juan shook his head and said, "No problems. If we keep up this pace, we could make maybe twelve miles today without pushing too hard." He broke into a big grin and asked, "Did you find the stream or were you too busy taking a siesta?"

Jared laughed. "It's a couple of miles ahead and it's just a gentle little stretch. Shouldn't be any trouble to cross and there's some good grass on the other side where the herd can graze. If you don't get'em lost between here and there, we should be fine."

"Bueno, amigo," Juan replied, "If you found it once, I think maybe I won't have any trouble finding it a second time. You want to take a break and have some biscuits and coffee?"

"I like the sound of that," Jared said. "You get ol' Ned turned out to graze a bit and I'll go let Miguel know what we're doin'. I reckon the fellas won't mind a little grub."

Jared rode back toward the wagon, passing Felipe and Patrick O'Reilly on the way. He hollered at them to get the herd settled and come on in for some grub. Felipe nodded and Patrick bowed elaborately in his saddle. Miguel saw him coming and anticipating his order, had already reined in his mules. He was climbing down when Jared arrived beside the wagon.

"Hey, compadre, I was thinkin' some biscuits and Arbuckle coffee are just what this outfit needs to get us up for a good push this afternoon." Jared smiled at his good friend and Miguel responded in kind.

"I made extra biscuits this morning. I'll get a fire going to heat up the coffee," Miguel responded. "The boys are working pretty hard. I think they've earned a break."

Jared noticed a fleeting frown pass over his friend's face after he made the statement about the crew's hard work. "Somethin' on your mind, amigo? You and Juan and Felipe have been droppin' hints for a couple of days, maybe you oughta go ahead and say what you're thinkin'."

"I'll tell you straight out, Jared, that Stallings boy is no good." Miguel straightened up from his task of piling kindling for the fire. "He complains about anything he's asked to do and then does a poor job of it once he gets around to doing it. The other night, I saw him looking in one of the other hand's saddlebags when he wasn't around. He stopped when he saw me looking at him and tried to pretend that he wasn't up to no good. But he was looking for something to steal, sure enough."

Jared took off his hat and scratched his head. "I been gettin' the same feelin', Miguel. We can't hardly spare any hands but if things don't change, I may have to send that boy packin' for Cimarron." He grabbed a couple of dry branches and threw them on the pile Miguel was assembling. "I reckon, to be fair, I oughta have a talk with him to see if he can straighten up. Maybe I'll pull him aside after we've had chow."

"I don't think it will do any good, amigo, but you're probably right, it's the fair thing to do. Sometimes a vaquero just needs a strong rein to get on the right track." Miguel knelt down to get the fire started and said, "At least you'll know you did the right thing, even if he doesn't come around."

Jared chuckled. "It wasn't that long ago that I was takin' some wrong turns and needed help gettin' straightened out. There's a bunch of folks, you included, who cut me some slack. Who knows, maybe this kid will surprise us."

"Maybe," Miguel said, "but I don't think he's cut from the same cloth as you. Still, you won't know unless you try."

Jared heard the other cowboys bantering among themselves as they rode over to get some grub. He reached over and gave Miguel a friendly pat on the shoulder. "Well, amigo, I sure enough appreciate all the times you've stuck by me." He shook his head and said, "We've been in some tough spots, ain't we? Reckon we're lucky to still be ridin' up the trail."

"You're right about that, compadre." Miguel had the coffee heating on the fire and he turned to get the biscuits from the wagon. "Now, enough of this talk, let's get some chow in these cowboys."

The cowboys dismounted and came on over to the wagon to get their grub. There was some milling around, then they lined up and Miguel dispensed the biscuits.

Patrick O'Reilly looked at his ration and said, "Say, Miguel, these rocks smell pretty good. Where might you have been pickin' them up?"

Miguel drew himself up with dignity and said, "If you don't like my biscuits, senor, you are welcome to cook some for yourself."

At that, the young Irishman laughed and said, "Sure and I'm just having fun with you. These are the best biscuits I've had since . . ." he paused, then chuckled, ". . . since yesterday."

Miguel muttered under his breath about the lack of respect with which he was treated but it was obvious that he enjoyed the banter and was fond of the young cowboy. Jared observed the interplay and reflected that every cow outfit he'd ever been around had always had at least one prankster who kept everyone in a light-hearted mood. It appeared to him that Patrick O'Reilly was to be their clown. His brother, Sean, would provide the music.

Thinking about the way the cowboys worked together in the outfit and the different holes each one filled reminded him that he needed to speak with the Stallings boy. He looked around and saw him sitting alone, a bit distant from the rest of the hands. He looked like he was about done eating, so Jared walked over to where he sat and crouched down beside him.

"I need to have a word with you, Tom. Why don't we walk over toward the remuda and chew the fat for a minute."

Stallings looked at him suspiciously but got up without a word. Jared began walking toward the horses and the young man followed him. When they got far enough away to be out of earshot, Jared turned and looked the boy in the eye. "Pardner, you don't seem very happy so far on this drive. I'm wonderin' what I can do to turn that around."

Stallings looked away for a second, then looked down at the ground. "I ain't quite sure what you're talkin' about, boss."

"I'm talkin' about the fact that you do a lot of complainin' about the things you're asked to do," Jared said. "I know it ain't much fun ridin' drag but every cowboy here has taken his turn doin' it. Right now, it's your turn. That's just how things are done."

"Well, it don't seem fair to me," Stallings said. "I can cowboy as well as them other waddies and it seems like they ought to suck some dust from time to time, too."

Jared felt himself getting impatient and struggled to hold his temper in check. "Like I said, Tom, them boys have already ridden the drag and they've earned their spurs. Maybe you think you're a top hand but the fact is, you ain't put in the time yet. It don't just happen over night. We all got to pay our dues."

For the first time, Stallings looked Jared in the eye and he saw the resentment there. "That just don't seem fair to me, boss. If I can do the job, I think I should get a break. Those Irish micks ain't had much more experience than me and they get the flanks. I don't think it's right."

Jared took a deep breath to calm himself before he responded. "You're entitled to your opinion but like I told you before, on this drive, I'm the boss. You've had your say but now it's time to do what you're told. If you can live with that and do your job without complainin', we'll get along. If not, then you might want to think about drawin' your pay and headin' for home."

It was obvious that Stallings was struggling to control his temper now. He looked around and fidgeted for a moment, then said, "I need this job. Reckon I'll go along. Still, that don't mean I think it's right."

He had hoped this conversation would go better but Jared sensed that this was the best he would get out of the young cowboy right now. He nodded and said, "Your thoughts

83

are your own but I expect you to keep'em to yourself. If you think you can do that, we're square."

Stallings seem to be struggling to come to a decision. Finally, he looked up at the sky and said, "Yeah, boss, I reckon I can do that."

"All right," Jared said, "let's head on back and saddle up. We got a ways to go before we bed'em down tonight."

Jared frowned as he watched the young hand ride to the back of the herd. He wondered what his story was and why he seemed so bitter. He shook off his irritation with the boy and speculated that this is how Nathan Averill, Ned Kilpatrick and others may have felt toward him only a few years ago. *I reckon what goes around, comes around,* he thought with wry amusement.

After they got the herd moving again, Jared rode ahead to scout out a spot to make camp for the night. He found a place out on the flats about four miles up the trail that looked like it would do. It was about a mile short of where he had hoped to make before they stopped, but it was level ground with plenty of grass for grazing, so he decided it would work. He looked around the area one more time to see if he was missing any potential trouble, then rode back to the herd.

Juan kept them traveling at a steady pace and they were able to make camp well before sundown. Tomas got the remuda secured and Miguel got their evening meal of beans, jerky and coffee ready as the cowboys got the herd settled in. Patrick and Joe took first watch and Jared rode out with them to keep an eye on things for a bit. He could hear laughter and talking from the campfire area and knew that some yarns were being spun.

Once he was satisfied that the boys had things in hand, he rode back to camp as the cowboys began breaking up and heading for their bedrolls. There was a three quarter moon in the sky and it was clear except in the area to the southwest that he'd been watching earlier. As far as he could tell, the clouds hadn't moved in their direction. He ordered Sean O'Reilly and Tom Stallings to take the next shift with the herd, noticing with some satisfaction that Stallings said "yes, sir," with no apparent hint of resentment.

Juan was checking the campfire to make sure the coals were burning down with no danger of setting off a grassfire. Jared walked over to his side and said, "Things are goin' pretty smooth, compadre. Makes me a might nervous, I got to admit, but I'll settle for smooth as long as I can get it."

"You're the boss, it's your job to be nervous." Juan chuckled. "Don't worry, something will go wrong pretty soon, then you can relax."

"I know I can always count on you to help me get my thinkin' straight," Jared replied. "By the way, I spoke with Stallings and I think maybe he got the message. I reckon we'll see one way or the other." He looked around at the blue roan sky above one more time, then said, "Guess I'll turn in. See you at daybreak."

Jared awoke with a start, realizing that it was the sound of thunder that had snatched him out of a deep sleep. He shook his head to clear away the fog of sleep and noticed that it was dark as pitch. When he'd laid out his bedroll earlier, he'd had to use his hat to keep the moonlight out of his eyes. He looked at the sky and realized that the clouds had rolled in from the southwest and were threatening rain. As he looked up, he was blinded by a flash of lightning, followed a few seconds later by another round of thunder.

Looks like Juan was right, he thought to himself. *Somethin's goin' wrong.* He rolled

86

out, pulled on his boots and grabbed his slicker figuring the nighthawks could use his help if the herd got spooky. He was in the process of saddling his horse when another flash of lightning struck a tree just to the rear of where the herd had gathered for the night. Jared heard loud bawling from the cattle and saw them begin to mill around, working themselves into a frenzy. He knew trouble was imminent and mounted up to ride out just as the cattle bolted. He shouted, "Stampede!" to the camp and immediately rode for the lead, wondering if one of the cowboys was up front making a circle. Out of the corner of his eye, he saw Juan saddling up and rousing the other cowboys as a hard rain began to fall.

The cattle were just building up a head of steam as he got up to the front. Another brilliant flash of lightning revealed a cowboy whose horse was crow-hopping around in confusion. To his dismay, he saw the horse begin to buck, taking two quick jumps to the left, which unseated the hand. He flew through the air in what seemed like slow motion to Jared before landing in the brush right in the path of the oncoming herd. Without a second's hesitation, Jared spurred his horse into a gallop and headed for the fallen cowboy. He hollered out to get his attention but his words were lost in the thundering hoof beats. He wasn't sure if he could make it in time to prevent the hand from being trampled but luckily, the boy had pulled himself out of the brush and was attempting to stand. He looked over in Jared's direction and saw him galloping toward him with his right hand extended so he was ready when Jared's horse got even with him. Jared thought to himself that this was going to be close but the cowboy was able to grab hold and let the momentum swing him up onto the horse behind the saddle. Jared had slowed down just a bit to make sure his hand didn't slip because of the rain as he made the grab. As soon as he felt the cowboy settle in on the back of his horse, he hollered, "Hang on!" and spurred his mount into a full gallop.

Even as his horse hit full stride, the lead cattle appeared to be gaining on them and Jared felt a stab of fear in his gut that they would both suffer the horrible fate of being trampled. Time seemed to stand still as their lives hung in the balance. All at once, Jared felt his mount put on a burst of speed, hitting a dead run and outdistancing the terrified cattle. As soon as he thought they had sufficient distance from the stampede, he began to look for a clear path off to the left so he could get outside the herd's path and find a safe spot to unload the cowboy. He heard gunshots behind him and knew that Juan and probably Felipe were doing all they could to turn the herd and get them milling.

Through the downpour, Jared could just make out a rise off to his left and he slowed his pony as he headed up in that direction. He figured if they made it up to the top of the hill, they would be out of harm's way. As he made his way through the brush, he could hear the sound of the stampede diminish just a bit and he figured he'd calculated correctly. He took a deep breath and waited for his heart to quit thumping.

He topped the rise and spoke over his shoulder. "I reckon you can let go and dismount, pard. You'll be safe up here. I need to get back down there and help'em turn the herd."

The hand seemed reluctant to loosen his grip and Jared wondered if he had heard him. Then he slowly let go, swinging off to the left and stepping forward to stand next to the saddle. Jared looked down. Tom Stallings stared up at him with eyes the size of saucers. Stallings stammered for a moment. "You saved my life, Mr. Delaney."

"It's what a cowboy does, amigo," Jared said. "I expect you'd have done it for me, too." Stallings continued to look up at him with wide eyes. "I've got to get back there and help Juan get'em calmed down. You wait here until you see'em millin', then head on over to the chuckwagon and report in to Miguel."

Jared spurred his horse again and rode back toward the herd. He could see that Juan had managed to turn ol' Ned to the right and was starting to get things under control. Most of the cattle were following the lead steer although a few continued running to the north. Jared knew that meant they'd have to send out a couple of hands at daybreak to round them up, but he considered himself mighty lucky if only a few head got scattered. As he rode up to the head of the herd, the cattle had slowed to a gentle trot and seemed to be calming down. Within minutes, they stopped. He rode up to Juan and said, "Looks like you got'em turned. Good job."

Juan said, "We need to get some hands to hold'em so they don't make another break. I don't know where the rest of the boys are."

Just then, Felipe rode up. "You two stay here," Jared said. "I'll ride back to find some help and we'll get these critters calmed down." Jared galloped back in the direction of the chuckwagon and before long, he saw a couple of cowboys galloping in his direction. When he got closer, he recognized Joe Hargrove and Patrick O'Reilly and ordered them to ride up ahead to hold the herd. As soon as he saw that they understood his directions, he rode back to where Miguel was waiting with the wagon.

Miguel saw him coming and stepped out to meet him. "Juan and Felipe, they got those steers turned, que no?"

Jared stayed in the saddle and replied. "Looks like they got'em under control for now. We need all hands out there to hold'em, though. They're still pretty spooked and it wouldn't take much to get'em goin' again."

"I can saddle up pronto if you need me," Miguel said.

"Why don't you stay here with the wagon. Is Tomas with the remuda, or did he head out with the rest of the boys?"

"I told him to stay with the horses," Miguel said. "I figured we didn't need them taking off to follow the herd."

Jared allowed himself a tight smile in appreciation of Miguel's wisdom and experience. "You called that one right. The last thing we needed was for all our animals to take off hell bent for leather." He looked around the camp. "I reckon the boys could use Tomas now, though, to help hold the herd. Maybe you can spell him at the remuda and send him on over."

Miguel nodded and said, "I'll get right over there. Looks like we won't be getting any more sleep this night."

"I'm afraid you're right about that. We'll see what this weather does." Jared glanced up at the night sky as he turned to head back to the herd. "Sometimes it comes in fast and passes just as quick. Maybe this'll be one of those times." As it turned out, though, Jared was wrong.

CHAPTER 8

Nathan was walking from his office to the St. James Hotel, planning to grab a cup of coffee and a piece of apple pie when he saw Christine Johnson headed his direction. He gave serious thought to turning around and heading back as if he'd forgotten something, then thought, *Nathan, you old fool, you're just imaginin' things.* Taking a deep breath, he continued on toward the hotel.

As Christine approached, Nathan stopped and tipped his hat. "Mornin' Miss Johnson, how's the world treatin' you on this fine Saturday?" He tried to strike a casual tone.

Christine smiled a big, sunny smile at him and said, rather breathlessly, "It's a wonderful day, sheriff. I've spent the morning planning my lessons for this next week and I was considering taking a little ride out in the country this afternoon." She cocked her head a bit saucily and said, "I couldn't persuade you to join me, could I? I thought

I might take a picnic lunch, maybe with some fried chicken."

Flustered, Nathan sputtered a bit before responding. "Uh, I'd love to, Miss Johnson, but I've got some paperwork I've got to finish up at the office and it needs to be ready by Monday mornin'." He smiled a bit sheepishly. "Maybe some other time."

"Why, sheriff," she said, "I'll just hold you to that." If Nathan wasn't mistaken, she had a mischievous glint in her eyes. "No one should work all the time. A fella needs a little relaxation, don't you think?"

Nathan pondered what she might mean by that statement. "I reckon you're prob'ly right about that, Miss Johnson." He tipped his hat again. "Well, good day to you."

"And a good day to you, sheriff."

Christine walked on past him and down the street. Nathan resisted the urge to turn and look at her. He took off his hat and scratched his head, puzzled. If he didn't know better, he'd swear that Christine Johnson, currently the school marm and formerly Christy Quick, the "soiled dove," was flirting with him. That didn't make much sense to him though, as she was a fine figure of a woman and he was probably about twice her age. He knew she was grateful for his kindness toward her when she had risked her life by sharing vital information about Morgan O'Bannon's plan to ambush him and Jared Delaney. She probably also appreciated that he'd been very supportive of Eleanor Coulter's decision to bring her on as assistant teacher at the school over the protests of some of the town's more uppity citizens. Still, it seemed to him that there was more than just simple appreciation going on here. Once again, he thought to himself, *Averill, you're the worst kind of a fool . . . an old fool.*

When he walked into the dining room at the St. James, Nathan immediately spotted Eleanor Delaney and walked over to her table. "Mornin' Eleanor. Mind if I join you?"

Eleanor looked up, and seeming a bit distracted, said, "Please do, Nathan. I needed to talk to you anyway."

Nathan noticed that she appeared pale. There was a haunted look in her eyes that he'd never seen before. "What's the trouble and what do you need me to do?"

With just a hint of a smile, she said, "Not much gets past you, does it, Nathan?"

"More gets past me than it used to but you look like you seen a ghost. You wanta tell me about it?"

Eleanor took a deep breath, then told him

95

about the unwelcome visitor she'd had. She explained about his talk of representing important interests who wanted to buy the ranch but left out the part about his threatening to take advantage of her. From her tone, the sheriff was able to read between the lines, however, and Eleanor could see him becoming agitated.

"It was that Barwick fella, wasn't it?" Nathan said angrily. "He's lurkin' around here, up to no good. I know he's just a hired gun for Tom Catron and Bill Chapman but he's dangerous as a rattlesnake, nonetheless."

Eleanor looked down and then away at the window. "You're right, it was Barwick." She shuddered. "After all we've been through, you'd think I'd be braver, but the man makes my skin crawl."

Nathan started to say something in response when suddenly Eleanor burst into tears. He'd known her since she was a little girl and had only seen her cry twice before . . . once when her mother died, and later when her father was murdered by gunmen hired by the vicious Santa Fe Ring. He reached out to touch her hand and asked, "What is it, Eleanor? It's me you're talkin' to."

She took a minute to collect herself, wiping her tears away with a kerchief. Finally, she spoke, again without looking him in the eye. "Nathan, I always thought I was brave but now I know I'm just a craven coward." It appeared she might begin sobbing again, but with an effort, she regained control. "I begged him not to hurt me, Nathan. If Maria hadn't shown up with her shotgun, I don't know what I would have done." A sob bubbled out. "Oh, I'm so ashamed."

Nathan was puzzled. "Maybe I'm missin' somethin', Eleanor, but I don't know what you're ashamed about."

Eleanor wiped her eyes. "Nathan, I've never begged anyone before. I was so afraid he was going to hurt me and the . . ." She stopped.

Nathan cocked an eyebrow. "You were afraid he might hurt you or what?"

"This is a horrible way to break what should be happy news to you but it looks like I'm going to have a baby." Eleanor managed a brief smile. "Jared doesn't even know yet. By all rights, he should have been the first but these are strange times."

Nathan didn't know whether to hug Eleanor or go into a rage at Barwick's audacity. "Well, that's wonderful news, even with everything else that's goin' on." He frowned. "I understand even more now why you would have been afraid. Barwick's a snake and you have even more than your own life to look after. What I don't get is what you think you have to be ashamed about."

Eleanor couldn't seem to meet Nathan's questioning gaze. Finally she said, "Nathan, I've always respected you more than anyone in the world. I'm a woman but I've tried to pattern how I conduct myself after what I see you do." She took a deep breath, then continued. "I've never seen you act afraid before. I feel like I let you down."

The sheriff contemplated what he'd heard. After a moment, he shook his head and grinned. "What you said is the absolute truth." When Eleanor looked confused, he continued. "You've never seen me *act* afraid. Fact is, I'm afraid a lot of the time, I just don't show it."

"I don't quite understand, Nathan."

"Well, here it is, Eleanor. If you're standin' across from someone and you know they might be interested in gunnin' you down, you'd have to be a fool not to feel fear. Bein' brave don't mean you're not afraid, it means you do what you need to do anyhow."

Eleanor contemplated his words. "I just always thought you weren't afraid. It never occurred to me that anything could scare you."

Nathan laughed. "You met me when you were a mere sprout. I reckon I did look pretty powerful to you back then. Fact is, though, there's been plenty of times when I've been quakin' in my boots." He chuckled again. "If a man's gonna last as a peace officer, he's got to get pretty good at foolin' folks. The trick ain't to not be scared, it's to not let'em *see* that you're scared."

Eleanor shook her head in wonder. "I feel so silly. That makes sense. It's the way any rational person would look at things. I can't imagine why I saw it in such a childish fashion."

"Eleanor, you're still bein' pretty hard on yourself. You first looked at me through the eyes of a child and like I said, I'm pretty good at foolin' folks into thinkin' I'm fearless. Maybe the way you acted with Barwick was pretty much the way anyone with a lick of sense would have."

"Maybe you're right," she said. "I'll have to think some more about it now that I know your secret." She smiled at him as she thought about what he had told her. "You probably want this conversation to stay just between the two of us, don't you?"

"Darn tootin'," he said, a big grin on his face. "I don't need folks callin' my bluff at this late stage of the game." Nathan hailed the waiter for more coffee. Once his cup was filled, he turned back to Eleanor. "We still got us a problem, though. With Barwick skulkin' around, it means Catron and Chapman aren't too far off. I had a suspicion this Santa Fe Ring business wasn't over. Much as I like to be right, I wish I'd been wrong in this case."

Eleanor looked distressed. "Oh, Nathan, you think they're after the ranch, don't you."

"Eleanor, they're after all the land they can snatch up. I don't reckon it's just your spread they're after, but it's prob'ly one of several they got their eyes on." Nathan gazed out the window for a moment. "Looks like I better track down Mr. Barwick and have a friendly chat with him."

Since the troubles with the O'Bannon clan had been settled, the Colfax Tavern was no longer the den of iniquity it had been in those times. However, it was still the center for activities that the more upstanding citizens of Cimarron frowned upon and as such, it was the place to start looking for someone of disreputable character. Nathan wasted no time walking down the street to the tavern to see if a certain Gentleman Curt Barwick was present. He didn't see him when he first walked through the swinging doors. As his eyes adjusted to the shadowy interior, he noticed a lone figure at a table in the corner, seated where he could survey the entire room. With a nod to the bartender, Tom Lacey, Nathan slowly walked over to Barwick's table.

"Mind if I have a word with you, Barwick?"

"Good morning to you, too, sheriff," Barwick said, an insolent grin on his face. "I'm fine, thank you."

"I ain't here to exchange pleasantries," the sheriff said through gritted teeth. "I'm here to give you a message."

Barwick's grin remained in place though his eyes were flinty. "What message would that be, sheriff?"

"There's two parts to it," Nathan said, "so listen careful. Here's the first part. Your bosses ain't gonna have any more luck grabbin' land around these parts than they did when Morgan O'Bannon was their hired gun. If they're as smart as they think they are, they shoulda figured that out by now."

"That's the first part," Barwick replied evenly. "What's the second?"

Nathan leaned forward in his chair, his clenched fists on the table. "This is the second part. If you harm a hair on the head of Eleanor Delaney or any of the other good

101

folks that live on the Kilpatrick spread, I'll kill you."

Barwick's smile faded. Nathan could see a pulse pounding in his forehead. In a quiet yet menacing voice, he said, "Why sheriff, I thought you were an officer of the law. That sounds more like you intend to take the law into your own hands."

Nathan returned his steady gaze. "You take it any way you like, Barwick, just as long as you believe me."

Barwick's cocky grin returned. "Oh, I believe you mean it, sheriff. I just don't believe you can do it. You're a bit long in the tooth to be making threats, now, aren't you?"

Nathan stood up slowly. "You don't want to find out, Barwick. If you're smart, you'll head on out of here pronto." With that, he turned on his heel and walked out the door without a backward glance.

Once he was out on Main Street, Nathan exhaled long and slow. The truth was that he had a sneaking suspicion Barwick might be right. He might be too old and slow to take a hired gun of Barwick's caliber. He smiled ruefully as he thought about his earlier conversation with Eleanor. *Don't ever let'em see that you're scared,* he thought to himself.

CHAPTER 9

The sky seemed to have sprung a leak and the rains showed no sign of slowing down. Jared knew his young cowboys were struggling to stay in the saddle, much less to keep the herd moving northeast. He also knew from his own experience that these were the times that separated those who would become top hands from the ones who just had a pipe dream of being a cowboy.

The outfit had been able to keep the herd calm and there were no further incidents the night before. No one was seriously hurt, although Sean O'Reilly's horse went down with him as he chased the herd and had collected some bumps and bruises. Typically, he took it in stride and seemed no worse for the wear. They could hardly tell when dawn broke because of the heavy clouds and pouring rain. Once it became clear that the storm wasn't going away anytime soon, Jared and Juan made the decision to push on in hopes of outdistancing the bad weather. Unfortunately, it seemed to be following them as they made their way northeast toward the town of Raton. The next stream they came to was swollen and rushing like a runaway stagecoach. Although they hadn't lost any hands or beeves in the crossing, it had been touch and go for a time. Their pace slowed down considerably as they slogged on through the mud and it soon became evident to Jared that it would take them three days to make it to Raton. He chafed at the delay but there was nothing he could do about it. *You can take control of some things but the weather ain't one of'em,* he thought.

Jared rode up to the point where Juan was plodding along on his horse. He had to yell to be heard above the downpour. "I hope we don't float away."

Juan glanced over at him and said, "We'll sure find out if we've got any fair-weather cowboys with us, que no?" He pulled a damp bandana out of his saddlebags and wiped his face with it, mostly just spreading the raindrops around. "Speaking of that, it seems like Stallings is making a hand. With all this bad weather, he could've gone the other direction."

Jared shook his head. "The boy does seem

to have come around. He's gonna drive me loony, though, if he doesn't quit thankin' me for savin' his life."

Juan looked pensive. "Maybe he never had anyone before who gave enough of a hoot about him to pull him out of the way of a stampede."

Jared thought about what his pard had said. "You could be right, amigo. If you are, I could see where that might've soured his disposition a bit." Jared laughed. "Still, just because I saved his bacon once doesn't mean I'm takin' him to raise. I just want him to do his job like the rest."

"Yeah, well, good luck," Juan said with a sly grin. "I think maybe you got yourself a new little brother."

Jared shook his head. "I hope not. I ain't got time for that sort of nonsense. We got to get this herd on up the trail if we're gonna meet our deadline. I thought we might be able to rest for a couple of days in Raton but it looks to me like I'll just be able to give the boys one night on the town."

"I reckon they can get in enough trouble in one night to make up for any lost time," Juan said.

"Prob'ly true." Jared stood up in his stirrups to get a better look ahead. "It's not showin' any signs of lettin' up, is it? Let's

105

just keep pushin' until it's too dark to see before we make camp. Maybe we'll finally get ahead of this weather." Jared chuckled. "Or maybe we'll just float away."

It took every bit of three days for the drive to make it to Raton. It finally stopped raining midway through the second day and Jared decided to make camp early to let the outfit rest up. Some of the cowboys were so tired they didn't even wait for Miguel to cook up some beans. They just ate a few soggy biscuits, laid out their bedrolls and dropped off to sleep. They were only about eight miles south of Raton, so Jared let them get a later start on the third day. He led them around to the west of town before calling the herd to a halt late in the afternoon. He had talked it over with Juan and Miguel and they had agreed to stay with the herd while the rest of the hands went into town. Jared would go along to keep an eye on them and try to head off any serious trouble that might arise if their hijinks got out of hand.

At Jared's insistence, the cowboys wolfed down the substantial meal that Miguel prepared for them. He knew they would have other things on their minds than eating once they got to town and would fare better on a full stomach once they started consuming large quantities of the cheap whiskey that was sold in the taverns. When they were done eating, they all did their best to shine up a little, putting on the cleanest, driest clothes they could find. Jared watched with amusement, then wandered over to the wagon where Miguel and Juan stood.

"You don't need to be acting like an old mother hen," Juan said to Jared. "Just make sure these boys stay out of dark alleys. They can spend their wages on bad whiskey and flash girls but we don't want them getting rolled."

"Listen to who sounds like a mother hen," Jared said. "I reckon they'll be all right without me lookin' over their shoulders every minute."

"Juan is right," Miguel chimed in. "There's some bad hombres in these cow-towns. Gamblers and thieves who'll slit your throat just as soon as look at you. You watch them boys and you be careful, too."

"All right, you convinced me. They'll think Father Antonio came on the drive with'em before the night's out." Jared laughed and clapped Miguel on the back. "I'll send'em over to the wagon to see you for confession in the morning."

Miguel shook his head and went about

cleaning up his pots and pans from the meal. Juan walked with Jared over to where his horse was saddled. When they were out of earshot, he stopped and cleared his throat.

"It's different from the last time I went up the trail, amigo. I was single and couldn't wait to get to town." He looked off at the sunset and sighed deeply. "Now all I can think about is getting back home to my Maria. I don't know if I want to do this too many more times."

Jared's thoughts had been running in the same direction but he was a little surprised to hear his friend say it right out loud. "I been thinkin' the same thing, compadre. I didn't mind roamin' all over when I had no roots but things've changed. I miss Eleanor more than I can say. Heck, I even miss Nathan."

Jared laughed at himself but Juan said, "I know what you mean. I used to like to wander but now, all I want to do is be close enough to the bunkhouse that I can come running when Maria bangs on her frying pan to let me know supper is on. It doesn't seem like a lot until you're away from it, then it seems like everything."

As he listened to his friend, Jared felt a wave of loneliness wash over him. It was so strong that it took the form of a pain in the pit of his stomach, and he had to bend over slightly to get relief from it. He glanced at Juan, hoping he hadn't noticed but Juan seemed lost in his own thoughts. The feeling reminded Jared of when he was a little boy, after his parents had been killed and his only true companions were the horses on the ranch where he worked as a lowly stable hand. The difference between then and now was that in his mind, he could clearly see the one he was missing and had every reason to believe he would be back in her arms in a few weeks. As he thought about that, the pain in his stomach eased a bit and he felt a gentle wave of optimism.

"Not much longer, pard, then we'll be back home." Jared checked his cinch and prepared to mount up. "We'll get this job done, then figure out how we can stay home for the rest of our lives." He laughed. "Eleanor and Maria will prob'ly get so sick of us, they'll make us head up the trail again."

Juan laughed as Jared rode over to the campfire and called out to the cowboys. "Who wants to go to town?"

CHAPTER 10

Nathan rode out to the Kilpatrick ranch the next morning under a crystal blue sky. The birds were singing and it was early enough that it was still crisp and cool with the scent of pinon gently tickling his nostrils. All in all, it was a great day to be out horseback except for the serious nature of the topic he needed to discuss with Lizbeth, Eleanor and Maria. He hadn't been this worried since the business with the O'Bannons had been settled a few years back. Now all those fears came flooding back, leaving him with a sickening feeling of dread. He intended to persuade the women to come into town for the next couple of weeks until Jared and his crew returned from their business up north.

As he jogged along, he thought ruefully, *I'll have to do some fast talkin' to convince'em it's the smart thing to do. You couldn't find three more hard-headed females in the entire territory.* Nathan smiled in spite of himself.

He respected courage and he figured three braver individuals, male or female, could not be found anywhere. Still, that didn't make his job any easier. Gentleman Curt Barwick was as dangerous an outlaw as he had seen in years. Not only was he good with a gun, he was a predator with no more regard for human life than a mountain lion. And unlike the lion, who only hunted prey for survival, Barwick had a mean streak. He liked to make people suffer and Nathan didn't want to think what he might do if he caught the women off guard. *Yes sir, there's nothin' for it but that those three'll come on into town for a spell. I'll just have to do some mighty fast talkin'.*

As he topped the hill and came into sight of the ranch house, Nathan saw Lizbeth and Eleanor on the front porch. They appeared to have recognized him as they were both lowering the shotguns they had held ready when they heard the dog's bark announce the coming of a rider. He was glad to see they were vigilant but he was afraid that might make it harder to convince them to go along with his plan.

"Mornin' ladies," he said cheerfully as he rode up to the house. "We got us a nice day workin' here, don't we."

"Mornin' back at you, Nathan," Lizbeth

replied. "What brings you out our way so early?"

Eleanor waited until he dismounted and then walked over to his side, giving him a sweet peck on the cheek. Like a lot of men, Nathan was not the most observant individual when it came to noticing details. But even he couldn't help but see that Eleanor had a shine about her. He'd heard that some women got that way when they were with child and it didn't surprise him to find that Eleanor was one of those women. "My goodness, Mrs. Delaney, you're positively sparklin' this mornin'. You'd put the aspens in October to shame."

Eleanor blushed then gave him a swift hug. "Thank you kindly, Sheriff." She stepped back and said, "Can we get you some coffee?"

Nathan figured maybe he could ease into the topic a little smoother over the kitchen table, so he said, "Coffee sounds good."

Lizbeth walked in first to get the coffee heated up while Eleanor and Nathan lingered on the porch. She took his arm as they looked out northwest at the mountains in the distance. Mist still shrouded the base but the trees at the top were sparkling as the morning sun hit the dew on the leaves. "I miss him, Nathan. I told myself I'd stay busy and the time would fly by but that's not how it is. The days and nights seem to last forever."

With a sideways glance, Nathan could see that her eyes were brimming with tears. Not knowing quite what to say, he patted the hand that was linked through his arm. She turned her head and smiled at him. He smiled back and shrugged. In a moment, they turned and walked inside. Nathan hung his hat on the rack and they sat down at the table where Lizbeth had set out their coffee.

"I expect you ladies are keepin' busy, what with the men folk on their lark up north." The sheriff laughed. "Course I always suspected you did most of the work anyway, so you might not have even noticed they were gone."

Eleanor laughed along with Nathan but Lizbeth looked sideways at him. "Nathan, it ain't like you just to drop in to brighten our day." She took a sip of her coffee and asked, "What did you really come out here for."

Nathan shook his head and breathed a sigh of exasperation. "Dang it, Lizbeth, I was tryin' to ease into the topic and you're just rushin' me."

Lizbeth didn't say a word, she just looked at him and waited. Finally, he said, "Well, all right. Here's the thing of it. We've had some trouble with that fella, Barwick, and I've been encouragin' folks to stay a little closer in towards town. Shoutin' distance, if you know what I mean."

Eleanor now joined Lizbeth in staring at the sheriff who was becoming increasingly uncomfortable. After a lengthy pause, Lizbeth said, "No, Nathan, I'm afraid I don't know what you mean. Could you spell out what stayin' in shoutin' distance of town means?"

Nathan shifted uneasily in his chair and stared down into his coffee cup for a moment. He looked up and said, "Well, you know, I was just thinkin' maybe you ladies might want to come in and spend a week or so at the St. James. Just until things settle down a bit, you know? I expect I could get the town council to pay for it."

To Nathan, it seemed as if the temperature in the ranch house had dropped several degrees since he first entered. Eleanor looked at him stonily and asked, "How many other ranch folks have you made this offer to, Nathan?"

The sheriff cleared his throat and said, "Well, you're the first I've mentioned it to but I was gonna talk to some of the others pretty soon." He could see the disbelief and annoyance in their eyes and tried to smooth things over. "No, really, I was. I was headed out to see Roberto Gonzales right after I left here."

"Were you now?" Lizbeth arched an eyebrow. "That's funny cause it's pretty common knowledge in town that Mr. Gonzales and his wife headed over to Taos about three days ago to take care of her sick sister."

Nathan silently cursed himself for forgetting that piece of local gossip. "Now that you mention it, I reckon I had heard that. I just forgot." He tried a cheerful smile and said, "But you know, that just makes one less family I got to talk to about this."

They heard footsteps on the porch and a moment later, Maria Suazo entered the front door. "Hola, Senor Nathan, que paso?"

Before Nathan could say anything, Lizbeth spoke up. "Maria, the sheriff seems to think we ladies are too delicate to look out for ourselves. He wants us to come stay at the St. James until Jared and Juan get back so he can look after us like we was newborn calves and he was an old mamma cow."

Nathan protested. "Now, Lizbeth, it ain't like that."

"Yes, sir, it is!" Lizbeth slammed her hand down on the table. "You and I both know you weren't plannin' on speakin' to anyone else about comin' to town."

"Well, shucks, Lizbeth, I'm just worried sick about y'all, that's all." The sheriff threw up his hands. "I don't think you understand what a bad hombre this Barwick is. He's already been out here threatenin' Eleanor and she's got a baby on the way. You need to be reasonable."

At the mention of Eleanor's pregnancy, the women were quiet for a moment. Lizbeth turned to Eleanor. "Much as I hate to give this old sidewinder credit for anything, he might have a point." Lizbeth got up, went to the stove and poured a cup of coffee, which she handed to Maria as she walked back to the table. "It might be best for you to spend a few days in town. Maria and I can handle things out here. That's another thing Nathan was right about," she chuckled. "We shoulder more than our share of the load around here so we're used to it."

Eleanor had begun shaking her head even before Lizbeth returned to the table with the coffee. "I'm not leaving the two of you out here by yourselves with a violent outlaw on the loose. Three sets of eyes are better than two and you know I can handle a shotgun." She paused and shook her head emphatically again. "No, I won't hear of it.

116

I'm staying and that's that!"

Once again, Nathan threw up his hands. "You three beat all I've ever seen. Are you not listenin' to a word I'm sayin'?" He got up from the table and paced to the other end of the room and back again. "I'm tryin' to tell you this is a man that *I'm* afraid of. I been a lawman for thirty years and I don't know if I can take him, even in a fair fight. And I promise you, he won't fight fair!"

Lizbeth looked at Eleanor and Maria, then turned to Nathan. "I don't mean to be hard on you, Nathan, you just got me riled up. I know you mean well and don't want us to come to harm." She looked down at the tablecloth then looked up again. "When Ned was alive, we never once backed down from Morgan O'Bannon and his worthless brothers. I will *not* dishonor my husband's memory by backin' down now. That's my final word."

For the first time, Maria spoke up. "I will stay, too." She paused, taking a deep breath then blowing it out. "I say this, though. This Barwick fellow scares me bad. I had the drop on him with my shotgun when he came out before. Most people would be afraid but all I saw in his eyes was cunning like a wolf." She shuddered. "He was just looking for an opening so he could jump on me and tear my throat out."

The sheriff looked at the three women around the table. He started to say something then stopped and sighed, shaking his head. "I don't know what made me think I had a snowball's chance in Hades of talkin' you into seein' things my way." He chewed thoughtfully on his upper lip for a moment then said, "I reckon we need to come up with another plan, then. Would you be too offended if I deputized Estevan Mares and had him come out here for a while? That'd give you another set of eyes and another gun."

"Nathan, I don't mean to be hard-headed about this thing. I know you're worried for good reason and I appreciate it." Lizbeth looked from Eleanor to Maria, then back at the Sheriff. "I've got no problem with Estevan spending a little time out here. He's been helpin' out some anyways and one more mouth to feed ain't that much trouble." She laughed. "I reckon we don't want to get out of practice feedin' cowhands. Those two rascals who used to work here are bound to show up again sooner or later."

"My Juan better show up pretty quick or I'll go find me a new husband. I don't need a man who's always gone!" The twinkle in Maria's eyes belied her harsh statement.

"Senor Nathan, I thank you for looking out for us. I think you're right about that Barwick. He is un hombre malo."

Nathan rose to go, taking his hat from the rack. "Well, I still wish you ladies would consider my idea and come into town for a spell. I think it'd be safer there." He walked to the door then turned back. "If you ain't gonna do that, then you at least need to be extra careful and don't go far from the house, especially alone. I'll speak to Estevan just as soon as I get back to town and get him headed out this way pronto."

The women followed the sheriff out to where his horse was tied. The day had warmed up a bit but the sky was still a brilliant blue and there was an abundance of green in the landscape thanks to the recent summer rain. In the quiet morning, a horse whinnied over in the corral and birds were chirping in the thick stand of aspens up on the hill. Nathan tipped his hat to the ladies and Eleanor came over to give him a quick hug. He mounted up and set off in a long trot toward town. Hidden in the shadows of that thick stand of aspens on the hill, a lone figure on horseback looked down and surveyed the scene with the eye of a hawk. As the sheriff rode away, Gentleman Curt Barwick smiled.

CHAPTER 11

"Who wants to go to town?" Jared asked as
he looked down at the excited faces of the
young cowboys. He was struck by how
young and innocent they looked. Stallings
and Hargrove weren't much past seventeen
and the Irish boys weren't yet twenty-one.
Jared was only twenty-four but he'd done a
lot of living during that time, some of it the
kind that ages you fast. He remembered
staring down the barrel of Morgan
O'Bannon's six-shooter thinking his time
had come and an involuntary shudder ran
through him. When you come face to face
with your own mortality and survive, it can
give you a different and deeper understanding of the fragile nature of our time here on
earth.

"Mr. Jared, didn't you hear me?" Jared realized that Patrick O'Reilly had been speaking to him and was now looking at him
quizzically. "I asked if you would be doin'

us the courtesy of providin' an advance on our wages. We're gonna be needin' to finance this expedition, if you get my meanin'." The cowboys huddled around expectantly.

Jared dismounted and reached into his saddlebags to pull out a small sack. He turned to the cowboys and said, "I'll give each of you a five dollar gold piece but once that's gone, there'll be no more." The cowboys began whooping and Joe Hargrove threw his hat in the air. When their shouts died down, Jared continued. "Five dollars sounds like a lot but you'll find there's many different ways to spend it and you ain't gonna have enough money to try all of'em. Remember, beer's cheaper than whiskey, most of the card games are rigged and any time you spend with some calico queen is gonna go by faster than you think."

At the mention of the ladies of the evening, the cowboys let out another whoop and Patrick O'Reilly shouted out, "Here's to the calico queens . . . hip hip hooray!!"

Jared smiled in spite of himself, remembering his first cattle drive at the age of seventeen and that first town they'd come to up the trail. He'd been just as excited and made all the same mistakes these boys were about to make so there was little point

121

in his sermonizing about the pitfalls they might encounter. He waited for the noise to die down a bit, then said, "Listen up, cowboys, here's the plan. When we first hit town, we'll stay together and find the biggest saloon, one where I can get a steak. That'll be headquarters and it's where you'd better wind up around midnight. I ain't gonna follow you around but if I have to come lookin' for you, it'll spoil your evenin', I promise you!"

As he finished speaking, Jared realized that Felipe Lopez had walked away from the group and hadn't collected the advance on his wages. Jared walked over to where the vaquero stood and asked, "Ain't you plannin' to head into town with the rest of us, Felipe?"

Felipe looked at the ground and scuffed his boot in the dust. "No, senor Jared, I think I stay here with the herd. We got to leave pretty early in the morning and I don't want to fall off my horse tomorrow."

Something in his manner made Jared realize the cowboy was uncomfortable but he wasn't sure what it was. He was just about to question him further when Juan coughed over by the campfire. Jared glanced over at him and Juan jerked his head for him to come over. Jared walked over to the fire and said quietly, "What's goin' on with Felipe?"

"In case you hadn't noticed, compadre, Felipe is the only cowboy with brown skin in the bunch. I think he figures that could lead to trouble once folks get a few drinks under their belts." Juan pushed his hat back and looked at Jared. "Raton is a pretty tough town, amigo. Not everybody is as friendly as we are down in Cimarron."

Jared shook his head at his own lack of understanding. "You're right, pard, I don't know what I was thinkin'. I'll go let him off the hook."

Walking back over to where Felipe stood, Jared said, "Juan told me he needed you here to help hold the herd in case we don't get back until late. I hate to make you miss the party tonight but I'm afraid I'm gonna have to ask you to stay back."

Felipe looked Jared in the eyes for the first time and said, "Si, senor. If you need me here, I'll stay."

Jared could feel the tension pass as Felipe was relieved of the burden of having to explain his reluctance to go to town with the other cowboys. Nodding to the vaquero, he walked back over to where the eager cowhands stood. "All right, boys, it's almost time to get started. I'll tell you once more.

We got a tough haul over that pass tomorrow and you all need to be awake in the saddle. We'll pick a spot to meet up and you better be there at midnight or I'll leave you there in town."

Jared tried to accompany his last statement with a stern look and it seemed to work, at least momentarily, as the men grumbled a bit, then quieted down. Jared continued. "Now, let's mount up but I'm tellin' you, I don't want to race all the way to town. We can do a steady trot, if you please." His last words were drowned out as the cowboys began whooping it up again as they raced to mount their horses. Jared glanced over at Juan and Miguel, grinned and shrugged his shoulders. They just looked at him and shook their heads. Jared went back to his horse and mounted up, realizing that if he didn't hurry, he would be left behind.

It took Jared almost a half a mile to catch up with his crew. He pulled up to the lead and reined in, waving his hat at the bunch. They slowed down reluctantly and he turned to resume a slower trot. When they fell in behind him, he shouted over his shoulder, "Stay behind me until we get to town!" They trotted on for about fifteen minutes and during that time Jared had to shoot stern looks at several cowboys who showed signs of spurring their ponies and galloping for town.

Around dusk, they entered the main street of town on the north side and Jared immediately saw that the road was a quagmire of mud. He figured Raton had been pounded with the same thunderstorms they had endured a few days back and it still hadn't dried out. He stayed to the right side of the street where the wagon ruts weren't as deep and made his way about a quarter of a mile before he saw what he was looking for. Just ahead on the right was a sign that said "Wild Mustang Saloon" and above the name was a surprisingly artistic painting of a bronc breaking in two. Jared reckoned this would do and he pulled his horse up to the driest spot by the hitching rail. He dismounted and tied off his mount as the other cowboys did the same.

He held up his hand to get their attention and said, "Boys, this might be a good place for you to start out. You can grab a beer, and chances are you'll be able to find out more about what pleasures the town has to offer while you drink it."

No sooner than he finished speaking, the hands took off through the door. Jared moved at a more leisurely pace and when he entered the establishment, he saw that it wasn't a bad-looking place. Instead of a plank laid on top of sawhorses, they had an honest-to-goodness wooden bar and there were tables and chairs as well. Although there were quite a few men there already, it was early enough that there were still some vacant tables. Jared made his way to one and pulled up a chair. He glanced around and noticed that there were serving girls running back and forth, taking orders and bringing out large platters laden down with steaks, potatoes and beans. He leaned back in his chair and waited for an opportunity to catch the eye of one of the ladies. His patience was soon rewarded and a young woman approached his table. She was rather plain and thick-set, dressed in calico with her hair pulled back in a bun.

"What can I get for you, cowboy?"

"Good evenin', m'am," Jared said in his slow Texas drawl. "I think I'd like one of those steaks I see you carryin' out to folks. Also, I've got some questions, if you don't mind."

"What sorta questions you got?" the young lady said with some caution.

"Well, I'm kind of lookin' out for that herd of young cowboys over yonder at the bar.

They been out on the trail for a week and they're ready to kick up their heels." Jared grinned at the girl. "I just need to know where they might go to get into trouble so I know where to start lookin' to get'em out of it later on tonight."

The girl smiled at him and said, "Most folks is just lookin' to get into trouble. I don't run into many that are lookin' to get out of it."

"Well, I don't want'em to come to any harm and besides, I need'em to make it the rest of the way over the mountain and on to Pueblo." Jared tipped his hat to the waitress. "I'm Jared Delaney from down near Cimarron. We're herdin' three hundred head up through the pass tomorrow mornin'."

The young woman nodded to him and said, "I'm Ellie Rogers. My daddy is Big Jim Rogers. He owns this place. He could prob'ly answer your questions better than me."

When Jared heard the girl's name, he felt a pang of loneliness. In tender moments when no one was around, he sometimes called Eleanor by that name. "It's nice to make your acquaintance, Miss Rogers. After I get my steak, I'd appreciate it if you'd ask your daddy to come over so we could talk a bit."

"I'd be right glad to do that, Mr. Delaney. I'll get your order in to the cook right away." The girl hurried off to the kitchen and Jared looked around again. As before, he noticed that the place was crowded but with all that, it still had an air of calm about it. He'd spent time enough in saloons to develop a feel for level of tension. Some, like this one, seemed relaxed and friendly, while others felt like the air was charged with lightning and thunder, sort of like the moment right before a thunderstorm breaks. He halfway hoped his crew would stick to this location but he noticed that the ladies serving the food seemed to be just that . . . ladies serving food. It appeared that they had stumbled into a respectable place, which suited him just fine. However, he suspected his young charges were looking for something on the wilder side and would likely be moving on to more promising pastures before long.

Ellie Rogers brought Jared his steak, potatoes and beans, along with a large mug of beer. He took a big gulp and savored it for a moment before digging into his meal. He was just polishing off the last bite of steak when he sensed an imposing presence approaching the table. He looked up and saw one of the largest men he'd ever seen in his life walking up to where he sat. He was so surprised that he caught his breath and the last bite of steak got stuck in his throat momentarily. Luckily, he was able to choke it down without making a fool of himself.

"Howdy," said the giant in a surprisingly high voice. "I'm Jim Rogers. They call me Big Jim. I'm the owner of this place."

Jared stood up and stuck out his hand . . . well, he stuck it up, in truth. Even when he was standing, the man towered over him and Jared was not small by any means. "I reckon I understand why they call you Big Jim," he said with a chuckle. "I'm Jared Delaney from down Cimarron way. Pleased to make your acquaintance." The man took the hand Jared offered, and although he didn't appear to be making an effort to crush it, Jared felt his bones grind together. He was relieved when the man released his grip.

"My daughter, Ellie, said you had some questions for me. How can I help?"

Jared motioned to one of the other chairs and asked, "Do you have a few minutes? I just want to get the lay of the land so I know where to go lookin' for my hands if they don't show up when I told'em to."

"I reckon I could give you that information, pard." The big fellow took a stride and sat in one of the chairs. Jared heard it creak and was concerned that it might give way under the man's weight. He shifted his own chair a bit farther away so his foot wouldn't get crushed should that unfortunate event occur. "We got quite a number of saloons right here on First Street. Some of'em are respectable joints like this one here, but a few are good places to lose all your money in a crooked card game or get a knife stuck up under your ribs."

Although Jared was looking for information, he realized that he was hungry for a conversation with another human being that didn't revolve around the topic of cattle. He said, "I noticed right off that this is a pretty peaceful place . . . nice bar, tables and chairs, ladies waitin' on the customers. How long you been here, Big Jim?"

Big Jim rested his elbows on the table, which tilted a bit in his direction. "I been runnin' the Wild Mustang for five years now." He was quiet for a moment then he continued. "I came out here with my wife and daughter about seven years ago from St. Louis. I worked in the mercantile for two years and with the money I saved along with the stake I brought with me from back East, I bought this place."

"I met your daughter already," Jared said. "Is your wife in the back cookin' up these fine steaks?"

Big Jim looked down at the table. "My wife passed away three years ago. I think she must of got pneumonia, we never rightly knew. There was no doctor in town back then to try to heal her or even figure out what was wrong."

Jared felt foolish for thinking the man's wife was back in the kitchen cooking. "I'm mighty sorry to hear that, Jim. I've lost family myself and I know it ain't easy. My sympathies."

The big man looked Jared in the eye. "It is hard, no gettin' around it, but a man's got to carry on. That's what I've tried to do with Ellie's help."

Jared glanced around the place and said, "Well, it looks to me that you've done a fine job. This is a nice establishment. Right classy."

Big Jim beamed at Jared's praise. "That was real important to Annie. She'd appreciate your sayin' that. She didn't want it to be no low class place like some of the dives around town." Jim was momentarily distracted by a loud noise over by the bar, which turned out to be an empty plate being dropped by one of the serving girls. Once he determined that it was a minor occurrence that didn't require his attention, he turned back to Jared and proudly said, "I painted that picture of a mustang over the door my own self."

"Why Jim, that's a mighty life-like picture." Jared smiled. "I have to tell you, though, I'm havin' a hard time imaginin' a fella your size breakin' wild mustangs." Jared chuckled. "As I think about it, I reckon most of the mustangs I've seen would have a hard go of it buckin' with you sittin' astride'em."

Big Jim laughed along with Jared. "I don't ride much. I mostly watch and paint what I see. If I need to go a distance, I generally hitch up a team and take the wagon." He pointed over to the wall over the bar and said, "See them paintings up there? They're all mine."

Jared glanced over to where Jim was pointing and noticed for the first time a series of paintings hung above the row of whiskey bottles behind the bar. There were paintings of horses standing by a stream or running across the plains, and one of two stallions locked in combat while a group of mares anxiously looked on. They were all unbelievably life-like and were as good as anything Jared had ever seen in his travels through the southwest. "My goodness, Jim, you're an artist!"

"Well, thanks," the big man said. "I'd never really done anything like that before I painted that mustang above the door. Annie liked it and told me I should do some more. She said I had a knack for it." He stopped for a moment, getting that far-away look in his eyes again. "After she passed, I didn't paint for a long while, it just hurt too much. Then I figured out that she probably wouldn't want me to stop so I took it up again." He smiled. "Now when I paint a good'un, I think about Annie lookin' down at it from up above. I know she's admirin' it, noddin' her head and smilin'. It makes me feel good."

Jared shook his head with wonder. "Don't you beat all, Big Jim. To look at you, a fella wouldn't think you were an artist. I'd have an easier time imaginin' you knockin' rowdy drunks' heads together."

Jim laughed. "Oh, I can do that, too. When we first started here, we had our share of rowdies. Mostly cowboys just blowin' off steam but a few rough customers, too. The cowboys learned that they'd just have to behave if they wanted to come in. The food's pretty good and most of'em decided it was worth their while to act right." Big Jim's eyes got a hard look. "Those rough customers were another matter. It took

133

some broken bones to get the message across but now they pass on by our place and head down First Street for the rougher joints."

That reminded Jared that his original reason for wanting to talk to the man was to find out about the other places in town where his cowboys might wind up. "Speakin' of rougher joints, maybe you could tell me the location of some of'em? I reckon I'll prob'ly have to go fish a few hands out later in the evenin'." Jared grinned. "I figure the boys'll be lookin' for whiskey, girls and card games, most likely in that order."

"I'll not only tell you the location, I'll walk on down there with you when the time comes. We're mostly an eatin' joint, so we close up earlier than the other places."

"Why, I appreciate that, Jim. That'd be mighty helpful."

The big man leaned back in his chair and once again, it squeaked in a way that made Jared nervous. "We got some spots where a cowboy can find all those vices you mentioned. Cisnero's Saloon, the Monte Cristo, Blackwell's Saloon, those are the most likely places. If your hands ask a few questions, that's where folks'll direct'em."

Jared glanced around the Wild Mustang and realized that all his cowboys had vanished like smoke from a campfire. He'd been engrossed in his conversation with Big Jim and didn't know when they'd left but he figured they'd probably had a drink, asked the bartender where they might find some action and skeedaddled out of there. "Looks like that's just what they did." Jared grinned. "I reckon I can nurse a beer along, watch the people and give'em some time to sew a few wild oats."

"I need to go back in the kitchen and make sure they're keepin' up with the orders. We got some music startin' up in a little while. That might help you pass the time while you wait."

"I appreciate that, Jim. I don't want to keep you from doin' your job. What sort of music might you be havin'?"

"We got two fellas . . . one plays a banjo and one a mouth harp. They'll sing some of your favorite songs, I guarantee it, and they'll do'em up proper."

"I reckon I'll enjoy that," Jared said. "We do some fiddle playin' at the ranch and have a high old time."

Big Jim stood up and Jared could swear the chair gave a sigh of relief. "If that's the case, you're gonna like these boys. I'll check back on you in a while."

The big man walked away towards the

kitchen and Jared settled in to wait for his wild ones to have their fun. He had another beer and watched the customers with interest. He noticed that most of them didn't seem much different from the folks he knew in Cimarron. There were some loud ones and some quiet ones, but they were all generally respectful of one another.

After awhile, Ellie Rogers came out with a slab of apple pie and a big mug of coffee for him. Right after she'd served him, two men came in the front door and walked over to the corner of the saloon not far from where he was sitting. One carried a banjo and sure enough, the other fella pulled a mouth harp out of his pocket. Pretty soon, they were making some lively music and as Big Jim had promised, they played some of Jared's favorites. They did a nice version of "Sweet Betsy From Pike" and a rendition of "The Old Chisolm Trail" that included some of the bawdier verses. Before Jared knew it, several hours had melted away and Big Jim was walking over to his table.

"I'm about done around here. Do you want to head out and see if you can round up your strays?"

Jared drank the last swallow of coffee and stood up. "That sounds like a good idea. I'll follow you."

As they walked down First Street, Big Jim pointed out various locations. There was a bank on the opposite side of the street and a mercantile just a block down from the Wild Mustang. Just beyond the mercantile, Jared spotted a sign that read "Blackwell's Saloon."

"That's one of the names you mentioned up yonder. I reckon we ought to make our first stop there."

Big Jim eased his bulk along the wooden walkway. "That would be a good bet. Blackwell's ain't the roughest spot in town but they do have some sportin' gals. That would make it a likely place to start lookin'."

As they got closer to the swinging doors that opened out onto the boardwalk, Jared could hear whooping and hollering from inside the establishment. He went in first, followed by Big Jim, and glanced around the crowded saloon. The smoke was thick and cowboys were lined up double at the bar but in a moment, Jared's eyes adjusted to the dim light and he spotted the O'Reilly brothers leaning up against the long plank laid on top of saw horses that served as the bar. As he walked in their direction, he could see that they had a bottle and two glasses in front of them. As he got closer, he could see that Sean was leaning against his brother and seemed to be out on his feet.

Patrick O'Reilly glanced in his direction, squinted and then gave a big smile of recognition. In his Irish brogue that seemed to have thickened with the drink, he hollered, "Saints preserve us! If it ain't himself, Mr. Jared Delaney, the finest cow boss in the West Come have a drink with me and me drunken Irish brother." Sean's eyes were closed but he raised his head a bit and smiled.

The cowboys on either side of the brothers had looked at them with irritation when Patrick began hollering but when they saw Jared and Big Jim approaching, they backed away and looked in the other direction. "Faith and begorra," Patrick exclaimed. "Look, brother, Mr. Jared's gone and found himself a giant. If it's not Finn McCool, it's sure enough his cousin!" Sean opened one eye, smiled again and then nodded off.

Jared laughed in spite of himself. "This is no giant, Patrick, it's my new friend, Big Jim Rogers. And I reckon the last thing you boys need is another drink." He clapped a hand on Patrick's shoulder and said, "It's time to head back to the herd. I've come to round you boys up. I hope you had your fun and it was worth the headache you'll be ridin' with in just a few hours when the mornin' comes."

Patrick looked at Jared with mock indignation. "I'm beggin' your pardon, Mr. Jared Delaney. Irishmen don't get headaches from the drink."

He gestured wildly with his arms and when he did, Sean slipped off his shoulder and fell face first down on the bar with a solid thunk. Patrick looked over at his brother and turned back to Jared. "However, we sometimes get headaches from bangin' our heads on the bar." He seemed to think this was the funniest thing he'd ever seen and doubled over with laughter.

Jared shook his head and wondered about how to proceed. Patrick and Sean weren't in very good condition to travel but he needed to find Tom Stallings and Joe Hargrove. He was afraid if he left the brothers here, they would continue drinking or get in some worse shenanigans. He finally decided that a walk in the night air might do a world of good at sobering them up a bit. "Patrick, my lad," he said in his best imitation of an Irish brogue, "it's time for us to shove off. You walk with me and we'll let my new friend, Big Jim, assist your inebriated little brother."

"I appreciate your offer of assistance, kind sir," Patrick slurred, "but I'm quite capable of walking under me own powers." He took a step away from the bar and stumbled. Jared grabbed him under the arms and helped him stand upright. "Seems like the earth is shiftin' a might. Maybe it's not a bad idea for you to give me a hand after all."

"That's why I'm here, Patrick. Have you paid the bartender for this bottle?"

"Of course we have, Mr. Jared. We're not bloody Englishmen, after all. We spent our last coins on the bottle." Patrick smiled knowingly at Jared. "Not before we spent a few coins for some sport with the soiled doves who frequent this lovely establishment." This statement struck his funny bone and again, he doubled over with laughter.

"Well, good for you, Patrick. I reckon you boys had the time of your lives. Now it's time to get a move on back to the herd and we've got to find Tom and Joe. Any idea where they wound up?"

"We left them in a fine establishment called the Monte Cristo, just down the street," Patrick replied, carefully enunciating his words even as he slurred them. "I've no way of knowin' if they remained there or moved on to greener pastures. They spent some time with the ladies there but then Tommy boy said he wanted to find a game of chance so he could win his money back."

Jared looked over at Big Jim, who was helping Sean O'Reilly up. A small trickle of blood ran from his nose over his lip and Big Jim used Sean's arm like a napkin to blot it away. Sean once again opened one eye and looked around to see what was happening. When he saw Big Jim, both his eyes opened wide and he stared in disbelief. "Holy mother of God!" he exclaimed. "Sure and it's Finn McCool. Jaysus, Mary and Joseph!"

Jim helped Sean get his hat on straight and boosted him up so he was standing upright. He turned to Jared and said, "If those other boys went lookin' for a game, they most likely wound up at Cisneros." A worried look crossed his face. "That's the toughest place in town and they run some crooked games there. We might want to get a move on down in that direction."

Jared hailed the bartender to make sure the brothers had settled their tab. He walked down to where they stood and Jared asked, "Did my boys pay up on what they owe you, pard?"

The bartender smiled. "They paid up and I even spotted'em a couple of free shots of whiskey. That taller one is about as comical a fellow as I've been around in quite a spell.

He talks kinda funny so I didn't understand everything he said but what I did catch had me in stitches. Them boys are welcome back in here any time they feel like comin' in."

Jared laughed. "We're headed up the trail through the pass in the mornin', makin' our way to Pueblo. We'll prob'ly stop back by on the way back down to Cimarron so there's a good chance Patrick will get the chance to entertain you again. Thanks for lookin' out for the lads."

The bartender nodded and moved off down the bar to tend to another customer. Jared got a firm grip on Patrick O'Reilly's left arm and moved him out toward the door. Patrick started singing a song about Molly Malone and her wheelbarrow and a few of the patrons at the table nearest the door applauded as they were walking out. Patrick stopped to doff his cowboy hat and almost fell on his face. Jared was able to use his momentum to swing him around in the right direction and they headed on out the door.

Big Jim already had Sean outside and was headed south on First Street. He called back over his shoulder. "Cisnero's is a couple of blocks down this way. Let's get these drunken Irishmen down there, then I'll wait outside with'em while you fetch your other hands."

"Sounds like a plan," Jared replied as he struggled to help Patrick walk a straight line. Patrick continued to sing at the top of his lungs and was waving grandly with his right arm as they walked along.

"You're a good boss, Mr. Jared Delaney, did you know that about yourself?"

The last thing Jared wanted was to be having a conversation with a drunken Irishman on the streets of Raton just before midnight. "And you're a good hand, Patrick, and a mighty fine singer, too."

With this slight bit of encouragement, Patrick launched into another old Irish song, this one about an Irish martyr who was hung for opposing the British. Jared found the singing mildly annoying, but he figured it was better than trying to have a discussion with the inebriated cowboy. They were almost to Cisnero's Saloon and Big Jim was already trying to get Sean seated on a wooden bench a little ways up the walkway from the door. He leaned him back against the wall but Sean seemed to be listing to the right. When Jared got there with Patrick, he helped him get seated to the right of Sean. Sure enough, he listed to the left and the two brothers wound up supporting each other as they sat on the bench.

Patrick was still singing and Sean joined in without opening his eyes.

"Jim, you want to stay here with the lads while I go collect my other two boys?"

"I'll do it," Big Jim replied. "Holler if you need my help."

Jared walked away from Jim and the boys toward the door to Cisnero's Saloon. As he got to the door, it struck him that the atmosphere was much less boisterous than at Blackwell's place where they'd found Patrick and Sean. He walked in and saw that there were patrons lined up at yet another plank bar along the right side of the room. The rest of the room was filled with tables where men appeared to be playing cards. There was very little laughter like there had been at the other establishments he had frequented that night and quite a few of the men eyed him with suspicion or even outright hostility. The atmosphere was in stark contrast to what he'd experienced when he walked into the Wild Mustang Saloon. His thoughts flashed back to the first time he'd walked into the Colfax Tavern in Cimarron several years back. He had a clear memory of that sense of tension, like a bronc that's getting ready to break in two. Considering how that encounter had played out, the association was not one designed to give him comfort. He looked around the room and saw Joe Hargrove walking toward him rapidly, looking like a cat whose tail had been set afire.

"You need to get over here pronto, Mr. Jared." The young cowboy's words came out in a rush. "Tommy's in a heap of trouble!"

"Slow down there, Joe. Tell me what's happenin'."

"He got himself in a game with some card sharks," Hargrove said. "Them boys been cheatin' all night, I seen'em deal from the bottom of the deck with my own two eyes." He stopped for a breath. "I didn't say nothin' though cause they're rough customers. They're packin' six shooters and they look like they know how to use'em."

"Has Tom been losin'?" Jared asked.

"He's about ten dollars down, I reckon," Joe replied. When Jared started to protest, Joe anticipated his question. "I know, he didn't even start out with that much. They been givin' him credit, actin' all friendly like." Hargrove looked down at the floor. "They been askin' him about the herd, Mr. Jared. I got a hunch they may be plannin' some mischief for later on. Tom told'em where we're camped for the night and everything."

Jared shook his head in disgust. He won-

145

dered to himself whether Stallings planned these calamities or whether they just happened to him naturally. "That just takes the cake. Well, let's see if I can get him out of this mess without it turnin' ugly." Jared looked over to where Stallings sat with four tough looking hombres.

"Mr. Jared, I ain't carryin' no weapon. What do we do if they start a play?" Joe looked around anxiously as if he thought more help might materialize.

Jared had already given this some thought and had come up with the best plan he could under the circumstances. "Joe, follow behind me while I talk to these fellas. If things get heated and you hear me say 'don't get your Irish up,' I want you to quietly turn, walk out the door and down the walk to your right about twenty feet."

"I couldn't just leave you alone, Mr. Jared!"

"Listen to me, Joe. Outside, you'll see a fella about twice your size. As quick as you can, tell him his new friend, Jared Delaney, needs his help inside and fast. Then you stay there with Sean and Patrick so nothin' happens to them." Jared looked into Joe's eyes to make sure he understood. "All right, then. Listen real careful and if you hear the words, 'don't get your Irish up,' do just what

I told you. You understand me?"

"I reckon so," Joe answered. "I just hope it don't come to gun play."

"Me, too, Joe," Jared said. "Me, too. If my large friend can get inside in time, we might be able to head off a shoot out. Now, be ready."

Jared walked toward the table as casually as he could manage with Joe Hargrove walking a few steps behind. He walked up behind Tom Stallings who looked up anxiously as Jared put his hand on his shoulder.

"Howdy, fellas," he said in the friendliest voice he could muster. "Looks like you been givin' my young hand here some lessons in poker. I hate to spoil the party but we ride out early and I need to get him on back to camp."

One of the men, a skinny fellow with a flat-brimmed hat, greasy black hair and a handlebar moustache looked up with a sneer. "Your hand still owes us a tidy sum, mister. I reckon he needs to stay and make good on his debts."

Jared noticed that the man was wearing a two-gun rig, which he took as a likely sign that he was a gunslinger. The other three men were all wearing gun belts with one pistol. He figured if push came to shove, Mr. Handlebars was the one he'd have to take out first and fast. He said, "Well, I reckon we can find a fair way to settle up but there ain't no discussion about when he leaves. I'm his boss and I say he leaves now."

Handlebars smiled a cruel smile. "You may be *his* boss but you ain't my boss, cowpoke. If that young rascal tries to leave now, y'all may have more trouble on your hands than you want."

Jared could sense the tension at the table rising. He felt his pulse quicken. Out of the corner of *his* eye, he saw two of the men slowly scoot their chairs back in preparation for the altercation they were anticipating. He decided it was time to change the odds a bit. "Now, don't get your Irish up, pardner." He sensed that Joe Hargrove had quietly turned and was headed for the door. Hoping to draw the gunslinger's attention away from this, he put his hands up in the air and smiled. "I'm sure there's some way we can work this out friendly like."

"I ain't Irish and don't be so sure about a friendly outcome here," the man with the two-gun rig said. "You go welshin' on your bets in this town, you're likely to wind up with a bullet in you and I'll have three witnesses that'll swear it was self-defense."

Tom Stallings was trembling slightly, whether from fear or anger, Jared didn't know. He figured things were going to hell in a hand basket pretty quick and he hoped that Big Jim wouldn't dawdle on the street. Jared had taken about as much guff from the man as he was willing to stomach. As casually as he could, he took a step off to the side so Stallings wouldn't be directly in the line of fire if the gunslinger made his play.

"That's pretty big talk from a cheatin' card shark," Jared said evenly. The man's eyes bulged out with surprise and anger. "I hear tell you been dealin' from the bottom of the deck. I reckon my hand don't owe you anything and consider yourself lucky we don't sic the sheriff on you."

With a concerted effort, the man got his anger under control. Jared could see him eye-balling the six-shooter he wore on his belt and calculating the odds. Clearly, they had the numbers on their side but they were all still seated while Jared was standing . . . and in a better position to draw and fire. "You're mighty brash, my friend, but I don't believe you can pull it off. You don't seem to know who you're messin' with here. I chew up cowboys like you and spit'em in the street." The man put his hands on the table and Jared anticipated that he was preparing to push back, jump up and draw.

He felt a surge of nervous energy mixed with fear.

"Hey there, Sam. How's the arm healin' up?"

All the heads at the table, along with Jared's, swiveled in the direction from where the high-pitched voice had come. To his relief, Jared saw that Big Jim was standing about ten feet away, smiling and holding a sawed-off shotgun, which was loosely pointed in the direction of the man with the greasy handlebar moustache.

"What's it to you, you big galoot?" Handlebars spat out. "I ain't lookin' for trouble from you, I'm just tryin' to collect what's owed me."

"Why Sam," Big Jim said with a big smile on his face, "everyone knows you're a cheat and a card shark. The way I see it, this youngster don't owe you nothin'."

Sam looked rapidly from side to side at his compadres. It was clear to Jared and apparently to Sam as well that they were fast losing their enthusiasm for an altercation. Jared put two and two together, realizing these were some of the rough customers who's bones Jim had broken in the past. "That's funny, Big Jim, I was just sayin' the same thing to old Sam here. I reckon if young Mr. Stallings will just get up real slow and walk toward the door, we can settle this without any further unpleasantness." With his hand, he nudged Stallings, who needed no further encouragement. He carefully pulled his chair out, got up and walked quickly toward the door.

Sam's eyes flashed like lightning. He ignored Big Jim and looked directly at Jared. "You're lucky you got backup, cowboy. That saved your bacon tonight. Just don't count on havin' old Goliath around all the time. When he ain't around, things'll be different, I guarantee it."

The fear Jared had experienced a moment before had transformed into a slow burning anger. He'd had his fill of being threatened by bullies and gunslingers in the past, and he wasn't about to stand for it from this greasy-haired rapscallion. "More big talk, pard, but talkin' don't get it done. If you come lookin' for trouble from me, that's exactly what you'll get and more of it than you can handle . . . and I *guarantee that!*" He continued to stare down the gunslinger, saying out of the corner of his mouth, "Let's head on out of here, Jim. I don't like the company."

Big Jim said, "You back on out and when you hit the door, I'll come on behind you. I got a feelin' one of these boys just might be a back-shootin' bushwhacker and I don't want to see my friend Cisneros get blood on the floor of his fine establishment."

Jared nodded and turned to walk out, looking carefully back over his shoulder as he went. Sam, the greasy-haired gunslinger, stared at him through eyes like slits. If he didn't know better, Jared would have sworn sparks of hate were flying out of those slits in his direction. He did his best to look unconcerned. When he got to the door, he stepped outside but stood where he could see in to make sure Big Jim made it out safely. He could see Jim speaking to the ruffians but couldn't hear what he had to say. In a minute, Big Jim turned as if he had not a care in the world and walked out the door.

"Where in the world did you come up with that sawed-off hog you're carryin'?" Jared asked breathlessly.

"I slipped in and spoke with my good friend, Henry Cisneros. He owns the joint and happens to be tendin' bar tonight. He's a pretty sharp fella and he'd already noticed the trouble brewin'. When he saw me, he just handed it right over."

Jared let out a sigh of relief. "I reckon it pays to have good friends, don't it?" He looked down the walk to where Tom Stallings and Joe Hargrove were watching them anxiously. "By the way, what did you say to those boys before you came out?"

"I just gave'em a friendly reminder of what would happen to'em if they tried to come back into my place and raise a stink." Big Jim chuckled. "Seems like they've got some painful memories from their last visit to the Wild Mustang. I reckon that'll make'em think twice about causin' any more trouble."

Jared said his thank you's and goodbye's to Big Jim, promising to stop in on the way back from Pueblo in a few weeks. He then turned his attention to the problem of how to get two drunken Irishmen and their horses back to camp. Patrick and Sean were where Big Jim had left them on the bench outside Cisnero's Saloon. Joe Hargrove and Tom Stallings had gone to gather the horses and were just now returning. As they pulled up to the hitching rail and dismounted, Jared walked over to them.

"Joe, you and Tom'll each have to take an Irishman on in front of you. Wrap your arms around'em and hang on tight so they don't slide off. I'll lead their horses and follow behind so if you do lose one of'em, I can get to him before too long." Jared noticed that as he gave his instructions, Tom Stallings was looking everywhere but in his eyes.

153

"Mr. Jared, you may have to hold them boys on while we get mounted up," Joe said. "I reckon they'd slip right off if you don't."

"I expect you're right about that, Joe. Let's start with Patrick. He was awake the last time I talked to him."

Jared walked over to where the boys were slumped over against each other and to his chagrin, Patrick had also apparently passed out. Jared called his name, to no avail, and then reached over and shook him roughly by the shoulders. "Patrick, come on, let's get movin'. We got cattle to drive."

"Comin', ma," Patrick muttered. "Give me just a minute."

"I'm not your ma, you drunken Irishman," Jared growled. "Let's go, up and at'em."

He reached down, grabbed Patrick's wrists and tugged him into a standing position. Patrick wobbled a bit but remained upright with one eye barely open. With Joe's help, they walked him over to Joe's horse. While Jared supported Patrick, Joe managed, with some difficulty, to get Patrick's left foot in the stirrup. With Joe pulling on Patrick's right leg and Jared shoving from underneath, they managed to swing him onto the saddle. The horse shied to the right in the middle of the process, causing Jared's

154

heart to leap into his throat but he was able to grab the reins and get him under control quickly so no harm was done. Once Patrick was on, Jared was able to keep him steady while Joe mounted up behind the saddle. He didn't look any too happy about how he was mounted but he didn't complain.

"I told you, ma, I'll be right there. Please quit screamin' like a banshee. Sure and you're makin' me head hurt."

"He ain't your ma, Patrick and no one's screamin' at you," Joe said with a giggle. "Just hang on tight and don't fall into no cactus."

Jared told Joe to wait there and walked over to where Tom Stallings was standing by his horse. Tom finally looked at Jared in the face and said, "Guess I made a mess of things again, Mr. Jared." He couldn't hold Jared's gaze and looked down again. "Guess I do that a lot."

Jared didn't speak for a moment, trying to maintain his composure. He knew Tom hadn't done anything wrong out of spite, and yet he feared that his association with those ruffians was going to be a problem again, maybe even before the night was over. "I know you didn't mean no harm, Tom, but you got to learn to pick your companions with more care. Those boys are some rough customers. I'm afraid we ain't seen the last of'em."

Tom looked up with concern. "You don't think they'll come out to where we're camped and start trouble, do you?"

"They might," Jared said.

Tom reacted as if he'd been slapped. "Mr. Jared, I told'em where we were camped. I didn't think about it, I was just makin' conversation." He took off his hat and raked his hand through his shock of brown hair. "They were actin' friendly, askin' questions and such. It never crossed my mind it would cause problems."

"Well, we don't know if it will or not," Jared said. "We just have to be ready for trouble in case it comes our way." He reached out and gave Stallings a firm pat on the shoulder. "If it turns out you've made a mess, you'll just have to do your part in cleanin' it up. Now, come on and help me get this other drunken Irishmen on your horse."

Sean proved to be more difficult to deal with than his older brother who was at least barely awake. Sean, on the other hand, was dead to the world. Tom and Jared had to lift him and lay him across the saddle, then Jared had to walk his right leg across the back of the horse while Tom tried to keep the horse from spooking and Sean from falling off. The entire process took quite awhile and Jared was feeling irritable as he thought about making the hard drive through the pass the next day after a short night's rest.

"We're gonna have to go slow, boys," Jared said as he grabbed the reins of the two Irishmen's horses and mounted up. "Like I said, you head out and I'll follow behind in case you lose one." *It'll give me a chance to watch out for an ambush, too*, he thought.

The trip back to camp was slow going. The nearly full moon rose majestically over the mountains, bathing the valley in moonlight and creating moon shadows around the boulders. The light made it easier for them to see their way, but also exposed them to rifle fire should anyone decide to take a shot at them. Fortunately, no one did, for which Jared was grateful. They were nearly back to the herd and Jared was just beginning to relax when he heard a number of rifle shots in rapid succession. He spurred his horse and as he rode by Joe and Tom, he shouted, "Stay here. Get those Irishmen out of the saddle and be on the look out for trouble comin' back your way.!"

He was almost at a full gallop when he crested the rise and looked down to see muzzle flashes coming from beneath the wagon. He figured Miguel and Juan had taken cover there and were firing at whoever had attacked the camp. Off to his right, he saw the silhouettes of four riders who were returning fire. As he looked closer, he saw that only three of the riders were shooting while the fourth was riding among the herd, whooping and slapping his hat against his leg in an attempt to spook the cattle. The steers were beginning to mill around and Jared realized that if he didn't do something quickly, this situation could turn into a nightmare.

Drawing his Winchester from its scabbard, he hollered as loud as he could. "Follow me, boys, we can take'em!" With a blood-curdling scream, he spurred his horse to a full gallop and began pouring lead down upon the interlopers. He saw one go down as the others looked his way. He continued shouting instructions to his imaginary followers as he emptied his rifle in their direction. He thought he might have wounded another one of the outlaws who jerked in the saddle, but things became increasingly confused as he drew closer to the herd. He heard the outlaws yelling at one another then saw them turn and gallop away from his approach off to the west. Jared saw more muzzle flashes from under the wagon and another one of the riders fell from his horse. He slowed his mount as he got closer to the wagon and hollered out, "Juan, Miguel, it's me . . . Jared. Hold your fire!"

The two men stopped firing and after a few seconds, he heard a voice say, "Nice of you to join us, amigo. You took your own sweet time getting here."

Jared chuckled in relief. "Juan, it's a long story and prob'ly not worth tellin' right now." He took his hat off and with his sleeve, wiped the sweat that had appeared on his brow in great quantity. "I've got to go back over the rise and get the rest of the boys back to camp before they get shot. Either of you fellas hit?"

Miguel stood up and walked out to where Jared sat on his horse. He was wearing his long johns. "No, I was sleeping under the wagon and when the commotion started, I just rolled over and grabbed my rifle." He looked around quickly and said, "Tomas raised the alarm but I don't know where he went. I'd better look for him."

"Juan, you need to check on those two rascals that went down to make sure they're not crawlin' around on their bellies like snakes lookin' to cause trouble. Don't let'em shoot Miguel while he's lookin' for Tomas. I'll go fetch the boys and come back

159

to help you sort out this mess."

Jared was just coming to the top of the rise when he heard gunfire coming from the direction of where he'd left the four young hands. The outlaws had doubled back to the south once they got some distance from the herd so they could head back toward town. Once again, he spurred his horse and drew his pistol but as he got closer, he realized the shooting had stopped. He hollered out to the boys that he was approaching and warned them not to shoot him. Joe Hargrove yelled back that they were holding their fire.

As Jared got closer, he could see one of the horses was down. He pulled up and dismounted. "Are you boys all right?"

Joe responded in a shaky voice. "I think we're all right but they shot one of the horses and it fell on Patrick."

Just then, Jared heard a groan and then the sound of laughter coming from the direction of the fallen horse. "Would someone please get this nag off me leg?"

Jared quickly surveyed the situation and turned to Joe and Tom. "What in tarnation happened here? How did that drunken Irishman let his horse fall on him?"

The cowboys looked at each other and shrugged. Joe said, "It happened pretty fast

160

so I ain't sure exactly how he did it. We took him off that nag and laid him out on the ground there. When the shootin' started, he sat up and looked around." Joe looked down at the ground. Then he looked up sheepishly. "When the horse got shot, it staggered around for a spell, then started to crumple to the ground. I guess it was right next to Patrick when it went down. I think he saw it comin' and tried to get out of the way, but he wasn't movin' all that fast and I reckon his leg got caught."

Stallings coughed. "Mr. Jared, things were happenin' real fast about that time, what with all the shootin'. We didn't have time to be lookin' out for Patrick, we were too busy shootin' and duckin'."

Jared looked from one cowhand to the other and shook his head. "I know that, boys. I think you did all right under the circumstances. We just need to get that horse off his leg and make sure nothin's broke." Jared walked over towards the dead animal. "Come on, give me a hand."

With the two cowboys grabbing the front and back of the saddle, they were able to shift the dead weight just enough that Jared could drag Patrick out from under. Patrick let out another groan of pain as he was pulled free. Once he got him clear of the horse, Jared said, "Lay still, Patrick and let me take a look at that leg."

Fearing the worst, Jared felt along Patrick's right leg, expecting at any moment to feel a bone protruding. To his relief, the leg seemed to be intact and relatively undamaged. "I think you're gonna be all right, big fella."

Patrick let out a sigh of relief. "Sure and I thought me leg was broke in two."

"Nope," Jared said. "It all seems to be in one piece but I expect it'll be awful sore for a few days, once you're sober enough to feel any pain. You're just lucky your ankle didn't get twisted up sideways underneath you when you fell."

Jared turned back to Joe and Tom. He noticed that Stallings hadn't said a word. "What happened, boys?"

Hargrove looked at Stallings, who remained silent, then he said, "We were just waitin' here like you told us to when out of the blue, these two fellas come a'ridin' all hell-bent for leather from the west. They started shootin' at us before we knew what was happenin'." He shook his head and spit on the ground. "Tell you the truth, I was so flustered, I dropped my gun pullin' it out of the holster. Tommy got his out though and danged if he didn't hit one of them rascals."

Jared turned to Stallings. In the bright moonlight, he could see that the young man was trembling and looking around in a dazed manner. "You all right, cowboy?"

Tom turned to look at Jared. His face was pale, perhaps from the moonlight and perhaps not. He said, "I never wanted to shoot no one, Mr. Jared. I didn't really mean to, I was just tryin' to keep'em from killin' us."

Jared reached out and put his hand on Stallings' shoulder. "Sometimes you don't have much choice. Looks to me like you did what needed doin'. That's all you can ask for in a man."

Stallings looked at Jared gratefully although he still appeared quite shaken. "I reckon you're right but I still don't feel any too good about it."

"I wouldn't think much of you if you did," Jared replied. "Takin' a life should never be cause for celebration but there's times it comes down to you or the other man and when it does, you got to make your stand. That's what you did."

"One of'em got away, Mr. Jared," Joe said. "He took off toward town. The other fella dropped off his horse just over yonder. Want me to go check on him?"

"Hold on," Jared said sharply. "Let me go

163

take a look to make sure he ain't playin' possum."

Jared crouched down as he glided silently in the direction Hargrove had pointed. Just ahead, he saw where the outlaw had fallen and he approached him with his gun drawn. He saw no movement and as he got closer, it was clear that the man was dead. He was sprawled out on the ground and his gun was several feet away where he had dropped it as he fell from his horse. Jared checked for signs of life and found none. He rolled the man over so that the moon shone on his face and realized that it was Sam, the greasy-haired gunman. He felt a brief twinge of pity for the lifeless figure, but then as he thought about the evil he'd been up to, he considered that maybe the man had gotten just what he deserved. *I don't know it word for word,* he thought, *but there's some-thin' in the bible about reapin' what you sow.*

Jared walked back to where the boys waited. "Let's head on back to camp, boys. I'll need Tom to help Juan settle the herd and Joe, I'm gonna need you to get a shovel and do some buryin'."

Joe looked crestfallen. He'd been anticipating spending a few precious hours in his bedroll before they started their long day over the pass. "Mr. Jared, these men were tryin' to steal your cows and fill us full of lead. Why would you bother with buryin'em?"

"Just cause they acted like savages don't mean we need to," Jared replied. "We'll do the right thing and the right thing is they get a burial, even if it is just a shallow grave with no marker."

"Yes sir," Joe said and shuffled over to mount up. He turned and asked, "What are we gonna do with Sean and Patrick?"

"You and Tom are gonna put'em back on your horses, ride over to Miguel's wagon and tell him I said to get some coffee brewin'. They're gonna sober up and help us out. They had their fun but now it's back to work and no slackin' allowed."

Jared heard a groan from the direction where Sean and Patrick were standing, but both lads gathered themselves and walked over to the horses without further complaint. Jared told the hands to mount up and get to camp pronto. Then he headed back to camp to get a better look at the damage and see what needed to be done before they began moving the herd up into Raton Pass. He didn't say anything to Joe Hargrove but he sympathized with the boy's disappointment about losing a night's sleep. He wasn't excited about it himself but he'd spent enough time on the trail to know that there were times when you just had to get tough and go on little or no sleep. *Looks like this is one of those times,* he thought.

As he approached the camp, he saw that Miguel had built a fire and was already brewing coffee. Miguel's son, Tomas crouched down by the fire with a mug in his hands. He rode up and dismounted. "You all right, Tomas?"

"Si, Senor Jared," Tomas responded with a grin. "They missed me this time."

As young as he was, Tomas Mares had been through some dangerous scrapes several years before when his father had stood by Jared in his battle with the O'Bannon clan. It did Jared's heart good to see the boy alive and well. He walked over to him and reached down to clap him on the shoulder. "Reckon it'll take more than a few cattle rustlers to take down the Mares boys, que no? You're some pretty tough hombres."

"You got that right, Senor Jared." Tomas grinned again. "I don't think those cabrones knew what they were doing though. I got to my horse and got around behind them and they didn't seem to know where I was. They were shooting off their pistols in the air but they didn't even come close to me." Tomas's grin faded. "I think maybe I hit one of them."

"Hard to know for sure," Jared said, "shootin' in the dark and all. We were all blazin' away. I believe there was four of'em and there's three down, which means one of those rascals got away." The thought of one of the outlaws getting away scot-free galled Jared and for a moment he considered pursuing the one survivor. "I hate to let him go but we just don't have time to spare to go chasin' after him. Maybe after what happened to his pards, in the future he'll think twice about tryin' to take what ain't his."

Miguel walked over to the fire from the wagon. As he got closer, Jared could see that he was scowling. "We got some bullet holes in the wagon but there's nothing to stop it from rolling out in the morning whenever you're ready."

"Better to have a few bullet holes in the wagon than in yours or Juan's hides," Jared joked. "Think what sorta bad humor you'd be in if you were all shot up."

Miguel didn't seem amused by Jared's joshing and ignored him as he went about straightening up his wagon. Jared took time to drink a cup of coffee then went out to supervise the hands as they gathered in the herd and surveyed the damage from the attack. Joe Hargrove got a shovel from Miguel and completed the unpleasant task of burying the three outlaws. When he returned to camp, he didn't speak about his chore but he appeared a bit green around the gills. Jared considered talking to him but decided against it, figuring he just needed to get back to work and move on from the harsh dose of reality he'd experienced.

Sean and Patrick O'Reilly joined the rest of the hands in getting the herd ready to make the trek across the pass. They were both moving a bit slower than usual and at one point, Jared saw Sean go off behind some brush. He heard retching sounds and knew the lad was paying the piper for his excesses of the night before. While he was sympathetic, Jared had no intention of letting the brothers slack off from their duties. Part of being a hand was doing your job whether you felt like it or not, and it was time for the O'Reilly brothers to learn that lesson, painful as it might be. Having been in the same position himself, Jared knew that a hangover was not a fatal condition and that the brothers would likely be wiser from the experience.

As the sun began peeking it's head over the mountains, the cowboys had the herd ready to go. Tired as they were, the mixture of rose and peach colors that were reflections of the sun's rays hitting the mountain slopes seemed to give them a burst of energy and inspiration. Jared and Juan rode out to the front of the herd and when Jared hollered "move out," he heard whoops of joy from back where Joe and Tom were riding drag. He smiled and thought, *maybe this'll work out all right after all.*

CHAPTER 12

Nathan was in a quandary. As if he didn't have enough to worry about with Barwick lurking around, he'd come back to his office that morning from making his rounds and found a fresh apple pie on his desk along with a note from Christine Johnson. He flushed with embarrassment when he remembered what she'd written in the note, that he needed more sweetness in his life or some such nonsense. It made him feel foolish to have a younger woman paying this sort of attention to him but if he was honest with himself, he also had to admit that he felt a bit of pleasure as well. *You durned old fool,* he thought, *she's got to be fifteen years younger than you, maybe more.*

The last thing he needed right now was to have his thinking muddled by a preoccupation with a woman. He'd been a bachelor all his life and had never been particularly bothered by that state of affairs. He wasn't prone to sitting around feeling lonely. There was always plenty to do and little time left over to think about what he might be missing. He'd always had friends and thought he was satisfied with the companionship that came with those friendships. He was surprised and a bit disconcerted to find that since Christine had been showing a romantic interest in him, he'd had passing thoughts about how it might be nice to have someone to greet him when he was finished with his day's work. He recognized the fact that Christine was an attractive woman, and spunky, too. She had a sharp wit and a good mind, qualities that would make her an excellent partner for someone who appreciated spirit in others. *And she **is** a fine lookin' woman, too,* he thought to himself.

With his thoughts thus engaged, it took him a moment to realize that he had walked right past the telegraph office, which had been his destination when he started out from his office. He cursed himself for a fool and backtracked, walking in to find Ben Martinez, the telegraph operator, standing behind the counter.

"Ben," he said, "I'm wonderin' if you got any messages for me. I'm expectin' somethin' from Santa Fe and I was hopin' it'd be here by today."

"Seems like I remember something coming in," Ben said as he turned to check his incoming box. "Yep, there's a couple of telegrams with your name on'em, Sheriff." He handed them to Nathan, waiting expectantly for him to open them and read them in his presence so he could ask him questions about the messages. "Ain't you gonna look at'em, Sheriff?"

Nathan knew that Ben was the local busybody and that spreading news in the form of gossip was his favorite pastime. Considering the nature of the information that was likely to be found in these telegrams, the last thing he needed was for their content to become fodder for the local rumor mill. He'd encouraged the folks at the other end of the telegraph line to be discreet in their responses and he didn't want to be pressured to explain the meanings of the messages. "Don't have time right now, Ben, I gotta get back to my office." Ignoring the disappointed look the telegraph operator sent his way, he said, "Thanks for your help."

"Any time, Sheriff," Ben said in a subdued voice.

As Nathan walked back to the jail, he noticed Lizbeth Kilpatrick stepping down from her wagon across the street at the mercantile. He waved and tipped his hat to her but because he was in a hurry to read his telegrams, he decided to forego crossing the street for a conversation. Lizbeth looked to be in a hurry as well. She smiled and waved in return but walked directly into the store, clearly interested in getting on with her business.

When Nathan got back to the jailhouse, he took off his hat and gun belt and hung them on the hat rack. Taking a seat at his desk, he tipped the chair back against the wall so that he had a clear view of the door and quick access to the top drawer where he kept a spare pistol. He proceeded to open the first of the two telegrams. It was from his old friend, the sheriff in Santa Fe. The telegram read: **Ring up to no good again stop TC and BC looking to grab up all they can stop Trouble headed your way if not there already stop Watch your back stop**

Nathan knew that TC was Tom Catron and BC was Bill Chapman, the leaders of the group known as the Santa Fe Ring. Although they had curbed their sleazy efforts to grab land from small farmers and ranchers over the last couple of years, he had suspected they were just biding their time waiting for the opportunity to get back in the game. This telegram confirmed his suspicion. He figured the "trouble headed" his way was the gunslinger, Barwick, although he couldn't rule out the possibility that the politicians had engaged the services of other rapscallions as well. Thinking about having to face off with these corrupt men and their henchmen yet another time left him feeling drained. He closed his eyes and leaned his head back against the wall. *When does a body get any rest,* he wondered? Almost immediately, he answered his own question . . . *It's the job you signed up for so quit your belly-achin'.*

Turning his attention to the second telegram, he saw that it was from the alcalde in Taos. It read: **Gentleman left Monday stop May be headed your way stop Had two compadres stop Don't know where they went but glad they ain't here no more stop Sorry if they coming to see you stop If it was me, I would consider getting some extra hands to help in case of trouble stop Good luck stop**

Nathan considered his friend's suggestion that he get help and shook his head in resignation. He knew that Jared Delaney felt this cattle business was a crucial step towards ensuring the financial future of the Kilpatrick ranch but right now was a terrible time for him to be gone, especially since he'd taken several of the most able-bodied hands with him. *Boys that'd do to ride the river with,* he thought, *but they ain't here so what good are they?* The alcalde's news was not a surprise, but it certainly confirmed his worst fear. One of the deadliest gunmen in the territory now might have help from two other ruffians who were most likely pretty handy with their six-shooters as well. Leaning his head back against the wall again and studying the ceiling, he wondered what else could go wrong.

Lizbeth had made a list of items she needed to purchase at the mercantile but she had that nagging feeling in the back of her mind that she was forgetting something. It was like an itch she couldn't quite reach to scratch and no matter how much she wracked her brain she couldn't put her finger on it. Forgetting something wouldn't be much of a problem if she lived in town, but since it was an hour's wagon ride either direction, she didn't want to leave something necessary out of her order that would require an extra trip back to the store. She'd thought of something earlier in the day that she didn't normally get when she came for supplies, but she'd be darned if she could remember what it was. *Annoyin' is what it is,* she thought.

She stopped in the aisle between the shelves of supplies, took a deep breath and closed her eyes, trying to go back to that moment this morning when she'd first had the thought. All of a sudden, it was clear in her mind . . . she needed molasses because she planned to make a special batch of cookies for Jared, Juan and the boys when they returned from their big cattle drive adventure. With a sigh of relief and a smile, she opened her eyes and nearly jumped out of her skin as she saw a man standing not two feet away from her.

"Afternoon, Mrs. Kilpatrick, I didn't startle you, did I?" The man had a smirk on his face as if he knew darned good and well that he'd scared the bejeebers out of her.

"My goodness gracious," she exclaimed although in her mind, she had a stronger epithet ready to let fly. "Why would you go and sneak up on a body like that? You nearly scared me to death!"

"Certainly wasn't my intention, Mrs. Kilpatrick," the man said smoothly, although his amused expression suggested that it was most definitely his intention. "I just wanted to talk with you about a business proposition."

As she collected her thoughts, it was beginning to dawn on Lizbeth who the man might be. "You have me at a disadvantage, sir. You know my name but I don't know yours and I'm sure we've never met."

"Curtis Barwick at your service, m'am," he said with a slight bow though Lizbeth noticed he didn't bother to tip his hat. "I wanted to speak with you on behalf of my associates about an offer to buy your ranch."

"Well, Mr. Barwick, I'm afraid you and your associates are wastin' your time. The ranch ain't for sale."

"Everything is for sale, Mrs. Kilpatrick," Barwick said, raising his eyebrow. "When you hear the offer, you'll see that it's in your best interests to take it and clear out."

Although the words he was saying sounded reasonable, there was a menacing tone to them that Lizbeth didn't like. "Mr. Barwick, I've got no intention of sellin' the ranch to you or anyone else and I ain't goin' anywhere. I'm sorry if you don't understand that but I reckon that's your problem. Now good day."

As Lizbeth started to walk past Barwick, he reached out and grabbed her roughly by the arm. "No, Mrs. Kilpatrick, it's you who don't understand and it's you who has the problem. Mr. Catron and Mr. Chapman will give you three thousand for your ranch, including both the land and the cattle, if you'll clear out right away. If not, your prospects for surviving through next winter are slim. Do you get what I'm telling you?"

Lizbeth shook her arm free and stepped back. "I understand that an offer like that is both an insult and a threat, Mr. Barwick. Now you'd better step back out of my way or I'll call for the sheriff."

Barwick threw his head back and laughed out loud. "Oh, I wish you would call for the sheriff. I'm looking forward to putting him in his place, a place that's dark and cold." He stopped laughing but continued to grin like a possum. "Unfortunately, now is not the time for that. I've been instructed to make this offer to you and give you twenty-four hours to consider it. I'll be out at your place tomorrow around this time with a contract for you to sign and if you have any sense at all, that's what you'll do. If not, you'll have more trouble than you've ever had in your life." He turned to go, then turned back. "And if you want to invite your friend, the sheriff, that would save me an extra trip back into town to deal with him."

Barwick turned on his heel and walked out of the mercantile without another word. Lizbeth realized that her heart was pounding and she was breathing rapidly. She took some deep breaths and tried to gather her thoughts. Having heard Eleanor's and Nathan's separate accounts about their encounters with Gentleman Curt Barwick, she knew that this was a serious threat. *Oh, Ned, why'd you go and get yourself shot? I sure do need you right now.*

CHAPTER 13

Jared couldn't remember ever being as cold in his entire life. The icy north wind cut right through his heavy coat, wool shirt and long johns and the bandana he had wrapped around the lower part of his face had frozen with the moisture of his breath. When they set out in the morning, it had been sunny with some high clouds but as they got up into the pass later in the morning, the clouds began rolling in. It was so cold that when they stopped to pay Uncle Dick Wootton his toll, the old man hadn't said much more than a couple of words to them warning them of the bad weather before he returned to his shelter.

Much to Jared's dismay and to the amazement of the young hands who'd never been through the pass before, it started to snow before mid-day. The flakes had gotten thicker as the day progressed and it was increasingly difficult to see. He'd huddled briefly with Juan and Miguel, and they made the decision to forge ahead rather than make a stop to have a quick bite to eat. Jared knew the last thing they needed was to get stuck on the downhill slope of the pass in darkness and a snowstorm. They reached the pinnacle of the pass in the early afternoon and he scouted ahead briefly. The snow was beginning to collect on the trail and he knew that if they didn't get on through pretty quickly, the drifts would get high enough to cause serious problems. *June blizzards,* he thought. *What next?*

Juan was on point and Jared rode up to him as he returned from his quick scouting expedition. "I'm a little nervous about this, compadre. We need to pick up the pace or we're gonna be spendin' the night in the snow up here on this mountain."

For once, Juan didn't have a humorous comeback. "You're right, amigo, we need to get a move on. If we get stuck up here tonight, I'm afraid we'll lose some cattle and maybe some hands, too. Got any ideas?"

"I reckon you could get that lead steer, old Ned, and see if you can light a fire under him," Jared said. "I'll ride back and get Felipe and Tomas. We'll fan out and start pushin' the herd a bit. We got to be careful to keep'em tight and not get'em goin' too

181

fast, though. It's gettin' slippery and there's some pretty serious drop-offs up close to the edges of the trail."

"Yeah," Juan said. "It's a fine line we'll be traveling but I think you're right. If we don't pick up the pace, we'll be in serious trouble."

"There it is, then," Jared said. "You get old Ned movin' and I'll get busy on the other end."

Jared rode back toward the rear of the herd, motioning to Felipe Munoz to follow as he passed him by. They stopped briefly on the left flank to let Sean O'Reilly know what they were about to do, then rode back to where Tom Stallings and Joe Hargrove were riding drag. Jared briefed both cowboys and could tell by the nervous glance they exchanged that they understood the danger they were in. He sent Felipe over to the right side at the rear of the herd to get in position and took Joe with him back to where Tomas was trailing the remuda behind the wagon. He explained the plan to Tomas, and leaving Joe with the horses, the two of them rode back up to the herd. As he passed Miguel and the wagon, he motioned that they were picking up the pace. Miguel waved back, indicating he understood what Jared was doing.

Once he'd positioned Tomas on the opposite corner from Felipe, Jared rode to a point square in the middle of the rear of the herd. He took a deep breath, stood up in the saddle, waved his hand to signal the other cowboys, who began whooping and urging the cattle to pick up the pace. At first, the steers were sluggish from the cold and reluctant to go faster, but soon they all warmed to the task and began moving along at a good clip. As the snow continued to fall heavily, the trick became not allowing the herd to get out of control. Jared spent much of his time the next couple of hours riding from one cowboy to the next with instructions to slow down or speed up, depending on his reading of the danger of the pace. He worked up a sweat in the snow as they covered a fair amount of ground and he was starting to feel a cautious optimism that they would make it out of the pass before nightfall. But this bit of optimism was tempered by his concern that the trail was becoming increasingly treacherous.

Jared had just given Tomas instructions to slow down and was riding over to the opposite side of the herd to give Felipe the same message. As he got closer, he heard Felipe holler in alarm but he couldn't quite make out what was happening through the thick snowfall. He spurred his horse forward and was able to see Felipe riding hot after a steer that had suddenly bolted out to the right side of the trail. As he got closer, he could just make out that the steer was headed for what appeared to be a drop-off at the edge of the trail. He had no way of knowing how far the drop was but he could see that Felipe had his lariat out and was right on the steer's heels, trying to keep it from going over the side.

The action seemed to slow down in Jared's vision. He saw Felipe's rope settle over the steer's head. As his pony pulled up to a stop, it veered a half turn to the left. Felipe had taken his dallies and because of the bad angle, the weight of the steer jerked his horse over on him. As Jared spurred his horse frantically in their direction, he saw Felipe release his dallies as the horse fell. The steer was on the edge of the precipice with only the weight of the horse holding it steady. As the slack shot towards the steer, it lost its balance and went over the edge. The horse struggled to get up. Jared heard Felipe scream in agony as its full weight bore down on him. Jared hollered over his shoulder for Tom Stallings as he spurred his horse again. Arriving at the spot where the horse had risen, he did a running dismount.

Felipe rolled over in the snow as his pony limped away toward the other horses. From the way the pony was walking, Jared figured she had a broken foreleg. He sighed as he knew this meant the horse would need to be put down.

Jared glanced to his right and saw that he was only a couple of feet from the drop-off at the edge of the trail. He cautiously inched over and looked down. Some twenty feet below, he saw the steer lying dead on the rocks with its head twisted at a strange angle. *That could be me or Felipe,* he thought. He shuddered . . . and not from the cold. Looking back over his shoulder, he surveyed the situation and determined that Felipe was badly hurt, as he was writhing in pain. He knelt beside the cowboy and said in a quiet voice, "Felipe, don't try to move yet, I've got to figure out where you're hurt before we do anything."

Felipe responded with another groan. Through clinched teeth, he gasped, "Senor Jared, I think my leg, she's broken. She hurts bad and it feels like something ain't right."

"Felipe, I've got to get help to get you to the wagon. I'm gonna ride over and get Miguel. You just hang tight and I'll be right back."

Jared mounted up quickly and as he started to ride back to where Miguel had stopped with the wagon, Stallings came galloping up. "Tommy, get that pony and tie her off to a tree," Jared said sharply. "I think she's got a broken leg but we need to tend to Felipe first. When you're done, get over to the wagon."

Without waiting for discussion, Jared turned and rode to the wagon. When he arrived, Miguel told him he had already sent Tomas up to tell Juan to hold the herd until they could get things straightened out. Jared explained the situation with Felipe and Miguel took the horse he'd been leading with the wagon to accompany him to the cowboy's aid. As they rode back, they met Stallings coming their way. Jared motioned for him to follow them.

When they got to the scene of the accident, they dismounted and hurried over to Felipe's side. What they saw was not encouraging. The lower part of his right leg was bent at an odd angle. Jared could tell from looking that Felipe would not be in the saddle any time soon. He bent over and whispered in the vaquero's ear. "Hang on, cowboy, we'll get you to the wagon and patch you up."

Stallings stepped back and surveyed the

situation. "Whew, this is a mess, Mr. Jared. What're we gonna do?"

Jared had been thinking about that. He turned to Miguel and asked, "Do you have spare blankets in the wagon?"

"Si," Miguel answered, understanding immediately what Jared meant to do. "I'll get one pronto and be right back."

As Miguel rode off, Jared turned to Stallings. "Tommy, we're gonna use the blanket to carry Felipe to the wagon and get him in where it's dry and a little warmer. Once we do that, we're gonna have to see if we can set his broken leg."

Stallings appeared a bit pale but steadfast nonetheless. "What do you need me to do, Mr. Jared?"

"We'll need your help gettin' Felipe to the wagon. Once that's done, I need you to get up to Juan and let him know what's happened. Tell him I said I'd stay here with Miguel and Felipe but he needs to get this herd down the mountain before nightfall." Jared glanced over at the mare lying pitifully in the snow and turned back to Stallings. "One more thing. Before you go, you need to put this horse down. Can you do that?"

Stallings looked crestfallen at the thought of having to shoot the horse. "I ain't never done that before, Mr. Jared, but I can see it needs doin'. I reckon I'll get it done."

Jared looked at the young cowboy and thought how much he'd changed from the surly malcontent who'd started the drive. "Good man, Tommy. I know I can count on you."

When Miguel returned with blankets, they did their best to gently lift Felipe onto one. They then covered him with the second blanket to keep him warm. The young cowboy was moaning softly and from his pale color, Jared worried that he might pass out. He knew they couldn't waste any time getting him back to the wagon and getting his leg set. Miguel and Tommy each took a corner by Felipe's head and Jared picked up the end by his feet. Slowly and carefully, they began trudging through the snow, trying desperately not to stumble. Each step was agonizing for Felipe and the few minutes the trip took must have felt like a lifetime to the cowboy. Finally, they arrived at the wagon. Miguel cleared a space out in the back and they hoisted him up, sliding him in head first. Miguel climbed into the wagon after him and produced a bottle of whiskey, the contents of which he forced down Felipe's throat in large gulps with the intention of deadening the pain as best he could.

Turning to Stallings, Jared said, "Time to get movin', Tommy. You ride on down there and tell Juan to get this herd off the mountain just as fast as he can. Comprende?"

"Yes sir, Mr. Jared, I'll take care of it." The young cowhand turned and walked down the hill. Jared had climbed into the wagon and was preparing to help Miguel with the gut-wrenching task of setting Felipe's leg when he heard a single gunshot. He bowed his head for a brief moment in respect for the animal that had given its life in his service. Then he turned his attention back to the job at hand.

Miguel had used his knife to cut Felipe's pants leg away and Jared could see that his lower leg was canted at an unnatural angle. Although he couldn't tell for sure, he thought the bone might have barely broken through the skin.

"Once the whiskey takes hold, I think we can stretch this leg and pop that bone back into line," Miguel said with a frown on his face. "If that works, we just need to bundle this boy up and get ourselves down the mountain. The lower down we go, the warmer it'll be but we need to get him next to a campfire as soon as we can."

With a good-sized dose of whiskey, Felipe seemed to be in a daze. He was muttering under his breath in Spanish but his eyes were closed and his head lolled back and forth.

Jared took a deep breath, let it out slowly and said, "Might as well get this done, amigo. It ain't gonna get any easier the longer we wait."

Miguel nodded and knelt down next to the cowboy's foot. He gently grabbed his ankle with both hands and looking up at Jared, nodded. Jared took a firm grip around Felipe's knee and said, "On the count of three, we'll give her a yank."

Jared looked at Miguel and counted to three. They both pulled at the same time and the leg bone snapped back into place with a loud cracking sound, which was nearly drowned out by Felipe's scream of agony. Miguel quickly looked over the leg and seemed satisfied that they'd gotten it set as well as they could. He looked around the wagon and in short order, produced a ball of twine and a couple of narrow boards that he kept for kindling. He emptied out a burlap flour sack that was nearly empty and cutting it into strips, wrapped the boards so they rested easier on Felipe's leg. Using the twine, he managed to apply a pretty fair splint that appeared to immobilize the broken leg.

"It's not pretty but I think it'll hold for the time being," Miguel said.

Jared surveyed their handiwork and nodded. "Yep, not bad considerin' we ain't doctors." He looked at the now-unconscious cowboy's face and shook his head. "What he needs, though, is a real doctor. We'd better not waste any more time. You ready?"

"Si, let's get this wagon moving," Miguel answered. "You try to keep him from rolling around back here and I'll make as good a time as I can without falling off the mountain."

The trip down the north side of Raton pass was hair-raising. Miguel got the team going at a pretty good clip, but one of the mules stumbled in the snow, jerking the wagon off to the left. This sudden motion threw Felipe against the side of the wagon and his screams filled the small enclosure. Jared got him settled finally and coaxed him to take another man-sized shot of Miguel's whiskey. Miguel started off again, this time at a more cautious pace and they began making steady progress. By mid-afternoon, however, the mountains were surrounded by clouds spewing an even thicker snowfall. It was as dark as night and Miguel had to slow the wagon down to a crawl. Jared grew concerned that Miguel would lose sight of the trail and unwittingly stray into the arroyo. He crawled on his knees up to the front of the wagon where he could speak to Miguel.

"Amigo, it looks to me like I need to walk ahead of you with a lantern so you don't drive off the side of this old mountain," Jared said in as light-hearted a manner as he could muster.

Without taking his eyes off the trail, Miguel slowly nodded. "Si, I'm afraid you may be right. I hate to ask you to do it. It's muy frio out there."

"I reckon I'd rather take my chances bein' cold than to take a tumble off the trail. Where do you keep the lantern?"

"It's hanging on a hook at the back of the wagon, on the left side," Miguel replied.

Jared looked but saw nothing. "I don't find it."

"No, it's on the right side, I get turned around from up here."

When Jared looked on the right side of the wagon, he saw the lantern hanging there. He took it down from the hook and checked to make sure it contained oil. He found matches in a small leather pouch hanging on the same hook and took them out in preparation to light the lantern. Steeling himself against the cold, he turned up the collar of his heavy coat, lit the lantern and hopped off the back of the wagon. The snow was thick and even though Miguel was moving at a snail's pace, it took him a minute to walk up ahead of the wagon. He forged ahead about fifteen feet in front then set his pace to match that of the wagon. The lantern burned brightly and he could see a fair distance ahead. What he saw both scared the pants off him and comforted him at the same time.

Jared walked back to the team and hollered up at Miguel. "I guess it was a good idea to check out the trail with the light. It makes a sharp turn to the right up there about twenty yards. If you don't make the turn, we'll go straight off into the canyon."

Miguel exhaled a heavy breath. "I'll go as slow as I can. You stay up ahead maybe fifteen feet and I'll do my best to follow you. I just hope nothing spooks this team."

Jared didn't respond to the last statement, not wishing to jinx their situation. He walked ahead a short distance and waved at Miguel to follow. They crept along and when they were almost at the turn, Jared swung the lantern several times toward his right. Miguel stayed on the right side of the trail. What he didn't know, nor did Jared realize until it was too late, was that the left side of the trail had eroded over time and was much lower than the right, a fact that was hidden by the drifted snow. Just as the team started making the turn, the wagon very slowly began to slide sideways on the trail. Jared heard Miguel shout and as he turned, he saw him crack the team with the lines. The horses responded immediately with a burst of speed, which gave the wagon sufficient momentum to move around the turn without sliding any further down the mountain. Jared dove off the trail into a snow bank to avoid the oncoming team and they just missed crushing his legs. Once he got on level ground, Miguel pulled up and hollered to see if Jared was all right. Jared extricated himself from the snow bank and dusted off. Picking up the lantern, he fumbled for matches in the pocket of his coat. After two failed attempts caused by his numb fingers fumbling the match, he was able to get it lit again.

"That was close," he said as he walked past Miguel to once again take up his position ahead of the wagon.

Seeing that his friend was unhurt, Miguel grinned. "You move pretty fast in that deep snow, compadre. You looked like one of them snowshoe rabbits I heard about." Jared contemplated a response but decided he was too tired and too cold. He just shook his head and kept walking.

They negotiated several more turns, though none as terrifying as the first. Jared found himself wishing his feet would just go ahead and get numb so the agony would go away. He had to force his mind to focus on marking the trail rather than thinking of his freezing feet. He plodded onward, one foot in front of the other, for what seemed like an eternity. He was so immersed in the task of finding safe passage that he lost all track of time and it took him a moment to realize that Miguel had closed the distance between him and the wagon. When he took his eyes off the trail and looked up, he saw that the snowfall was not nearly as heavy and things were not as dark as they had been. Miguel pointed off in the distance to the north and Jared saw a small break in the clouds. He thought he might have spotted a patch of blue in that break. Heaving a sigh of relief, he walked back toward the wagon.

"Guess we might make it after all, amigo," Jared said.

"It's looking much better now than it did up on that turn we nearly missed, that's for sure," Miguel responded. "I think in another half mile, maybe we'll get below this snow cloud. I hate to say it but you prob'ly need to lead me a little further before you get to come in from the cold and dry off."

"I think you're right. Now's not the time to be takin' any chances. Once we get below the clouds, I look for the snow on the trails to thin out. Reckon that'd be the time for me to get my frozen carcass back in the wagon." Jared took a deep breath. "Let's get to movin'. I think we can make a little better time now that the snow ain't fallin' so heavy."

Pretty soon after they started up again, the snowfall became intermittent and then stopped altogether. As they moved along down the trail, the clouds parted and ahead of them, Jared could see blue skies and sunlight illuminating the valley to the north. He stepped up the pace again and as they descended, he looked out to the northwest where there was a sight that made his heart soar. Spread out on both sides of a silver ribbon of a stream that was highlighted by the late afternoon sun, he saw his herd.

CHAPTER 14

Eleanor rinsed her mouth and spit the water off the porch. She was growing tired of getting sick in the mornings, although she knew it was just the natural scheme of things when a woman was in a family way. Still, it offended her sensibilities and her need to be in control. And it was difficult to feel in control when she was retching into a washbasin. She took several deep breaths to combat the nausea, then set out to the chicken coop to gather eggs. She took a couple of steps in that direction, then turned around and returned to pick up the double barrel shotgun that was leaning against the wall by the front door. At times, she thought it was silly to constantly be armed around the ranch house and it certainly made it more difficult to complete the chores that required both hands, which was pretty much all of them. When she had those thoughts, however, she would recall her encounter with Gentleman Curt Barwick, particularly the predatory gleam in his eye when he told her he liked to make women beg before he hurt them. The memory of that gleam sent a chill up her spine and kept her alert and focused as she went about her business on the ranch.

As the sun rose, the face of the mountains to the west turned a beautiful shade of reddish pink framed against the brilliant blue sky. This was her favorite time of the day. The beauty of the sunrise went a long way towards making up for the hardships in being so far away from town without the comforts and conveniences that came with town living. She was glad she had made the decision to give up teaching and spend her time with Jared out on the ranch. When she thought about her child having the chance to grow up free and unfettered out here with miles of open range to roam, she knew in her heart that she had made the right choice. She also knew that what they had was worth fighting for, and she made a silent vow to never give in to the evil men who pulled the strings of vicious puppets like Barwick.

Eleanor finished gathering the eggs and walked back toward the house. She could see Lizbeth moving around in the kitchen and could hear the coffee pot clatter as she set it on the stove. She knew she would be cooking up some eggs and ham, but the thought of food set her stomach to roiling again. She stopped and once again took several deep breaths, which seemed to be one of the few things that helped when she became sick to her stomach. Once her midsection quit doing flip-flops, she continued on into the house.

"You're lookin' a might green around the gills," Lizbeth said. "Still havin' that old mornin' sickness, I take it."

"I'm afraid so," Eleanor replied. She thought about the high level of alertness they were maintaining as they continued to watch for Barwick and she smiled ruefully. "I'm not sure I'm holding up my part of the responsibilities in keeping lookout." She thought about it for a second and her smile widened. "Perhaps if Mr. Barwick does make an appearance, I can be sick on his boots. He might ride off in disgust."

Lizbeth Kilpatrick laughed out loud. "I reckon that'd be one way to make lemonade out of lemons, wouldn't it?" She flipped the slices of ham over in the skillet and continued chuckling to herself.

Eleanor leaned the shotgun against the wall by the door and made her way to the table where she set the basket containing the eggs she had gathered. Pulling out a chair, she eased into the seat and watched Lizbeth cook for a moment. Finally, she spoke aloud what she'd been worrying about for several days now.

"Christy told me she'd heard from some of the girls at the Colfax Tavern that Mr. Barwick has been joined by two other ruffians. They've been drinking and gambling quite a bit and one of them threatened a girl."

"My goodness," Lizbeth exclaimed. "What did Nathan do about it?"

"Apparently, Tom Lacey, the bartender decided not to tell him. He was able to get the fellow calmed down without doing too much damage and he didn't want it to lead to bigger trouble." Eleanor frowned. "I suspect he didn't want to lose the business either. Those three men have been spending a lot of money there and bragging that once they take over this ranch, they'll have the run of the valley."

Lizbeth turned and smacked her hand down flat on the table, startling Eleanor and causing her to jump part way out of her chair. "I won't have it!" Lizbeth shouted. "I don't care if they send a hundred outlaws, I won't stand for it. In my heart, I made a promise to Ned that I'd keep this place goin' and I mean it, by God!"

Eleanor was almost as startled by Lizbeth's use of the Lord's name in vain as she was by the noise of her hand striking the table. She sat silently as Lizbeth stood there with her fists clenched. Finally, Lizbeth relaxed and pulled out a chair across from Eleanor. She looked down for a moment, then she sat down. When she looked up again, Eleanor could see that tears were flowing down her cheeks.

"I just miss him so much sometimes I don't know what to do," Lizbeth said through her tears. "He was cut down too soon by an evil man. I just can't abide the notion that those same evil men are still at their same old dirty deeds. It ain't right and it ain't fair."

Eleanor reached across the table and took Lizbeth's hands in her own. The ranch widow's hands were strong and rough, reflecting the life she led, but there was a gentleness in her touch as well. Eleanor recollected Jared's telling her that Lizbeth had been unable to bear children. It filled her heart with sadness that this good woman's strength and love could not be passed along to the next generation of Kilpatricks. After a moment, Eleanor spoke.

"You're right. It's not fair and it's just plain wrong. You know as well as I do that some people only care about what they want, and the needs of others are completely unimportant to them. They don't care who they hurt as long as they get what they're after." She gave Lizbeth's hands a gentle squeeze. "But some folks will stand up for what's right, even if it means fighting . . . yes, even dying for it."

Lizbeth looked in Eleanor's eyes from across the table and nodded. She squeezed Eleanor's hands back and without speaking they seemed to reach a pact between them about where they stood and what they stood for. Finally, Eleanor slowly released her grip and they sat back in their chairs.

Just then, they heard footsteps on the porch. The women looked at each other. Estevan was supposed to come out in the afternoon to check on things but they knew it was too early for this visitor to be him. Eleanor moved quickly out of her chair and grabbed up the shotgun. She felt as if her heart was in her throat and the first thought that raced through her mind was that her child might be hurt. The door opened and Maria Suazo walked in carrying a basket of vegetables from the garden. The friendly greeting she was starting to share faded on her lips when she saw Eleanor with the shotgun pointed in her general direction and she dropped the basket of vegetables.

"Madre de Dios!" she exclaimed.

Eleanor quickly set the shotgun aside and said, "Oh, Maria, I'm so sorry. We've been talking about Barwick and I'm afraid we're both very jumpy. Please forgive us."

Maria leaned back against the doorframe to catch her breath and slow her pounding heartbeat. "I forgive you but if you shoot me, I'm not sure Juan will be so forgiving." She wiped her brow, then said, "I'll forgive you more if you help me pick up these vegetables."

Eleanor immediately went over and began helping Maria put the vegetables back in the basket. Lizbeth had jumped up from her chair when Maria came in the door and now she sat back down at the table. She took a deep breath then she let out a heavy sigh.

"We're as jumpy as long-tailed cats in a room full of rockin' chairs." She looked from Eleanor to Maria and said, "Maybe it's time we think about takin' Nathan up on his offer to bring us to town."

Christy was unsure of what to do. She felt like she needed to share the information about Barwick's new sidekicks with Nathan, but she was afraid he might charge down to the Colfax Tavern and seek a confrontation in which he would be badly outnumbered. Truth be told, she was also worried that he would see her as pestering him or worse yet, that she was being brazen and forward. She had done her best to change her life when she became Eleanor Delaney's teaching assistant, but she knew there were quite a few folks in Cimarron who hadn't forgotten her days at the Tavern and who sure hadn't forgiven her. She didn't think Nathan fell in that group . . . after all, he had spoken up on her behalf when Eleanor had first brought up the idea . . . but he was awfully straight-laced. Supporting her attempt at bettering herself was one thing, but it might be that he found the thought of a romantic relationship to be distasteful. She didn't much care what most folks thought, but she had tremendous respect for the sheriff and lately she'd developed a strong attraction to him as well. The thought that he might find her disgusting filled her with shame and self-loathing. It was at times like this that she wished Eleanor hadn't made the move out to the ranch on a full-time basis.

Straightening up the chairs in the one-room schoolhouse, Christy then tried to concentrate on the lessons she would be teaching the youngsters the following day. Her mind kept straying back to her dilemma of whether or not to tell Nathan about the new developments with Barwick. Finally, she decided that he was likely to find out soon enough and it would be better if the news came from her than for him to be blind-sided by it on the streets. Having made up her mind, she got up and headed down the street toward the sheriff's office.

She knocked on the door and when she heard the sheriff call to come in, she entered. As usual when he was at the jailhouse, Nathan was seated at his desk doing paperwork. He looked up as she came through the door and she couldn't help noticing that as soon as he recognized it was her, he appeared to become nervous and slightly agitated. This was definitely not the effect she wanted to have on him. He stood up quickly and walked around his desk to greet her.

"Afternoon, Miss Johnson, how are you?"

"Afternoon, Nathan," she replied. "Don't you figure we've known each other long enough to be on a first name basis?"

The sheriff smiled sheepishly. "Well, m'am, I reckon you're right. I stand corrected. Let me start over . . . how are you this afternoon, Christine?"

"I'm all right, Nathan, and how are you?"

"I'm a might distracted with all this paperwork. It never seems to end. There's hardly any time left over to keep the peace what with all the forms I got to fill out these days." As he spoke, he walked around his desk and pulled a chair out. "Would you like to have a seat and visit for a moment?"

At another time, Christy might have come back with a sassy comment about perhaps wanting to visit for longer than a moment but she remembered the seriousness of her visit and restrained herself. Once she was seated and the sheriff had taken his place behind his desk, she spoke. "Nathan, I'm worried about somethin'. I didn't know whether to burden you with it or not, but I finally decided I'd better take a chance and tell you."

"Christine, it's my job to take on folks' burdens. If you think it's important, I'm willin' to listen."

Christy wondered how willing Nathan would be to listen if the message was personal and not related to his job, but she set the thought aside and proceeded. "I'm afraid Curt Barwick has two new pards down at the Colfax Tavern. A couple of rough lookin' hombres rode into town about two days ago and they been spendin' all their time with Barwick. I got word from some of my friends . . .". Christy paused and felt herself blushing. "Well, some girls I used to know at the Tavern and they told me they been talkin' about what they're gonna do about the Kilpatrick place. It's not soundin' good."

Nathan sat back in his chair and looked thoughtful. "I reckon I've been payin' way too much attention to this paperwork non-sense and not spendin' enough time out makin' my rounds. You say these fellas hit town about two days ago?"

"That's right," Christy said. "I don't know where any of'em are stayin' at night but they spend pretty much all of their wakin' hours at the Tavern." Christy cleared her throat and looked uncomfortable. "I heard they even got rough with some of the girls, but Tom got it smoothed over." Her eyes blazed. "Not that he did anything to stand up for the girls or try to make it right. He ain't Heck Roberts but he's still a snake!"

Nathan had clear, if not fond, memories of Heck Roberts, the shifty and dangerous former bartender at the Colfax Tavern who had been the right-hand man of Morgan O'Bannon. "You may be right about Tom, Christine. I thought he had a bit more spine than that but it looks like I was mistaken." Nathan chewed on the corner of his moustache for a moment. "Looks like all this is comin' to a head pretty fast. I'd better do somethin' to nip it in the bud before it gets any more out of control."

Christy sat forward in her chair with a worried look on her face. "Nathan, don't you go and do anything rash. There's three of'em and only one of you." She shook her head. "That's why I hesitated in tellin' you about this. I don't want you to go and get yourself hurt."

Nathan sat up stiffly in his chair. "Well, so far, Miss Johnson, I've been able to handle any trouble that's come along. Are you implyin' that I ain't up to the job anymore?"

Christy was puzzled for a moment at his change in demeanor but then she realized he thought she was saying he was too old. "No, Nathan, that ain't . . .". Christy stopped and corrected herself, wanting desperately for Nathan to see her as a school teacher rather than a former lady of the evening. "That's not what I meant at all. What I mean is that I worry about you because I care about you. I don't want to see anything bad happen to you."

"Well, thanks for your concern," Nathan said huffily, "but I can still do my job, thank you very much. I may be a little long in the tooth but I ain't all the way over the hill just yet."

His tone offended Christy. "Maybe you don't think my concern means much because of what I used to do, Mr. Nathan Averill, high and mighty sheriff, but I'll have you know I've changed my life and I ain't ashamed to look anybody in the eye now." Christy was mad as a hornet and she'd be hanged if she was going to go back and correct her grammar.

Nathan appeared stunned. He started to speak, shook his head, then started to speak again. Finally, he cleared his throat and said, "Miss Johnson . . . Christine, if I've given you the idea that I look down on you for how you used to make your livin', I apologize from the bottom of my heart. I know I'm an old fool but I still appreciate folks who try their best to do the right thing. I know how hard you've worked to better yourself and I respect you a great deal for your efforts."

Christy replied in a small voice, "You do?"

"Well, of course I do," Nathan said with feeling. "I think you're one of the finest young ladies I've ever met and worth a darn sight more than some of those priggish old busybodies that strut around town mindin' everyone else's business."

Nathan's praise made Christy feel shy. Good but shy. "Thank you, Nathan. That means a great deal to me, comin' from you." She gave him a puzzled look. "Why do you keep sayin' you're an old fool, though? I think you're just hittin' the prime of your life."

Now it was Nathan's turn to blush. He looked down at the papers on his desk. "I don't know. I guess bein' around a handsome young woman such as yourself has a way of makin' me feel my age."

Christy leaned forward. "Look at me, Nathan." Nathan slowly looked up from his desk and looked in her eyes. "First off, I'm not as young as you seem to think I am, and I don't think you're as old as all that. The second thing is somethin' I learned from livin' a hard life. There's a lot of bad in the world and sometimes you find yourself knee-deep in it. If you can get out of it and happen to find somethin' good, you don't ask too many questions or waste time findin' fault over things that just aren't that important."

Nathan looked thoughtful. "Are you sayin' that if you and me was to spend a little time together . . . say we was gettin' coffee and some apple pie at the St. James Hotel dinin' room . . . you wouldn't feel the least bit silly bein' with an old goat like me?"

Christy sat back and smiled coyly. "Why Sheriff Averill, you wouldn't be askin' me out like a proper suitor, now would you?"

Flustered, Nathan responded. "Well, ain't that what you were talkin' about?" He looked around as if there were help to be found somewhere in his office. Seeing none, he blushed beet-red. "Why, I'm sorry Miss Johnson, I believe I've misunderstood your intentions. Please accept my apologies."

Christy laughed out loud. "Nathan, I'm teasin' you! If there's any chance we can make this work between us, you're gonna have to relax and understand that I like to josh with folks."

Nathan shook his head and smiled ruefully. "You'll have to excuse me, Christine, I'm out of practice when it comes to courtin'. I can't remember how long it's been since I had the pleasure of spendin' time with a lovely lady such as yourself." This comment drew a smile from Christy. "Let me start over. Miss Johnson, would you do me the honor of joinin' me for some coffee and apple pie down at the St. James?"

"Why, Sheriff Averill, it would be my pleasure."

Nathan rose, grabbed his hat and walked

around his desk to where Christy sat. He offered his hand and she took it, rising from her seat. As they turned and walked toward the door, she linked her arm through his. She felt him stiffen just the tiniest bit, then he seemed to relax and they headed down the street to the St. James Hotel. Christy noticed the stares from a number of the townspeople but if Nathan did, he gave no indication.

Christy and Nathan spent the better part of the next hour making conversation over their coffee and pie. She noticed that as he began to relax, he exhibited a sharp sense of humor that she found very attractive. He noticed that she was an extremely bright woman and had clearly formed opinions about a number of issues related to state politics that he would not have expected of her. She knew about the territorial legislature, the new governor and quite a bit about the Santa Fe Ring. Finally, as they touched on the Ring, their conversation came back around to where it had started when she entered his office earlier in the afternoon.

"Nathan, where do these rascals come up with ruffians like Barwick? I suppose I understand the greed that drives men like Catron and Chapman but where do they find the hard men to carry out their dirty work?"

Nathan shook his head and made a wry face. "In my experience, Christine, whenever men with evil motives and plenty of money need assistance, they don't have much trouble findin' it. Men like Curt Barwick crawl out from under their rocks and are more than happy to do the deeds."

"But what rock does Barwick come out from under?" Christy persisted, reaching out and covering Nathan's hand with her own. "It seems like it would help for you to know more about the man before you have to take him on."

"I expect you're right about that, Christine," Nathan said. "I've tried to find out a bit about him but I haven't come up with much. One story I heard was that he was the mystery man in a gunfight up in Kansas back in '71, in the Hide Park district. Word was that some kid appeared out of nowhere when some cowboys went after a railroad man named McCluskie. Shot four of'em down, then vanished. No one knew who he was or why he even got into the fight."

"That doesn't make much sense, Nathan," Christy said. "Why would he join in a fight that wasn't his?"

"Some men are just naturally mean,

213

Christine. They just seem to arrive in this world with a tarnished soul and they don't need much of a reason to engage in violent actions. I don't know if that's the case with Barwick or not but it might well be." Nathan took a sip of his coffee. "Those men are the most dangerous kind. They're not fightin' for a cause or even really for the money they make. They're just lookin' to destroy the lives of other folks cause it gives'em some sort of twisted pleasure."

Christy shuddered. "That's awful scary, Nathan. Now do you understand why I was nervous about tellin' you about Barwick's compadres?"

Christy still had her hand on Nathan's on the table. He turned his hand over and clasped hers. "Of course I do." He grinned a bit shyly. "I reckon I understand a lot better after we had the chance to talk a bit and spend this time together. But what you got to understand is that it's my job to deal with these types of men when they come to threaten our town and the people that live in and around it."

Christy was distressed. "I know that, Nathan, but I can't help bein' afraid even so. Most times, you can count on men like Jared and Miguel to stand with you when there's trouble but now they're up in Colo-

214

rado and who knows when they'll be back."

"That does make it dicey," Nathan said. "Still, this ain't a situation that can wait around. I'll have to do somethin' about it but I promise you, I'll be careful." He smiled at Christy. "I didn't make it this far by bein' foolhardy. I'll sure watch my step."

Christy grinned back at the sheriff. "Well, you'd darned sure better, Nathan Averill. After I finally got you to ask me out on the town, it'd just be wasted effort if you went and got yourself killed."

For most of the afternoon, Gentleman Curt Barwick's two compadres held court at the Colfax Tavern, drinking, playing cards and from time to time, fondling the girls who worked the tables. The regular crowd at the Tavern was a bit on the rough side, but they were still taken aback at the bad manners exhibited by the two newcomers. They bluffed and bullied their way through card games, raking in winnings most of the time even when it wasn't clear they held a superior hand. The girls tried to steer clear of their table as much as possible, but whenever one got close enough, she was pinched, insulted and on one occasion, pushed to the floor. The girl, young Mollie, a recent emigrant from Ireland, looked around for assistance but found none available. All the men focused their attention on other objects of interest around the bar rather than come to her aid. With a look of disgust, she got up, dusted herself off and moved out of range.

Through it all, Barwick remained aloof and impassive. He didn't participate in the abusive behavior, nor did he intervene in any way. Unlike his comrades, he was unfailingly polite to the working girls and the other patrons. As dusk approached and Tom, the bartender, went around lighting lanterns, Barwick rose and motioned for his friends to follow him to a secluded table over against the wall farthest from the swinging doors at the entrance. Folks watched with a mixture of curiosity and relief as the men huddled for their conference, but no one said a word.

Tom approached their table and asked deferentially if they would like for him to light their lantern. Barwick responded politely that they would prefer to sit in the shadows, but would appreciate his bringing a bottle of his good whiskey and three clean glasses. Barwick waited patiently until the bartender returned with the whiskey and glasses. He filled all three, then turned to his companions.

"Boys, I think it's time we make our move. I got a telegram from Chapman in Santa Fe this morning and he's tired of waiting around. He dispatched a rider yesterday who's carrying papers that'll make it legal to buy that Kilpatrick ranch for what he likes to call a reasonable sum." Barwick flashed a cold smile. "I think you understand that means dirt cheap." He chuckled. "What it boils down to is we got to get a signature from that widow woman and our job here will be done."

Dick Cravens was short and slender and he possessed a nervous energy that kept him fidgeting constantly. He had a scar extending from just below his left eye down to his chin, a reminder of a barroom scuffle that hadn't started well for him. But as he recalled, it ended far better for him than the other fellow. There was wisdom in the saying that one should never bring a knife to a gunfight.

"From what you told me, Curt, she ain't all that willin' to sign away her land. You reckon she might need some persuadin'?" His grin turned into a leer as the left side of his face didn't move while the right side went up. This interesting facial feature tended to make folks uncomfortable, but Dick didn't seem to mind that at all.

217

Barwick nodded slowly. "I'm anticipating some resistance from the widow Kilpatrick, Dick. That's why you and Pancho are here."

Francisco "Pancho" Vega had been leaning back in his chair, his attention apparently focused on the patrons in the bar. When he heard his name, he turned his head and put all four legs of his chair back on the floor. In contrast to Cravens, Pancho was tall and bulky, although people were always surprised and on occasion, dismayed, to find that he moved with the speed and grace of a mountain lion when he was aroused.

"Dick can take care of that old widow. I got plans for those two young senoritas livin' out there on the ranch with her." He turned and spit chewing tobacco on the floor, ignoring the spittoon that was two feet to the side. "I been watchin' them for the last couple of days and I like the way they look."

"What makes you think you get both the young ones, you greedy rascal," Cravens sputtered.

Vega smiled. "Because I'm bigger and meaner than you, Dick, and if you don't shut up, I'll cut your heart out and eat it for dinner."

Barwick leaned into the table. "Easy boys,

there'll be plenty of time for that sort of fooling around and plenty to go around, too. First, though, we've got to get that name on the contract so this appears legal. Chapman was clear about that and we don't get any more money until that's done."

Vega grunted. Cravens was more vocal. "Let's not waste any more time then, Curt. I'm ready to ride out there right now if you want."

Barwick's eyes narrowed. "Slow down, Dick. We got a little problem here in town we need to get taken care of first."

This time, Pancho Vega spoke. "You're talkin' about that old sheriff, ain't you, Curt? He's got a reputation from here down to Las Cruces as a tough old cuss. How do you want to handle him?"

Dick Cravens snorted. "Hell, he may've been tough in his day but it's plain as the nose on your face that he's past his prime now. I don't reckon he'll be a problem." Barwick stared at Cravens until he became uncomfortable and started to squirm in his chair. "What, Curt? Don't just stare at me like that, it gives me the willies." Cravens' fidgeting became so pronounced that he almost turned over his chair. "Okay, if you think we need to take care of him, we'll take care of him. I's just sayin' I don't think he's so tough, that's all."

Barwick remained silent for another moment, letting Cravens squirm a little longer, then he continued as if Cravens hadn't spoken. "I don't want to kill him just yet. He knows an awful lot about the ranchers in this territory and I think we might be able to use that information. What I want to do is knock him in the head and keep him out of sight for awhile." Barwick flashed his cruel smile again. "Once he's out of the way, there's nobody in this town with the sand to stand up to us."

Pancho Vega leaned back in his chair again. "You got a plan, amigo?"

"As a matter of fact, I do," Barwick replied with a smug grin. "We're going to arrange for the sheriff to come on down and join us for a little get together right here at the tavern. I guarantee you he won't like how it turns out."

"How we gonna do that, Curt?" Cravens was almost bouncing up and down in his chair.

"Just like this, Dick. You see that cowboy over there leaning back in his chair? You were playing cards with him earlier as I recall. When I give you the word, you go over there, kick his chair out from under him and accuse him of cheatin'."

Cravens looked puzzled. "But he wasn't cheatin', Curt. Matter of fact, I won about ten dollars off of him." Cravens' puzzled look changed to one of amusement. "Matter of fact, I was the one cheatin'."

"None of that matters," Barwick continued patiently. "He won't be eager to fight you and will probably try to back out of it. You keep egging him on but don't draw. I want this to take a little time." Barwick took a sip of his whiskey. "Pancho, as soon as Dick gets this ruckus started, you grab one of the ladies and tell her to go get the sheriff pronto. If you have to threaten her to get her movin', that's fine but don't hurt her so she can't walk or talk."

"I can do that," Vega said. "Then what?"

"Then," Barwick said, "You go stand off to the side of the doors. Take this ax handle with you." Barwick reached down beside his chair and brought up a solid oak ax handle.

Vega looked surprised. "Where'd you get that, Curt?"

"I've been planning this for two days. I saw it behind the bar yesterday. I figure the bartender uses it to restore order on occasion." Barwick grinned. "I just told him I'd be needing his ax handle if he didn't mind and you know what? He didn't mind at all." Barwick's grin got wider. "When Averill comes busting through the doors to see what all the fuss is about, you crack him on top of the head. Be careful not to break his skull, we need him to come to after we get him all trussed up and in a secure location."

"I suppose you got a rope, too, since you got all this planned out," Vega said with a smirk.

"Actually," Barwick said with a smirk, "I've got some leather straps that should do the job nicely. We'll get his hands and feet bound then wet the straps down so they tighten up. He won't be going anywhere once we do that."

"Where you gonna keep him?" Cravens was fidgeting so much now that he bumped the table and the whiskey bottle almost fell over.

Vega grabbed at it with lightning speed and managed to catch it before it spilled a drop. "You spill that whiskey, Dick and you and me is gonna have a dust-up, never mind that cowboy over there!"

Cravens gave Vega an indignant look but wisely chose not to say anything smart in response. He turned to Barwick instead and said, "So . . . where do we take the old cuss once we get him knocked out and hogtied?"

Barwick leaned forward and put both elbows on the table. "You know where the livery stable is at the end of town? Right back of the stable, there's an abandoned adobe hut. I already checked it out and it'll do to keep the sheriff out of sight."

Vega nodded slowly while Cravens' head bobbed frantically. Barwick looked from one to the other. "Well," he said slowly, "let's get busy."

It took a second for his meaning to become clear to Cravens. Once it did, he smiled, got up and turned to saunter across the barroom. As he got closer to the table where the unsuspecting cowboy sat tilted back in his chair, a number of the patrons seemed to sense the menace in his walk and became silent. As the silence spread, the cowboy became aware of it and looked up to see Cravens begin striding purposefully toward him. Confused, he looked around the table at the other card players. He glanced back in Cravens' direction just as the gunslinger arrived at the table and proceeded to kick his chair out from under him. He fell with a squawk.

"You dirty, double-dealin' card shark," Cravens yelled, "you thought you could cheat me, did you?"

The cowboy was trying to disentangle himself from the chair and get to his feet. "What in the Sam Hill are you talkin' about, mister?" He responded with a mixture of indignation and fear. "You're the one who took my money. How could I be cheatin' you?"

Cravens hauled off and kicked the cowboy in the side. "Don't you lie to me, you slimy sidewinder! I saw you dealin' off the bottom of the deck."

Confused now as well as indignant and scared, the cowboy gave it another try. "You musta been mixin' loco weed with your whiskey, pardner. I didn't do nothin' of the kind."

"Now you're callin' me a liar, you sidewinder!" Cravens kicked the cowboy again.

"That ain't what I meant to do," the cowboy gasped.

Cravens let loose with yet another kick. "Stand up and fight me, you yellow-bellied coward!"

The rest of the patrons at the table jumped up and backed away. Pancho Vega approached one of the bar girls who was edging her way towards the door and grabbed her by the arm, digging his fingers into her flesh until she squealed in pain.

"Look at me," he barked at her. She looked up at him with terror in her eyes. "You get yourself down the street as fast as your pretty little legs can carry you and you bring that old sheriff back. If you're not back by the time I count to twenty, I'll break those little legs. You understand?"

She stared at him for a moment, then shook her head in acknowledgment. He let go of her arm and she raced out the door. Vega turned back to the barroom and watched Cravens' performance with amusement.

"Get up and take your lickin' like a man or I'll shoot you like a dog where you lie," Cravens bellowed.

The cowboy scooted back several feet as he continued to try to get upright. "Wait a minute, mister, I ain't lookin' for no fight. All I'm sayin' is that I didn't cheat you."

"And I'm sayin' you did, you numbskull," Cravens shouted again. "We're gonna settle this here and now or my name ain't Dick Cravens."

The cowboy was clearly baffled at how the situation seemed to be spiraling out of control. "Mister, I ain't even armed. You wouldn't shoot down an unarmed man, now would you?"

Cravens smiled at the terrified cowboy. "I might. In fact, I have a couple of times before." Cravens stomped his right foot on the floor, startling the cowboy and causing him to jump. "If you don't get a move on and find yourself a sidearm, I might just lose patience and gun you down right where you stand."

"I don't want to fight you over somethin' I didn't even do," the cowboy said. "That just ain't right."

"Right be damned," Cravens hollered. "I'm spoilin' to fight somebody and you're the one I elected. Quit wastin' my time and let's get busy."

Like Vega, Barwick was enjoying Cravens performance as well but he figured that enough time had elapsed that he needed to be alert. He turned his attention to the swinging tavern doors and saw that Pancho Vega was in position just off to the right side. He waited and watched for another minute when his patience was rewarded.

Nathan Averill pushed through the doors with authority and shouted, "What's goin' on here?" He started to say something else but before he could get the words out, Pancho Vega gave him a tremendous clout on the head with the ax handle. He fell like a stone.

CHAPTER 15

As the ground leveled out, the wagon rode more smoothly on the trail. Jared had been holding Felipe Munoz to try to ease the agony he was experiencing from the jolting of the wagon wheels, but now he laid him back down on the blanket. Felipe appeared to be unconscious and Jared thought he didn't look any too good. He was deathly pale and Jared was afraid his body was shutting down. He'd known of men dying even when their injuries hadn't appeared to be life threatening, as if their bodies couldn't stand the shock of what had happened to them. He was worried sick about the young cowboy and was anxious to make camp so he could get him situated on softer bedding near a fire. He went to the head of the wagon and spoke to Miguel.

"Soon as we get to camp, we need to get Felipe warmin' up by the fire and get a better splint on that broken leg. We need to get some coffee in him, too."

"He doesn't look so good, no?" Miguel used his hand to shade the late afternoon sunlight out of his eyes and then pointed. "Look, we got company."

Jared saw two riders heading their direction from camp. At a distance, he couldn't make them out but he figured one would be Juan. Sure enough, in a couple of minutes they were near enough for him to recognize Juan and Tomas.

"You fellas get lost?" Juan grinned as he rode up to the wagon. As he pulled up alongside and fell in step, he saw the troubled expressions on Miguel's and Jared's faces. His grin faded.

"Felipe's hurt pretty bad, Juan. Horse fell on his leg and it's busted up somethin' awful. He's freezin' cold and I think his body may be shuttin' down. We got to get him to camp as fast as we can. Do you have a fire goin'?"

"They gathered some wood but we haven't got it started yet." Juan turned to Tomas. "Tomas, you hustle back to camp and get that fire started. We got a cowboy down."

Without a word, Tomas turned his horse, spurred him and lit out at a gallop for camp. From a distance, they could just make out when he arrived, dismounted and got to work on the fire. As they rolled on towards camp, Jared recounted to Juan the events that had transpired on the mountain including their hair-raising journey down the steep hairpin curves.

"Here I am leadin' the way through the snow for my amigo, Miguel, so he don't drive the team right off the side of the mountain and he goes and tries to run me over."

Miguel snorted in amusement at Jared's description. "That is not exactly how it happened, Juan, but I will tell you this much. Your friend here can jump like a jackrabbit when he feels the need to. You never saw him move that fast in all the time you've known him."

Juan laughed along as the tale was spun but he could read between the lines and knew how dicey the situation must have been. He knew his friends were just letting off steam the way cowboys do, making light of a dangerous incident.

"Hey, I believe you, Miguel," Juan said. "I saw him jump for some biscuits one morning. He jumped right over my horse to get to the pan where they were. I know he can move pretty quick when he wants to."

"You're just still hot cause you wanted those biscuits," Jared said. His expression became serious again. "Did you boys have any trouble makin' it down the trail?"

Juan shook his head. "We were moving pretty good when Stallings came riding up like his horse's tail was on fire. He told us you boys were having a rough go up above us but he didn't have time to tell us the details. He said you told him to tell me to get off the mountain pronto. That's what we did." Juan heard a moan from inside the wagon and craned his neck to try to see Felipe. He shook his head then continued. "That Stallings, he's turned into a pretty good hand. He got behind the herd and made one heck of a commotion. He was riding from side to side, keeping them in check but we were sure making good time."

Jared nodded his approval. "Yeah, I didn't know if that boy had it in him or not but he sure came through when the times got tough, didn't he?"

"Remind you of anyone?" Miguel looked sideways at Jared, then directed his gaze back down the trail.

Jared heard Juan chuckle. "You boys are real funny." He thought about what Miguel had said and gave a chuckle himself. "It is a little odd to be on the other end of it, dealin' with a young fella learnin' the ropes. Lucky I'm so patient."

Miguel and Juan both snorted with derision at this. "You're the one who's funny, amigo," Juan sputtered. He laughed even harder. He started to say something, then waved his hand, shook his head and continued to laugh. In a moment, Jared joined in the laughter. They rode on toward camp.

As Miguel pulled the wagon into camp, the cowboys rushed over and began peppering them with questions all at the same time. Jared barked out an order to quiet down.

"We got a man hurt real bad here and we need to get him set down over by that fire as gentle as we can right away. I'll fill you in once we get that done but right now, we got to move fast and careful." Jared motioned to Patrick and Joe. "You boys are pretty stout, get over here and give me a hand." He turned to Sean and said, "Run grab some more blankets and spread'em so we got a soft bed for him to lie on."

They got Felipe out of the wagon and carried him as gently as they could over to a spot a few feet from the fire that Tomas had started. Jared noticed Patrick and Joe stealing glances at Felipe and could tell from their expressions that they were alarmed by his appearance. Jared was alarmed as well. The cowboy was unconscious but still

231

moaned in pain as they carried him over. Once they got him on the blankets, he lay motionless.

Miguel came over with more blankets. "We need to do a better job of setting and splinting that leg or it will never heal up right."

Jared nodded grimly. He was thinking that it might not matter as he wasn't sure Felipe would make it through the night. "Let's get that done and get him covered up."

The rest of the hands milled around a little distance away as Jared and Miguel went about setting Felipe's leg. The young cowboy screamed in agony during the process and Juan could see that the hands were getting worked up. He knew he needed to get their minds occupied on other things so he directed them to go about their chores, getting their bedrolls in place and making sure the remuda was secure. He told Tomas to build a cook fire over by the wagon and get some beans and coffee heating up. Finally and mercifully, Jared and Miguel finished their agonizing chore. Jared left Miguel to watch Felipe and walked over to the wagon where the cowboys were seated in a circle eating their beans.

"Boys, Felipe's havin' a pretty rough go of it. If you haven't already heard the tale, he had his horse fall on his leg and it's broke pretty good. Miguel and me, we did the best we could to get it set but we ain't doctors so I don't know how this is gonna shake out." He looked around the group. "Best thing we can do is push on to Pueblo and make the best time we can. The sooner we get there, the sooner we can get him to a real doctor. You boys got any questions?"

As Jared looked around at the young faces, he could see that they were scared and exhausted. The last twenty-four hours were a blur to him and it took him a moment to recall the uproar they'd gone through the previous night, with the wild time in town followed by the violent intrusion of the rustlers. None of the cowboys said anything. Jared realized that what they needed more than anything was a decent night's sleep with no excitement. He also realized that they needed for him to take a firm grip on this cattle drive and get things back on solid ground.

"Well, here's the plan, fellas. You boys need a good night's rest so Juan and I will take first watch tonight. Miguel and Tomas will take second." Jared saw their faces brighten up immediately. "Don't get used to this," he said with a laugh. "This is a special occasion that ain't likely to come along again for quite awhile. We'll get you boys back out on nighthawk tomorrow, you can count on it."

When Jared and Juan rode out to check on the herd, they left the cowboys gathered around the campfire talking in subdued tones. If Jared had been a betting man, he would have wagered every bit of the money he hoped to make off this cattle drive that the hands would be in their bedrolls before the moon was over the mountain. As he slowly made a circle, Jared considered the events of the past twenty-four hours and thought that he should be exhausted. However, his mind was racing and he felt a surge of energy that kept him alert in the saddle as he watched over the herd and passed the time. Now that they were out of the pass, it wasn't quite as cold and his heavy coat kept him warm enough.

The clouds had cleared out and when the Colorado moon came up, it was so full and bright that Jared thought he could have read a book if he'd had one handy. It looked close enough to reach up and touch, like his dream of making a success of the ranch for his family and the ones he loved. Silently, he took a vow on that moon, swearing that he would do everything within his power to take hold of that dream and make it a reality.

The herd was spread out for the night, and while he couldn't see Juan, he knew his friend was on the other side looking out for dangers. He figured they'd had more than their share of troubles to deal with in the past day and a half, and he was hoping they'd get a break before the next challenge presented itself. Still, it was a comfort to know that he had compadres like Juan and Miguel to count on when things got tough. A cowboy couldn't ask for any better hands to ride with, that was for sure.

Thinking about his friends led his mind in the direction of family and got him started missing Eleanor. He'd been so caught up in everything that was happening that he hadn't had time to think about her since the day before. It occurred to him that if someone had asked him three years ago if he could see himself missing someone like this, he would have laughed in his face. Now he was incapable of imagining life without her.

Riding nighthawk gave a cowboy time to think . . . sometimes *too* much time to think. It could get you to feeling lonely before you knew it. He wondered if Felipe had a sweetheart back home or family that was worried about him. He felt guilty that he didn't know the answers to those questions and vowed to ask Felipe in the morning, assuming he would be in any kind of shape to answer questions.

When he figured that they'd passed half the night, Jared whistled to signal Juan. He rode back to the wagon and where Juan soon joined him.

"Quiet night, que no?" Juan said.

"We could sure use a quiet night, don't you reckon?" Jared replied. He dismounted and led his horse over to where the remuda was grazing. He unsaddled and took the time to brush him down before heading back over to the campfire where Miguel was looking over Felipe.

Miguel had been kneeling next to the bedroll where Felipe lay, but when he saw Jared approaching, he rose and stepped a few paces away from the fire. "He's not doing so well, Jared. First he's on fire with fever, then he has chills. That's not a good sign. He's mumbled some words but he's been out of his head most of the time."

"What do you think I need to do for him?" Jared asked anxiously.

"Not much you can do except keep him covered up with blankets. If he comes to, try to give him some water. We can't let him get dried out."

Juan came in from putting away his horse and heard the end of the conversation. "Jared, you need to get some sleep or you won't be worth a hoot in the morning. Let me stay here with Felipe, you go roll up in your bedroll."

"Juan, I'm the trail boss, it's my responsibility to look out for the hands. I reckon you're pretty tired, too."

"I'm tired but at least I got a little rest last night before you brought those cattle rustlers down on us." Juan chuckled. "I'm tougher than you anyway." Turning serious, Juan said, "You're right, you're the trail boss and that means you're responsible for the whole mess, not just one cowboy. You know the plan better than anybody and you've got to be awake to lead us. Go hit the sack."

Jared realized that his friend was right and he also realized that exhaustion was finally catching up with him. "I reckon you're right . . . except for that part about bein' tougher than me," Jared said with a laugh. "You wake me if anything happens. Otherwise, I'll be up before first light."

Miguel walked off to rouse Tomas and take over night herd. Jared gathered his bedroll and spread it fairly close to the fire. Once he was in it, he gazed up at the full

Colorado moon and the shining stars for a few minutes, contemplating what the next day would bring. He wondered if Eleanor had been looking up at the same moon and stars earlier in the night. But he didn't wonder long. Soon enough, sleep overtook him.

Jared awoke with a start and realized that the sun was already over the mountain. He heard an unfamiliar noise coming from the other side of the wagon, which is what had awakened him. Shaking the cobwebs out of his head, he got his boots on and went to investigate the noise. As he walked, he was aware of the cowboys, up and moving around as they tended to their morning duties. None of them looked in his direction, which he thought was odd but he attributed it to their being embarrassed that he had slept in. He was a bit shame-faced himself but he figured he must have needed the rest. Anyway, he was the trail boss. It seemed like he should have some privileges. As soon as that thought crossed his mind, he rejected it, knowing that as trail boss, he should expect more of himself than he did of all the other cowboys.

Rounding the back of the wagon, Jared was shocked to see Juan shoveling dirt out of a hole that he was digging. It took a second for it to register on Jared that it was a grave and another couple of seconds for him to realize the significance of that. He walked up to Juan, who leaned on the shovel and looked at him.

"He didn't make it, did he?" Jared asked the question even though he could already see the answer in Juan's eyes.

"No, amigo, he passed in the night," Juan answered quietly. "He didn't make a fuss, he just quit breathing. He'd been groaning and at first, I thought he had gone to sleep." Juan looked off toward the mountains for a moment. "Maybe that's just what he did. He went for a long sleep."

Jared shook his head and searched for something to say but nothing profound came to him. "He was a good hand," he said finally. "I wish I'd known more about him. He didn't talk much about himself or anything else, for that matter. He just did his job."

"That he did, amigo," Juan said quietly. "That he did."

They stood there silently for a spell, then Juan spoke again. "I don't mean to sound hard, but we need to get him buried so we can head on up the trail. We still got these steers to move and Pueblo is not getting any closer."

Jared nodded slowly. "You're right. I reckon we ought to gather everybody around and pay our last respects. That's the least we can do for a good cowboy."

"He was that." Juan started to dig again and spoke over his shoulder to Jared. "You think you could say a few words over him?"

Jared wasn't sure what words he might say that would make any difference but he knew Juan was right. It was the least he could do. "All right, I'll think of somethin'. I'll get Miguel and Tomas to wrap him in his blankets and bring him over. I'll let the boys know what we're doin' so they can get ready."

After speaking to Miguel and Tomas, who went over to get Felipe's lifeless body, Jared went among the cowboys, telling each one of them individually what had happened and what they would be doing. Some took the news without comment while others expressed bewilderment that Felipe had died from a broken leg. Jared patiently explained that the shock of the injury plus the intense cold had caused his body to shut down in spite of their best efforts to revive him with the warmth of the fire and liquids. He could see the confusion and fear in their eyes as the awareness of the danger they lived with daily became a harsh reality and replaced the last vestiges of the romantic daydreams they'd had about a cattle drive. He knew that the sooner they got the formalities of the burial out of the way and headed on up the trail, the sooner things could get back to a routine. The best medicine for these boys was to get back to work.

When Jared passed the news to Sean O'Reilly, he asked the young Irishman if he would be willing to sing a song over Felipe's grave.

The boy nodded solemnly. "There's a song I learned from me ma, it's called 'Amazing Grace.' I'm thinkin' it would be a nice one to send him off with, don't you know?"

Jared smiled briefly. "That'd be a good one, you're right about that."

After he had spoken with each cowboy, Jared went over, gathered up his bedroll and then saddled his mount for the day. When he finished those chores, he glanced over and saw that Juan, Miguel and Tomas were ready for them at the graveside. Signaling the hands, he walked over to where they stood and waited until the cowboys joined them. Once they were all gathered, he spoke.

"There ain't any right words to say at a time like this, yet it don't seem right to let it pass without sayin' somethin'. This is

241

what I got to say." Jared looked around at the very young faces waiting expectantly for him to make sense out of this tragedy. "I wish I could say I knew Felipe well but I didn't. Truth is, we never had much of any conversation. I'd tell him where to go and what to do and he'd do it." Jared paused to collect his thoughts and then he continued. "But that right there says a lot about a cowboy. Felipe came to do a job and he did it well. He was in the right place at the right time and you could count on him every time. That's a man to ride the river with, for sure."

Jared thought for a moment but couldn't think of anything to add. Finally, he said, "Let's have a moment of silence for Felipe."

Everyone closed their eyes and looked down at the ground. When Jared felt like the time was right, he opened his eyes and saw that Sean was watching him. He nodded. Sean began singing, quietly at first but then his voice gathered strength as he moved into the second verse. Jared saw Miguel make the sign of the cross. Juan dumped shovels of dirt on the grave as the young Irishman sang from his heart. There was a haunting quality to his voice, and Jared got chill bumps as he listened to the words. He noticed some of the boys trying to wipe away tears without being seen. He knew there were times and events on the trail that would propel young boys into manhood, and he reckoned this was one of those times. Their comrade had fallen and lay in a shallow, unmarked grave. They would grieve and then they would get on with their jobs. It was hard but it was the way of the world.

Jared let the silence hang in the air for a minute, then he spoke. "Boys, we got a job to do and Felipe's dyin' don't change that fact. Let's break camp and get movin'."

The next several days went off without a hitch. The weather was good with clear blue skies and temperatures that led to the cowboys' taking off their coats and tying them behind their saddles. They made good time, and Jared anticipated getting to Pueblo within three to four more days. He was eager to get there and transact his business and head for home.

Since he and Eleanor had gotten married, he'd never been away from her more than a few days at a time when she would stay in town to work with Christy and the children at school. This separation seemed different somehow. For one thing, it was a much longer time than he was used to. But there seemed to him to be more to it than that. Felipe's death had hit him hard. His head told him there was nothing he could have done to prevent it, but his heart told him otherwise. He felt a duty to look out for his cowhands and an even greater duty to protect his family. Felipe's accident had driven home with great clarity the fact that dangerous things happen in the West, most often with little or no warning. He had an uneasy feeling that something was amiss back in Cimarron and while he could think of no rational reason to believe this to be the case, it still left him unsettled.

Jared spent the morning scouting ahead of the herd, making sure the water crossings were passable and looking out for trouble. A little bit before mid-day, he came upon an abandoned encampment that showed all the signs of being the recent temporary home to a band of Indians. Judging from the condition of the camp, he guessed that it hadn't been used in more than a week and he figured it had likely belonged to a small band of Ute foraging across the plains. This was comforting to him, as the Ute were generally not hostile to the cattle drives. This was in stark contrast to his first cattle drive across the northern part of Texas when they were constantly on the lookout for

Comanche, the most ferocious fighters in the West. Fortunately, Charlie Goodnight had established a reputation as a pretty fierce warrior himself, so they hadn't been bothered on that trip.

Riding back to the herd, Jared began to get the feeling that he was being watched. He reckoned that if it was the Ute, he wouldn't see them until they chose to show themselves and he didn't think they would be prone to attack. He remained even more alert than usual, however, since you could never predict with complete accuracy how the plains Indians would act. He approached the herd from the northwest and rode in alongside Juan, who was riding point.

"We might have some company pretty soon, compadre."

Juan nodded and scanned the hilltops ahead of them. "I wondered if we might not see some of our Ute friends up this way. They're not usually warlike but they'll most likely want to dicker for some beeves."

"You speak Ute?" Jared wiped the midday perspiration from his brow onto his shirtsleeve.

"No, but I speak Spanish. Some of these fellas know a few words and I hear tell you can carry on a pretty decent conversation that way."

"Well, be ready. If they're comin', I expect it'll be pretty soon. They'll likely want to powwow and you know that could take awhile. They generally don't get in a big hurry when they're tryin' to talk you out of some cattle." Jared stood up in the stirrups and looked ahead for signs of company but saw none. "I'll go let the boys know what might be happenin' so they won't get panicked, thinkin' we're bein' invaded by hostiles."

Jared had just turned his horse and started to head back to alert the crew when Juan hollered at him. "You're a little late, amigo, they're already here."

Turning his horse back to the north, Jared saw a group of Indians coming over the nearest hill to the northeast of them. They were still a little distance away, but it looked to Jared that there were perhaps twenty braves on horseback with squaws and children walking a distance behind. When they got to within about fifty yards of where Juan and Jared waited, they stopped and two braves continued on at a slow pace. At about ten yards distance, the older of the two raised his right arm in a greeting. He was a powerful looking old warrior and most likely the leader of this band. Jared responded in a similar manner, raising his hand in greeting and the two rode up to within about ten feet of them. The same brave who had waved the greeting spoke to them in what Jared thought was most likely the Ute language.

"We don't savvy your tongue, chief," Jared said. "Don't reckon you speak English, do you?"

The warrior looked confused and shook his head in response. Jared spoke to Juan out of the corner of his mouth. "Try some Spanish on him and see what he does."

In Spanish, Juan greeted the brave and asked him what his business was. There was a look of recognition on the Ute chief's face. He nodded to them and held up his hand as if to tell them to wait. He spoke to the other brave who turned his pony and trotted back to where the rest of the Ute were waiting. In a moment, he rode back, followed by a third young brave. They stopped in front of Jared and Juan and the third brave offered a greeting in what might have been Spanish, although he spoke in guttural tones that were hard to understand.

Juan looked at Jared and said, "I'll give it a try." He turned back to the young brave and in Spanish, he asked, "What is the meaning of your visit?"

The young Ute spoke to the older warrior, who stepped down from his horse and proceeded to make a lengthy speech in the Ute language. When he was done, the young Indian translated it into Spanish. Juan listened carefully, then he explained it to Jared.

"He says this is Ute hunting grounds and it sounds like he thinks we are intruders. He says they are mighty hunters but the white man has slaughtered the buffalo. He says his people are hungry because the buffalo no longer roam in numbers like they did in the past." Juan chuckled. "I think he's going to demand some beeves to make up for all the buffalo the white man shot."

"Tell him we are sorry for his people's hunger but we've shot no buffalo," Jared said quietly. "Tell him we're in a hurry to get to Pueblo and don't have time to pow-wow."

Juan translated Jared's message into Spanish, and the young brave translated it to his chief. The older man looked agitated and spoke again at some length. The young man translated for Juan.

"He says he has long counseled the younger braves in his tribe in the ways of peace. But he says they are angry about the slaughter of the buffalo and sometimes they seek revenge." Juan turned his head and spit on the ground. "He's trying to see if he can threaten us into giving him some cattle."

Jared knew the Ute had staged an uprising up near White River a few years back but since their great chief, Ouray, had died, they had been fairly subdued. "You tell him it would be a big mistake for his young warriors to attack our band. Tell him we're seasoned fighters and have killed many Comanche in Texas."

When the chief received the translation, he held up both hands and nodded quietly. Again, he made a speech, which was translated into Spanish and conveyed to Juan who passed it to Jared in English.

"He's backtracking now, amigo. He wanted to see if he could bluff us but I think he got your message before I ever relayed it to the young buck. He says his squaws and children are hungry and have been crying for many nights. They hunt but the buffalo are gone and game is scarce."

Jared nodded thoughtfully and looked directly at the older warrior. He took the measure of the Ute chief and it seemed to him that his last statement was, in fact, a true one. It occurred to him that if his family were hungry, he would go to whatever lengths necessary to put food in their mouths. When you love someone, you protect them and keep them safe, even if you have to beg, steal or even lay down your life for them. He'd come by this knowledge only recently in his young life when he fell in love with Eleanor and became friends with Nathan Averill, Lizbeth Kilpatrick and the others in Cimarron whom he now considered his family.

"Tell him we know the Ute are mighty hunters and brave warriors. Tell him we come in friendship and don't wish for his squaws and children to go hungry. Tell him we'll give him a steer as a token of our friendship."

Juan nodded and said, "I'll do it but mark my words, he'll want to dicker with us to try to get more cattle."

"I expect you're right," Jared said. "I'll let go of three steers but no more."

Juan spoke in Spanish again and as he had predicted, the warrior translated that the chief demanded five steers. Juan translated the message to Jared who held up three fingers. The old chief looked at Jared for a long moment, then nodded solemnly. Jared nodded back and told Juan to ride back to the herd and cut out three steers.

As Juan was turning his horse, Jared heard a commotion behind him and saw the chief and two young warriors look up in alarm.

He turned and saw Tom Stallings apparently having an argument with Tomas. Stallings was shouting at him and trying to get his horse around Tomas and ride out to where Jared was parleying with the Ute.

"Juan, stay here and try to keep these boys calm. I'll get back there pronto and see what's going on."

Juan did his best to pacify the Ute braves as Jared turned and spurred his horse back to the herd. As he rode, he saw that Joe Hargrove had joined Tomas in trying to restrain Stallings, who now appeared to be trying to free his Winchester from the scabbard on his saddle. Jared reined in his horse right next to the boy who was yelling at the other hands at the top of his lungs. He was so distraught that Jared could barely make out what he was saying, but he heard random words like "savages" and "I'll make'em pay." He knew he had to do something fast before the Ute band got spooked and decided to attack.

"You stop right where you are, cowboy," Jared shouted in an authoritative voice, "or I'll shoot you out of that saddle." As he spoke, he drew his pistol, cocked it and pointed it at Tom Stallings.

"You got no call to talk to me that way, Mr. Jared," Stallings yelled, although he began getting his horse under control as he spoke. "I'm gonna kill those no-good Injuns before they try to take our scalps."

Jared reached out and grabbed the reins from Stallings so he would quit jerking the horse's head around. Once he had the reins, the horse calmed down and stopped tossing his head. "They ain't interested in our scalps, you nincompoop, they just want a few beeves. The only reason they might attack us is if you keep raisin' cane and threatenin' them. Now stand down!"

Stallings stopped yelling but his eyes retained a wild and angry look and he stared at Jared. "You just gonna let'em steal your cattle like this?"

Jared returned his stare until the young hand looked down under the intensity of his gaze. "How I handle this situation is my call, not yours, mister. I thought I'd made that clear as a bell to you before we started up the trail. Now you get yourself under control and ride back to the wagon. You stay there and we'll deal with this after I get this Ute band on their way."

Jared turned to Tomas and Hargrove and said, "You boys ride back with him and make sure he stays there. If he shows signs of makin' any more trouble, Tomas, you shoot him, you got me?"

Stallings' face took on the sullen look that Jared hadn't seen for the past couple of weeks but without another word, he turned his horse and rode off toward the back of the herd, where Miguel had halted the wagon. Tomas and Hargrove rode after him.

Jared figured the best way to calm the situation with the Ute warriors was to get them their cattle quickly and part company as soon as possible. He quickly cut a steer out of the herd, driving it back up to where Juan waited with the three Ute warriors. As he rode, he spoke to Juan.

"Tell'em one of our cowboys got a burr under his saddle blanket but everything is all right now. I'll go cut out two more beeves and we'll get these people on out of here."

Jared waited until Juan had spoken and the chief received the translation. He saw the chief nod in understanding and visibly relax. With that, he turned and rode back to get the other two steers that they had agreed to share with the Ute tribe. When he got the cattle back to where they waited, the chief spoke and one of the braves began driving them over to where the rest of the band waited. The chief looked at Jared for a moment, then he spoke at some length. When he was done and his words were translated into Spanish, Jared saw Juan smile.

"He says he thinks your cowboy didn't get a burr under his saddle blanket, he thinks he's been smoking some of the loco weed. He says he can tell you are a powerful chief by the way you forced the boy to listen and obey you. He says the Ute are your friends and appreciate your gift of the cattle to make up for intruding on their hunting grounds. He says that we can go our separate ways in peace."

Jared nodded to the chief. "Tell him I'm glad for the friendship of the Ute and hope we can continue to live on this land together in peace."

Juan relayed the message back. The chief listened to the translation, then nodded back at Jared. Turning his pony, he rode back to his band without another word. Jared and Juan sat on their mounts and waited as the band of Indians headed back over the hill in the direction they came from.

"What was that all about with Stallings?" Juan asked.

"I don't know yet," Jared said with frustration, "I haven't had a chance to sort it out." Jared slapped his leg so hard that his horse started. "I'm ready to do just that right now, though, I promise you."

Once the Indians were out of sight, they turned and rode back to the wagon. Jared was fuming but he realized he needed to calm down so he could get to the bottom of the disturbance with Stallings.

"I don't know what to make of this, Juan," Jared said with frustration in his voice. "I thought Tommy was comin' around to make a hand. He did a man's job up in that pass and he's been a hard worker for weeks now. What in the world do you figure got into him?"

"I don't know, amigo, but maybe that's a good question to ask him . . . *before* you yell at him or fire him."

Jared thought about Juan's advice. He remembered several years ago when Ned Kilpatrick had lit into him without trying to understand why he'd acted the way he did. The memory was still painful for him, as if his friend had punched him in the stomach. It had taken them quite a while to work out their differences, but luckily they had been able to do so before Ned's untimely death. He resolved not to make the same mistake with this young cowboy.

Jared chuckled. "You know, Juan, you can't ride worth a hoot but sometimes you almost make good sense."

Juan laughed out loud. "You're right, compadre. And who would have ever thought you would learn to listen?"

They arrived back at the wagon to find Tom Stallings standing alone looking down at the ground. Jared dismounted and walked over to him.

"I'll take my pay and pack my things, Mr. Jared," Stallings said in a subdued tone.

"Are you quittin' on me?" Jared asked.

Stallings glanced up with a puzzled look in his eyes. "I figured you were gonna fire me."

"I haven't decided what I'm gonna do, Tommy," Jared said. "I don't know what you were thinkin' or why you acted the way you did. I thought I'd let you say your piece before I made up my mind."

Stallings' eyes still reflected puzzlement but there was a hint of relief as well. Jared said, "Let's take a walk and get to the bottom of this thing."

They walked for quite a ways before Stallings said anything. Finally, without looking at Jared, he said quietly, "Injuns killed my family, Mr. Jared."

"Is that a fact?" Jared said. "I'm real sorry to hear that."

"Yes sir, it's true. I was eleven years old and I'd gone with my uncle to his place to help'em with a gather. When we got back home, we found my Ma and Pa and my little sister dead." Stallings took a breath. "They'd scalped'em, Mr. Jared. I could hardly recognize'em."

Jared knew from his own experience that there was nothing anyone else could say that could take away the pain. "That's hard, Tommy. That's real hard."

"You don't know what it's like, Mr. Jared, losin' your family to a bunch of savages. It makes you hate everybody."

They walked on in silence, then Jared spoke. "Truth is, Tommy, I do know." Stallings' head whipped around and he stared at Jared in disbelief. "My folks were killed by outlaws. I was nine years old at the time. And you're right, it can leave you all torn up inside."

Stallings looked hard at Jared. "So what do you do? With the hate, I mean."

Jared didn't respond at once, giving some thought to the question. "I don't have an easy answer for you, Tommy. Time helps some . . . but not much." He paused again, choosing his words carefully. "I know this. I shut people out for a long time and that didn't help at all. Lucky for me, I found some folks who saw past the hate and didn't give up on me, even though I gave'em some good reasons to. I guess I finally figured out that even though there's terrible things that happen in this world, there's some mighty good things, too. Hate was in the way of me seein' the good things. I guess I finally saw the light." Jared smiled. "I had a lot of help to see that light, though, pard. I sure couldn't have done it on my own."

"I lost my head, Mr. Jared, when I saw those Injuns. All I could think of was revenge. I never wanted to kill someone so much in my whole life."

"I know the feelin', Tommy, but the fact is, those weren't the Indians that killed your family. If you kill them, I don't reckon you're any better than the savages that killed your folks."

"I guess I didn't think about it like that, Mr. Jared. Fact is, I didn't think at all." Stallings tried to speak but he choked up. He waved his hand at Jared who didn't say anything. Finally, Stallings was able to speak. "My parents was God-fearin' folks, Mr. Jared. They read to me and my sister from the Bible. They always said to do unto others as you'd have 'em do unto you. They didn't raise me up to hate but sometimes the feelin's just too strong."

"Sometimes it is, Tommy, you got that right." Jared paused. "When it happens, though, you got to find a way to let it pass

258

without doin' any harm to yourself or anyone else. When you get back to thinkin' right, you got to remember what your parents would have wanted you to do."

"I'm pretty sure they wouldn't want me to kill innocent folks, even if they was Injuns." Stallings looked at Jared and he could see that the boy had tears in his eyes. "My folks were good people, Mr. Jared. They didn't deserve what they got."

"No, they didn't, Tommy. But how do you think they'd feel knowin' you grew up to be filled with hate and went around spewin' it on innocent folks?"

"I don't reckon they'd like it." Stallings shook his head. "Sometimes I just forget."

"Well, I'd be the first one to tell you that none of us is perfect," Jared said. "Like I told you, I had friends who didn't give up on me even when I gave'em cause to." Jared put a hand on Tommy's shoulder and gave him a gentle shove. "I don't guess I'll give up on you, either."

He looked at Jared with relief and gratitude. "You're gonna give me another chance?"

"Yep." Jared laughed. "We need every hand we got. I ain't givin' you an easy out."

Stallings reached out and grabbed Jared's hand, which he pumped enthusiastically. "I appreciate this more than you'll ever know, Mr. Jared. I give you my word as a cowboy that you won't be sorry you made this decision. I'll make you proud."

"I know you will, Tommy," Jared said. "And I know somethin' else as well."

"What's that?" Stallings asked.

"I know your parents would be proud of you, too. It's clear they taught you right from wrong and that's somethin' you carry with you all the time."

"Thanks, Mr. Jared," Stallings said gratefully. "You won't be sorry."

"I think you're right about that, Tommy. Now let's get back to the herd and see if Miguel has some chuck for us before we get these cattle movin' again."

CHAPTER 16

Mollie watched the scene with Cravens unfold . . . something about it didn't seem right to her. She was a bright girl and even though she'd already led a hard life in her seventeen short years, it hadn't clouded her ability to think clearly. As soon as the sheriff walked through the doors and the big Mexican clouted him on the noggin, she knew something bad was happening.

Few people had treated her well during her time on earth. Her Mum had died when she was a wee child and her Da was in love with the drink. He would start out pleasant enough in the cool Irish mornings but by noontime, after imbibing mass quantities of what he called "Nancy whiskey," he would grow increasingly grumpy. By the time supper rolled around, he was looking for someone to inflict his rage upon. She'd been on the receiving end too many times to count, and this had figured prominently in her decision to leave Ireland and come to America. That and a brother who wanted to come out West and be a cowboy. She'd tagged along and found herself working in a saloon in a little town where half the people spoke a language she was unfamiliar with . . . and *that* was the folks who spoke their Western slang version of the Queen's English. Much of the time, she just smiled and nodded when customers spoke to her, which caused her difficulties in getting their drink orders right.

Tom the bartender had tried to have his way with her when she first started at the Colfax Tavern. When she resisted his advances, he'd given her the dirtiest jobs in the kitchen. Eventually, his unwelcome attentions shifted to a new girl and she'd gradually moved up the ladder to serve food and drink to the customers. For a time, her strict Catholic upbringing had outweighed her desperation and she hadn't followed the path of the working girl. Times were hard, though, and money was scarce. She'd given in and now made her wages on her back but in her mind, she saw this as a temporary setback. She did her best to cling to her self-respect and every penny that came her way.

Some of the customers treated her with kindness, or at least indifference, but these three outlaws whose performance she was currently witnessing had been particularly cruel. She already knew they were a bad lot, and their attack on the sheriff scared her to death. Clearly, they were taking their dirty deeds to a new low.

The sheriff was one of the townspeople who had been friendly and courteous to her. He'd treated her with respect and had even asked her questions about the old country on occasion. She felt like she should do something to help him, but she was at a loss. What could a skinny Irish lass do against three experienced highwaymen?

Mollie pulled back into the shadows and watched the three gunmen. After the big Mexican hit the sheriff in the head, some of the cowboys in the bar had jumped out of their chairs as if to come to his assistance. Quick as a snake, the leader . . . the one they called the Gentleman . . . pulled his six shooters and ordered everyone back in their seats. To Mollie's disgust, all the cowboys quickly complied. Remembering their lack of action when she'd been flung to the floor earlier, she was not surprised.

The Gentleman went over and whispered something to the big Mexican and Cravens. They laughed and then they each grabbed an end of the sheriff, lifted him up, and began walking out the door of the tavern with him. Mollie was overcome with panic. She had no idea where they were taking him or what they might do with the sheriff once they reached their destination, but she knew that if she were to be of any help at all, she must discover where they were going.

Without stopping to think any further, she slipped out the back door of the tavern and came around through the alley to the front of the building. She peeked around the corner and saw the two ruffians coming her way down the boardwalk. They were laughing as they carried the sheriff and didn't see her as she quickly pulled her head back. She waited until they were a good twenty paces ahead of her, and when she was reasonably sure that the Gentleman wasn't following them, she crept out on her tiptoes and snuck along behind them keeping to the shadows.

She followed along behind the two men, glancing over her shoulder from time to time to make sure the Barwick fellow hadn't come out of the tavern and overtaken her. They seemed to be heading for the north edge of town where the livery stable was located. She wondered if they had a wagon waiting and were planning to take the sheriff out into the canyon to dispose of him. When they finally reached the stables, they walked around the corner and seemed to be heading someplace out back. She crept as quiet as a rabbit behind them and peering around the corner, she saw them set the sheriff's body down roughly and struggle to open the door of a mud shack.

Mollie pulled back and tried to think of what to do next. It appeared to her that they planned to keep the sheriff prisoner. If they were going to kill him, they could have done it at any time, and if they wanted to dispose of his body, they would likely have taken him out of town. Clearly, the sheriff was still in mortal danger but she was guessing that she had time to enlist someone's help. The question was . . . who?

She pondered the question and an idea came to her. There was a lady all the girls at the tavern talked about and whom Mollie had met a few times. They said she had worked at the tavern but now she was the schoolteacher. The girls laughed about how this seemed to "put a bee in the bonnet of the respectable folks" but there was also admiration and envy in their voices when they talked of her. She'd found a way out of the sordid life they were leading and it gave them hope. Mollie knew this lady was a friend of the sheriff's and she might have an idea about how to help. She wasn't sure what one more woman might do against these brutal killers, but she didn't have a better plan. She set off to find Christy Quick.

Christy was just dozing off when she heard the rapping at her door. She woke up with a start and immediately reached for the short gun she kept on the nightstand by the bed. Jared Delaney had given her that gun when she was still working at the Colfax Tavern, and although it was a .22 caliber and only contained two bullets, it also contained the element of surprise and could make the difference between life and death in a pinch. She had no idea who might be trying to wake her and she figured she was better safe than sorry. Moving off to the side of the door to the room in the back of the schoolhouse where she kept her quarters, she called out, "Who's there?"

"It's Mollie, miss. Irish Mollie from the tavern. We met once awhile back."

Christy remembered the young Irish girl but had no idea why she would come calling on her after bedtime. "What is it, Mollie? Can't it wait until the mornin'?"

"No, miss, I'm afraid it cannot. We've got a terrible problem. You've got to help."

Reluctantly, Christy opened the door.

266

"Come in, then and tell me what you need."

The girl rushed in and Christy shut the door behind her. She was out of breath and clearly upset. "There now, Mollie, have a seat and calm yourself. Catch your breath and then tell me what's wrong."

"No time, Miss Christy," she said breathlessly. "We've got to do something fast or he's a goner."

Christy frowned in confusion. "Who's a goner? What are you talkin' about, Mollie?"

"The sheriff, miss, that's what I'm trying to tell you, saints preserve us!"

"The sheriff!" Christy felt her pulse quicken. "What's the matter with the sheriff?"

"They knocked him in the noggin, miss, and carried him down to a shack behind the livery."

"Who did, Mollie? Who knocked the sheriff in the head?" Christy felt her head begin to swim and she sat down on her bed in an effort to clear it.

"Those bad men at the tavern, miss. The ones that just rode into town last week. You know the ones I'm talkin' about?"

Christy's mind raced out of control for a moment, then she was able to calm herself. "Do you mean Mr. Barwick and those other two gentlemen, Mollie?"

"I do, miss, I do, but they're no gentlemen if you're askin' my opinion."

"Right you are, Mollie," Christy said patiently. "They're bad men. Now, slowly tell me what happened so I can decide what we need to do." Christy reached out and took Mollie's hands in hers. "Slowly, girl."

Mollie took a deep breath and then recounted the story of the ruse she saw played out. When she described the Mexican hitting Nathan in the head with the ax handle, Christy choked back a sob. Mollie stopped and looked at her, but Christy waved to her to go ahead with the story. The girl continued, describing how she'd followed the two men who carried the sheriff's body into the mud shack behind the livery stable. When she was done, she looked at Christy and waited expectantly.

"You said the sheriff was alive, Mollie," Christy said as calmly as she could. "What makes you think that?"

"Why, I heard him groanin' as they carried him, Miss. A couple of times, clear as a bell. Dead men don't make noises, miss." Mollie looked frightened. "Leastwise, not unless they're spirits or banshees, miss, but I don't think the sheriff is a spirit yet." The girl crossed herself. "Though if we don't hurry, he might become one sure enough."

Christy wasn't sure why Barwick had chosen to let Nathan live, but she figured this was only a temporary condition. Once he got whatever information he sought from the sheriff, she knew his life wasn't worth the mud in the streets. On the other hand, she knew she couldn't take these men on alone. She would need help and Nathan's survival depended on her taking the time to secure that assistance. She quickly reasoned out her next step and spoke to the girl.

"Mollie, you're a brave lass and thanks to you, we may have a chance to save the sheriff's life. Now I got to know . . . are you willing to continue helping?"

Although she still looked frightened, the girl's eyes narrowed to slits and her jaw jutted out. "That I am, miss. I've had a belly full of bein' pushed around by bad men. I may not be much but it's sure that I don't have to tolerate such malarkey. I didn't come all the way to America just to keep bowin' and scrapin' to the man!"

Christy was taken aback by the girl's grit. "You're a scrapper now, ain't you?" Without thinking, Christy had lapsed into the manner of speaking from her previous life. "If you're with me, here's what I want you to do."

"Just tell me, miss, and I'll do it."

"I need you to be my eyes and ears, Mollie," Christy said. "I've got to get some help as fast as I can and while I'm doin' that, you need to keep an eye on these rascals so we'll know where the sheriff is and if he's all right. Can you do that, Mollie?"

"Sure and consider it done, miss." The girl looked down shyly, then asked. "If you don't mind me askin', miss, why are you so willin' to be riskin' your life for this sheriff fella?"

Christy looked at the girl. "Because he's a good man, Mollie. You said there are bad men, and you're sure right about that, but there are good men, too. The sheriff is one of the best." She smiled. "And I love him."

Nathan wanted to shake his head to clear it but the ache was so intense that he didn't dare for fear that he would pass out again. He had a vague recollection of one of the girls from the Colfax Tavern rushing into his office and telling him there was trouble and he needed to come quickly. He'd grabbed his gun belt and strapped it on as he ran down the street.

As he entered the doors of the tavern, he'd caught a glimpse of Gentleman Curt Barwick against the back wall and heard another man talking in a loud and aggressive voice. This was followed almost immediately by a flash of light. He was out before he hit the floor. He also had a blurry memory of feeling like he was floating as he passed in and out of consciousness. He guessed that he was being carried to the location where he currently lay trussed up like a hog. His hands were bound behind his back and his feet were tied as well. A piece of cloth, most likely a bandanna, was tied around his mouth, presumably to prevent him from yelling out for help. To the extent that the cloth gag allowed, he smiled a grim smile at that thought. He figured he could howl for help all night and get nothing for his efforts. There was no one in town he could count on for help.

Nathan was still trying to make sense of his predicament when the door to the adobe hut was shoved open. The man whose voice he'd heard as he entered the tavern stood over him. The darkness in the hut obscured his features, but Nathan heard the sneer in his voice.

"Guess you ain't so tough after all, are you, Mr. High and Mighty Sheriff Nathan Averill." He cackled with laughter. "I told'em you wouldn't be no trouble but they was worried anyway. Looks like old Dick Cravens knew what he was talkin' about,

271

didn't he?"

Nathan's head was gradually beginning to clear although the pain was still sharp. His vision didn't seem blurred and he took that as a good sign. He looked up at the shadowy outline of the man standing over him and thought about what he had said. The name, Dick Cravens, rang a bell and he remembered seeing it on a wanted poster that had been sent over from Taos. As best he could recall, Cravens was a hired gun who was brought in as an enforcer. He figured he was one of the two men that Christy had reported to him who had joined Barwick. He wondered who the other one was. He struggled against his bonds and grunted his frustration.

"What's that, Sheriff?" Cravens taunted him. "I couldn't quite make out your words. Oh, wait, looks like you're gagged, ain't you." He laughed at Nathan's predicament. "Here, let me help you with that. I think I'd like to hear what a brave old lawman like yourself has to say."

Cravens reached over and untied the bandanna around Nathan's mouth. In a voice that sounded raspy and far away to him, Nathan spoke. "Those other two fellas ain't all that bright, are they? They're not planners like you, Dick. Who'd you say they were?"

"I didn't say, mister, but I don't mind tellin' you, even though I know you're tryin' to trick me. Pancho Vega and Gentleman Curt Barwick is who they are and they're a couple of rough hombres." Cravens cackled another evil laugh. "They was wrong about you but they ain't often wrong. And I don't mind tellin' you their names cause you ain't gonna be alive long enough to do anything about it."

Nathan had definitely heard of Pancho Vega. He was a sadistic hired gun who had murdered quite a number of men in cold blood. He would back-shoot you as soon as look at you, and he was fast with his pistol in a straight up fight as well. Nathan knew he would have had his hands full dealing with this trio, even if he weren't bound and gagged. With another grim smile, he calculated the odds considering that he was, indeed, bound, although no longer gagged. It didn't look good.

"Curt's got a few questions for you, sheriff. I reckon he'll wait til tomorrow to ask'em. Give you time to clear your head." He laughed. "You'd better have a lot to say cause as soon as you're through talkin', I'd wager you're a goner."

Nathan had never felt so helpless in his life. He strained at his bonds again but found them to be so tight that they were cutting into his wrists. Cravens noticed his struggle.

"Good luck gettin' out of those leather thongs, sheriff. We wet'em down after we tied you up. They're only gonna get tighter."

Nathan had always stayed on the right side of the law but he knew that if he had been free at that moment, he would have killed Dick Cravens with his bare hands.

"You yellow-bellied coward, you talk big while I'm tied up." Nathan continued to struggle with his bonds, grunting with the effort and with frustration. "You're nothin' but a piss ant! If I was free, I'd squash you under my boot."

"Coward, am I?" Cravens leaned over and yelled in the sheriff's face. "You just might still get a chance to find out about that, old man." He straightened up. "Dick Cravens is as tough as they come," he shouted. Then he kicked Nathan in the head. Everything went black again.

As soon as Mollie left, Christy quickly changed into her riding clothes and went out to the little stable behind the school-house. She hitched up the bay mare to the buckboard and as quietly as she could, headed out of town towards the Kilpatrick spread. The moon was full and she made good time. Within an hour, she pulled up in front of the ranch house.

"Halloo the house," she cried out at the top of her voice. "It's me, Christy. We've got big trouble and I need your help."

She waited to see if she'd been able to rouse anyone and within a minute, she saw a lantern being lit inside. The door opened and she saw a hand reach out and set the lantern on the porch. A voice that sounded like that of Lizbeth Kilpatrick directed her to step into the light and stop. She realized that they suspected someone was using her as bait and were being cautious. Quickly, she stepped up to the edge of the porch.

"Lizbeth, I'm alone. Nathan's in big trouble. We can't waste any time. Please trust me."

After a pause, the door opened. Lizbeth stepped out onto the porch. "Are you all right?"

"I'm all right," Christy said quickly, "but Nathan's hurt bad and those scoundrels have taken him prisoner. We've got to do somethin' to save him."

"Well, come on in and tell me what's happened so we can figure this thing out."

Christy rushed into the house and saw that Eleanor was standing by the window where she'd had a Remington double barrel shotgun trained on her just a moment before. She was strangely comforted by that fact, as it told her the women were prepared for trouble. Lizbeth escorted her over to the table while Eleanor put a pot of water on to boil for some coffee. As soon as she got the stove burning, she joined them at the table.

"Barwick and those two other ruffians bush-whacked Nathan at the Colfax Tavern." The words poured out of Christy in a rush. "They took him down to that old adobe shack behind the livery stable and left one of'em there to guard him." She paused to catch her breath, then continued her account. "Best I can figure, they want to try to get information out of him. I'm afraid that once they're done, they won't have any further use for him." She didn't elaborate but the look on her face made it plain to the other two what she meant. "We don't have a lot of time."

"Speakin' of time," Lizbeth said quietly, "I'd say Jared and the boys picked a rotten time to go on a cattle drive. I'm not sure what we can do up against hired killers."

Eleanor had been silent up to that point. Now she spoke up and her voice had a tone in it that neither woman had heard from her before. "What we'll do is exactly what Nathan or Jared would do under the circumstances. We'll treat these men like the savages they are. We'll stalk them, set a trap for them and when the time comes, we'll leave them dead in the dust."

Both women looked at Eleanor for a moment without speaking. Then Lizbeth nodded her head and said, "That sounds right to me." She pulled away from the table and said, "I'll go get Maria. We're gonna need her help, too."

When Lizbeth left to bring Maria into the fold, Eleanor got the coffee made and poured. By the time she had four mugs set up, Lizbeth and Maria arrived and took their places at the table. They engaged in an animated discussion for about half an hour. At the end of that time, they had a plan.

Mollie watched the mud shack from a small grove of trees about thirty yards away. She'd heard noises that sounded like an argument earlier, but it ended abruptly and it had been quiet since that time. Her eyes were beginning to droop when a sound startled her. In the light of the full moon, she could make out the figure of Dick Cravens as he stepped out in front of the shack and lit up a smoke. She could hear him muttering to himself and occasionally laughing in his nasty cackling voice. Something about this seemed evil to her and she shivered with a mixture of disgust and fear at the sound. She recalled her earlier comment to Christy about banshees and spirits, and thought to herself that maybe there were evil spirits around this night after all.

Christy had told her to be her eyes and ears but hadn't said how long she would need to serve in that capacity. Mollie was worried that with the light of dawn, she would be unable to observe without being seen. Momentarily, she was tempted to return to the room that she shared with two other girls above the Colfax Tavern. Then the memory of being pushed to the ground by one of Barwick's men . . . she didn't know if it was Cravens or the Mexican . . . came back very clearly and she felt her Irish temper rising. She thought to herself, "I said I'll bow and scrape no more and I mean it!" She settled in to keep up her vigil.

Mollie's eyes blinked open and she was momentarily disoriented in the darkness. She glanced around rapidly to determine where she was and why she was so cold. It didn't take her long to regain her senses and realize that she was in the grove of trees not far from the mud shack where the sheriff was being held prisoner. As her eyes adjusted to the dim light of the moon, she felt herself flush with shame for having fallen asleep on her job of reconnoitering for Christy but she reasoned that if she was still alive, she must not have been discovered.

As these thoughts were crossing her mind, she realized that she had been awakened by the noise of someone approaching from the street in front of the livery stable, headed back to the adobe hut. Whoever it was, they were making no attempt at stealth. She waited and in a moment, she saw a smallish figure who appeared to be a woman walking up to the entrance of the hut.

"Hello in there," the figure called out. "I've come for the sheriff."

Dick Cravens walked out of the hut and said, "Who is it and what in blazes are you talkin' about, you've come for the sheriff. He ain't a bag of feed you can just come pick up when it suits your fancy." He peered through the darkness to get a better look at the mystery person.

"It's Christine Johnson and I heard the sheriff needed medical attention. I've come to take him to Doc Adams so he can see about him."

Cravens stepped further away from the door, lit a match for his smoke and squinted at Christy. As he recognized her, a malicious grin appeared on his face.

"You're that school teacher, ain't you? The one they say used to be a workin' gal down at the tavern before you got all high tone." He chuckled and then took a draw from his smoke. "If my memory serves me, you're quite a looker."

Christy put her hands on her hips and looked Cravens up and down. "And you're a silver-tongued devil. A girl could get light-headed with all your sweet talk." She snorted in derision. "I'm not here to listen to you babble about my looks, I'm here to get the sheriff."

Cravens took a step back and looked Christy up and down. "Hold on there, Miss Smarty Pants. I reckon you don't under-stand the situation you walked into, dar-lin'." He took another drag of his smoke. "The sheriff's my prisoner. Why in tarna-tion would I want to release him to you?"

"Maybe because you realize that if you don't, you're going to be in more trouble real quick than you know what to do with."

Now it was Cravens' turn to snort in deri-sion. "Honey, I was born to trouble and I've caused nothin' but trouble my whole life. I don't reckon there's any kind of trouble you could bring me that I ain't already seen and handled."

Christy didn't respond but watched Cravens intently. She could almost see his brain working as he arrived at the conclusion she had anticipated. He grinned lasciviously at her.

"Say, I got an idea that might work out to both our benefits," Cravens said. "I won't give you the sheriff but I might go with you to take him to see the doc so he can fix him up a bit." He paused and grinned even wider. "Thing is . . . you got to give me somethin' I want in exchange."

"And what might that be," Christy asked, although she already knew the answer.

"Well, here's what I was thinkin', Miss Goody Two-shoes school teacher lady. I was thinkin' me and you could mosey around back of this shack, find us a nice place to relax and see if you can remember some of them tricks from your former trade. How does that sound?"

Christy didn't have to fake the disgust in her voice as she replied. "And why on earth do you think I would do something like that?"

Cravens chuckled. "Cause that's the only

way you're gonna get that old sheriff out of this hut alive, missy. That's my deal. Take it or leave it."

Christy pretended to consider his offer. Finally, she shook her head and said, "I don't like it but we're wasting time. Let's just get this over with."

She began walking around the adobe hut and Cravens followed a few steps behind like a puppy dog. She continued on towards a clump of underbrush, keeping just ahead of the man. She could hear his breath quicken in anticipation and she felt like her stomach was tied in a huge knot. When she got to the bushes, a figure stepped out and Cravens heard the unmistakable double click sound of a shotgun being cocked. Off to his left from behind the other side of the hut, another figure stepped out and he again heard the deadly double click.

"What the Sam Hill?" Cravens looked from person to person and a look of astonishment flashed across his face, followed by an evil grin. "So, that's how you want to play, is it? Well, I don't mind it rough."

Cravens stood there for a moment, looking from one to the other, the grin still on his face. Suddenly, he reached over his left shoulder and pulled a wicked looking knife from a scabbard slung over his back. He lunged at Christy who was a step too slow in getting out of the way. He slashed at her and although she tried to dodge, he left a deep gash on her left arm near the shoulder. She screamed as her sleeve was immediately soaked with blood. She fell backwards and simultaneously, there double booms from two directions. Cravens' body was picked up and flung backwards.

Maria Suazo approached Cravens cautiously but his body lay still. Two dark stains had appeared on his shirt and were growing as he lay there. In the moonlight, his face seemed to have a look of surprise on it. As she walked over to him, she reloaded both chambers of her shotgun. She kicked his left boot and got no response. Eleanor raced over to where Christy had fallen.

"Let me look at you, Christy! How bad is it?"

Christy groaned and held her arm. "He cut me pretty deep, Eleanor, but it's just my arm. If he'd been a step closer, it would be a whole lot worse."

Eleanor bent down and looked at the cut on Christy's arm. She straightened up and turned to Maria. "I'll tear some strips of material from my dress and try to bind this wound. You go fetch Lizbeth and have her bring the wagon up. We've got to get Nathan out of here fast! Those shotgun blasts will alert the whole town that something is going on."

"You keep an eye on this cabron, Eleanor. I think he's dead but I can't say for sure." She kicked his boot again, harder this time, and said some unflattering words in Spanish.

"We don't have time to wait, Maria," Eleanor said. "You need to get moving now. I'll keep one eye on him while I tend to Christy."

Eleanor approached Cravens carefully and saw where his knife had fallen in the dust. Watching Cravens closely for any signs of life, she picked it up and returning to Christy's side, began cutting strips of cloth from her skirt. When she had enough material, she began wrapping it around Christy's injured arm, pulling it tight enough to stem the flow of blood. Christy gasped in pain as Eleanor tied off the ends of the bandage.

"Sorry, Christy," she said with concern in he voice. "I don't mean to hurt you but we've got to get the bleeding stopped."

"I know," Christy answered. Then she turned away from Eleanor and emptied her stomach. She gagged for a moment, then turned back and wiped her mouth with the sleeve of her good right arm. "I'm sorry. I couldn't help it."

"You have nothing to apologize for, Christy," Eleanor said. "I just wish I'd moved quicker before he had time to cut you. Besides, pain can make a person sick to their stomach."

Christy took several deep breaths. "I don't know if it's the pain or the thought of doin' what he wanted me to do. When I left the tavern, I swore I'd never do that again, yet here I was walkin' someplace to lay down with a man so he could get what he wanted from me. It made me feel shameful."

"Christy, honey, you were setting a trap for him to save Nathan's life," Eleanor said emphatically. "You never intended to do what he asked and you put yourself at risk to save a friend. I'd say that's brave behavior, not shameful."

"I know you're right," Christy said, "but it still feels wrong." She looked down shyly, then looked Eleanor in the eyes. "Besides, Nathan's more than a friend."

Eleanor couldn't hide her surprise. She realized that her mouth was open and closed it. Then she grinned. "Bless your heart, Miss Johnson, you and the sheriff? Aren't you the respectable one now!"

Christy felt herself blush although she figured Eleanor couldn't see it in the dim moonlight. "I don't know about that, Eleanor. I just know that Nathan's a fine gentleman and there's not too many of them around. A girl would have to be loco to let a chance to be with a real gentleman go by without giving it a try."

Eleanor patted Christy's good arm. "I'm just teasing you, honey. I think it's wonderful. You and Nathan are two of my dearest friends in the world and I can't think of many things better than the two of you being together."

The sound of a wagon approaching intruded on their conversation. Although she was fairly certain it was Lizbeth and Maria, Eleanor needed to be sure. Putting her finger to her lips to silence Christy, she jumped up and taking her shotgun, moved quietly and quickly around the side of the hut. She returned almost immediately.

"It's them," she said. "We've got to get out of here. Can you move all right?"

Christy groaned as Eleanor helped her to her feet. "It hurts but you're right. We can't waste any more time." As Eleanor led her around to the wagon, a thought struck Christy. Startling Eleanor, she suddenly called out. "Mollie, are you out there?"

As they continued walking toward the wagon, the women heard a rustling in the trees a short distance away. Soon after, a slight figured appeared and walked slowly in their direction.

"Miss Christy," the girl said softly, "are you hurt bad?"

"I'm cut pretty deep, Mollie, but I think I'll live. Have you been out there the whole time?"

"Yes, miss, I have. I was your eyes and ears, just like you told me." Speaking in a stronger voice, she said, "I think that gobshite in there hurt the sheriff. I heard'em arguin', then things got quiet." She looked down. "I wish I could have done somethin' but I didn't know what to do. I stayed here the whole time, though."

"You did just fine, Mollie. Thank you for your help. Come over here."

Mollie approached the wagon. Christy turned to the women and said, "Eleanor, Lizbeth, Maria, I'd like to introduce Miss Mollie . . . ?" She turned to the girl. "Why, I don't even know your last name, girl. What is it?"

"It's O'Brien, miss. Mollie O'Brien from County Kilarney."

Eleanor stepped over and reached out her hand, grasping that of the girl. "Well, Mollie O'Brien from County Kilarney, you're a brave lass. We're all indebted to you for your

287

assistance." She dropped the girl's hand and stepped back, looking thoughtful. "I'm afraid we need a bit more of your help."

"What would you be needin' now, miss?"

"We've got to get the sheriff out of here before those bad men come. He's a good-sized man and we could use another hand lifting him into the back of the wagon. Could you help us with that?"

"Sure and I'm far stronger than I look, Miss. I'd be happy to be helpin' youse."

With the fourth set of hands, the women went in the hut to get Nathan. They found him on the dirt floor, bound and unconscious, with dried blood on his forehead.

"I'm afraid if we move him, we may hurt him worse," Christy said.

"If we don't move him," Lizbeth said, "he's a dead man. Take your choice."

Lizbeth's observation had made the decision easy. They discussed who would grab which parts, assumed their positions and gently lifted Nathan and began carrying him to the wagon. Using her good arm, Christy gently cradled his head and shoulders while Lizbeth and Maria each took an arm. Eleanor and Mollie grabbed his legs. When they reached the back of the wagon, they gently slid him in part ways onto a blanket, which was laid on top of a bed of straw. Lizbeth hopped in the wagon and helped them slide him in the rest of the way. Ominously, he never blinked or uttered a sound as they loaded him in.

Once the sheriff was secure in the back of the wagon, Lizbeth looked at the other women. "I'll get the horses goin' and Eleanor will ride up front with me. She'll be armed. Christy, you try to keep Nathan from bouncin' too much as we go." She turned to Maria. "You get your shotgun and be on guard at the back of the wagon. Any sign of trouble, you blaze away and ask questions later. Same goes for you, Eleanor."

"What about me, miss? I'll go with you if you want." The young Irish girl waited expectantly.

Lizbeth turned to Mollie and handed her a folded slip of paper. "Are you sure nobody saw you follow those outlaws when they carried Nathan down here?"

"No, miss, I didn't make a sound."

"Then this is what we need you to do. As soon as the telegraph office is open in the morning, take this note to Ben Martinez. He's the telegraph operator. Tell him to send this right away to the name on the paper and to make sure he gets the message right. Tell him I said it was life or death. Do

289

you understand?"

"Yes, miss, I do. I can lay low until dawn, then I'll get right over there."

"All right," Lizbeth said. "Anyone else have any questions?"

There were no questions. Everyone took their positions and Lizbeth got the wagon turned around the side of the livery stable and headed north out of town. Luckily, they were already on the edge of town, and it didn't take long before they were at the top of the hill and almost out of sight.

Maria turned her head toward the front of the wagon and spoke quietly. "I see a lantern and some people moving around down in town. Do you want me to hop out and go back to see what is happening?"

"No," Lizbeth said, "just keep an eye out for anyone followin' us. We'll be turnin' off directly and we ain't goin' where they'll think we'd head anyway. It's been dry and our tracks'll get lost amongst all the others on the road. I don't believe they can track us in the dark."

They were over the hill quickly and Lizbeth clucked to the horses to speed up a bit. This made the ride rougher which increased the risk to Nathan, but as Lizbeth had pointed out, getting away from town was critical.

They rode along in silence for a while longer. Lizbeth glanced over at Eleanor. "Are you all right?"

Eleanor took a deep breath and held it for a moment, then she exhaled. She stared straight ahead. "No, Lizbeth, I don't think I am all right. I've never taken a human life before and I never imagined that I would. It's the most horrible thing I've ever endured."

"Does it help to recall that the life you took belonged to an evil man who was dead set on killin' Christy and then you and your baby if he could?"

Eleanor thought about it, then turned and spoke. "You would think it would make a difference, Lizbeth, but somehow it doesn't." Eleanor frowned as she pondered the question further. "I don't know how, but it seems like that's something else entirely. That man had to be stopped. Killing him was the only way to do it, but that doesn't make me feel all right about it."

They continued on in silence for several minutes. Lizbeth leaned forward in the seat, straining to see something. Then she sat back and relaxed visibly as she turned the team off the main road, heading west up a narrow trail that led up into the foothills. Once they were headed in the new direction, she turned to Eleanor. "I think maybe that's the difference between black-hearted scoundrels like him and decent folks. You did what you had to do but you took no pleasure in it. You know that human life is precious and it's a terrible thing when it gets snuffed out, whatever the reason." Holding the lines in her left hand, she reached out with her right and gave Eleanor a comforting pat on the shoulder. "I'm sorry you're feelin' bad about what you did but in another way, I'm not sorry. I don't know if that makes sense but that's what I think."

"It makes sense to me and it's some comfort, though I still feel . . . I don't even know how to describe how I feel," Eleanor said haltingly. She was quiet for a minute, then she said, "I know I'll never forget this as long as I live."

Lizbeth didn't know what else to say, so they rode on in silence, climbing higher up into the foothills. From in the distance behind them came the faint sound of hoof beats. Lizbeth stopped the wagon and they waited in silence until the sound faded in the distance. When they were once again surrounded only by the natural noises of the night, she continued towards their destination.

■ ■ ■ ■

"Dammit, Pancho, I think we lost them!" Barwick reined in his horse and pulled over to the edge of the trail.

Vega eased his horse to a stop next to Barwick. "I think you're right, Curt." He took off his hat and wiped sweat from his forehead. "They didn't have that big of a head start and we've come about three miles now. Reckon they turned off somewhere?"

"They must have, but I'm darned if I know where. There's any number of trails that lead off this main one and some of them are hard enough to find in the daylight." Barwick slapped his thigh in frustration. "We got no choice but to head back to town and wait for sunrise before we try again."

"Who do you think done this?" Vega asked.

Barwick was quiet for a moment. "I don't know but there's not too many possibilities. There's not many folks in this town I would peg to be willing to take such a big chance, that's for sure."

Vega made a low rumbling sound in his throat that sounded a lot like a growl. "Well, whoever they are, when I find 'em, they're gonna pay. Me and Cravens rode together for a long time. He was a mean little son of a gun and I can't say I liked him, but he was a tough hombre when trouble come along." Pancho chuckled to himself at some memory that crossed his mind. "Like as not, he woulda been the one that caused the trouble to come along."

Barwick didn't respond as he pondered the events that had transpired. Finally, he spoke. "Pancho, I got a hunch and we'll need to follow it in the morning. I want you to ride out to that Kilpatrick ranch when there's enough light and see what they're up to. I don't know how they could pull something like this off, but those women are the only ones I can think of that would be bold enough to try it."

Vega snorted and shook his head. "You don't really think a couple of women could outfight Dick Cravens do you?"

"Not outfight him, maybe, but they could sure outthink him. There's something rotten going on here and we need to get to the bottom of it."

When Mollie left the women at the livery stable, she crept back down to the Colfax Tavern and snuck into the little tool shed behind the building. She figured she would

294

rest until dawn and then take the message to the telegraph office. Before long, her eyelids grew heavy and she fell asleep on the dirt floor. Several hours later, she was rudely awakened by the sound of a bucket of water being thrown across the ground. It took her a moment to remember where she was but then it registered that she was in back of the tavern in the shed. The noise that had awakened her was caused by the old man who mopped up the floors every morning in the tavern after another night of revelry had passed. She waited until she heard the sound of the back door shutting, then she cautiously opened the door and peered out. The sun was well up.

Checking both directions to be sure no one else was lurking around, Mollie exited the shed and went around the corner to Main Street. Again looking both ways and seeing no one who looked like trouble, she walked quickly over to the telegraph office across the street. There was a sign on the door that read "open" and she walked into the office.

"May I help you, miss?" A man not much taller than Mollie sat behind the counter.

"Yes, please. Are you Mr. Ben Martinez? I have a message for you to send. Miss Lizbeth said to tell you it was important. Life or death is what she said, to be truthful."

The man look puzzled. "Lizbeth? Would that be Lizbeth Kilpatrick?"

"Sure and she didn't tell me her last name, sir," Mollie replied nervously. "She was with some other ladies . . . an Eleanor somebody and another one who looked Spanish."

"That sounds like Lizbeth Kilpatrick," Martinez said. "What's she got for me to send that's so all fired important?"

Mollie handed him the note. "I'm sure I don't know, sir. I don't go readin' other folks' mail." Mollie was embarrassed to tell him that she couldn't read.

Martinez took the note and opened it. He read its contents and a worried look crossed his face. "This is to a Mr. Wheeler in Pueblo. He runs the Colorado Coal and Steel Company. It says there's trouble and he needs to get word to Jared Delaney to get back right away."

Mollie nodded. "I don't know this Mr. Delaney but one thing I do know. There's surely a heap of trouble and if he can help, he needs to get here sooner than right away."

CHAPTER 17

As Jared rode back into camp, the sun sank part way below the foothills to the west, and the last light of day cast a rose color across the plains. He was tired but pleased with the results of his scouting efforts for the day, having located a shallow canyon in the hills that would serve as a pen where they could use the rocky walls on three sides to hold the cattle. It was only about eight miles southwest of Pueblo and he figured they could make it there by mid-afternoon of the next day. He planned to ride into town ahead of the herd and meet with Mr. Wheeler to inform him of the impending delivery and transact his business. Although Jared figured a deal was a deal, he didn't know this Mr. Wheeler. He didn't want to be sitting right outside the Colorado Coal and Steelworks Company with three hundred steers and no buyer.

"Juan," Jared said as he dismounted, "we

might just make it through this cattle drive alive if the earth doesn't open up and swallow us between here and Pueblo tomorrow."

Juan looked up at the heavens, then back at Jared. "Don't tempt fate, amigo. You know a lot of things can happen in a short time out here on the range and most of it is not good."

Jared laughed. "You accused me of bein' a mother hen back at Raton. Now listen to who's makin' cluckin' noises." Jared walked over to a water bucket by the wagon and dipped his bandanna in it, then proceeded to wash the dust off his face. "You're right, though, we can't be gettin' cocky. Cocky leads to careless and we sure don't need that now."

As they walked over to the wagon to get their chuck, Jared filled Juan in about the natural pen he'd found, and they made plans for an early departure the next day to ensure they had a good deal of daylight to set up their camp. Once all the cowboys got their food, Miguel joined them and they discussed the plan with him as well.

Darkness fell and the hands began to gravitate toward the campfire. The night was clear and a gentle west wind blew the smell of pinon pine through the campsite. The cowboys were holding quiet conversations and drinking coffee when Jared, Juan, and Miguel walked over to join them. Jared moved over and stood beside the fire, waiting until they noticed him there. A hush descended and they waited expectantly.

"Boys, we're just about done with the hard part. I found us a good place to gather and hold the herd a few miles south of town tomorrow and I'll head in to take care of business with Mr. Wheeler while you fellas set up camp in the afternoon. I expect he'll want to come out and see what we brought him but once he's done that and accepts these cattle, I figure we'll get our money and be free to head on our way."

"Will we be able to go into town, Mr. Jared?" Joe Hargrove sounded eager to have another night like he'd experienced in Raton.

"Joe, once we deliver the cattle, I'll give you your wages and you're on your own. Me, Juan and Miguel are gonna head on back to Cimarron, but you footloose boys can go whatever direction you like." Jared grinned. "You'd be welcome to ride along with us old married hands but I'd understand if you didn't."

For a couple of minutes, the campfire was abuzz with the animated discussion of possibilities to be found in Pueblo. Jared waited patiently before finally clearing his throat to get their attention again.

"I just wanted to say a couple of things. Then you can get back to your business of plannin' mischief." The hands all laughed and Jared smiled, too. "What I want to tell you is this." He looked from one cowboy to the next until he had looked into each pair of eyes. "When you left Cimarron, you were all pretty wet behind the ears. A cattle drive will naturally toughen a fella up, though, and besides, we've had some situations that were harder than your usual drive." He paused for a sober moment as their thoughts all ran back over the dangerous and sad events they'd been through over the past few weeks. "Here's the thing. You left home green but now you're not. What you are is cowboys. In my estimation, that's as high a callin' as there is. Whatever else happens in your life, you can always look another man in the eye and tell him you're a cowboy."

Jared thought for a minute but could think of nothing else he wanted to say. The silence continued for another moment, then it was broken as Patrick O'Reilly whooped at the top of his voice and threw his hat high in the air. The cowboys looked at him, then at each other and they all joined in, whooping and throwing their hats. Jared looked over at Juan who smiled back at him and shrugged. At that moment, Jared felt a sense of pride in his accomplishments, accompanied by humility, as he thought about the price that had been paid in human suffering. It had been hard, and only time would tell if it had been worth it. But for now, it was almost done.

Before first light, the cowboys were up and about, finishing their breakfast of coffee and tortillas and getting saddled up. They had a good laugh when Sean O'Reilly's horse got a little snorty and dumped him off near the wagon, but no one was hurt and they went about their business. Jared stood by the fire with Juan, finishing up one last cup of joe.

"I'll ride with you boys partway through the mornin', then I'll head on into Pueblo and meet with Mr. Wheeler. With any luck, I'll get him to ride out tomorrow mornin' and settle up with us so we can get on down the trail back home."

"That sounds mighty good, amigo," Juan answered. "I haven't been away from Maria this long since we got married. I hope she hasn't taken up with some other hombre."

"I've often wondered how she put up with you when you were there," Jared teased. "She may like you better when you're gone."

"The woman worships the ground I walk

on," Juan responded with mock dignity. "You're just jealous because she's a better cook than Eleanor."

Jared grimaced. As a cook, Eleanor was an abject failure and what's more, she didn't seem too upset by the fact. "Wish I could argue with you about that but I can't," Jared said. "Just don't tell her I said that!"

Juan laughed and they continued to banter back and forth for a few more minutes before saddling up and sending the hands out to their positions around the herd. They began the gradual process of getting the herd moving, and by the time the sun had fully cleared the horizon, they were on their way.

It was a cloudless summer day with little wind and the sky was a brilliant blue. Jared rode with Juan on point and took the time to enjoy nature's gift as they moved slowly along with the southern Rockies off to their left in the west. They talked about their hopes for the future, many of which were attached to the success of this venture. They went over what had seemed to work best on this drive as well as mistakes they might avoid in the future. Like most cowboys, they were reluctant to mention the loss of Felipe Munoz, but they talked at length about the way the young cowboys, particularly Tom

Stallings, had developed into good, dependable hands.

Jared glanced up and noticed the sun moving toward the middle of the sky. "Things are goin' smooth, Juan, so I believe I'll head on into Pueblo now. The spot I picked out is about five miles up the trail on your left. Even you can't miss it."

"If you found it, I'm pretty sure I can find it." Juan looked up at the sun, then glanced back at the herd trailing behind them. "Maybe you want to get a couple of tortillas from Miguel."

"Good idea," Jared replied. "I'll go do that and then ride."

As Jared started to turn his horse to ride back to the wagon, Juan called out. "Amigo."

Jared turned. "What now?" He asked with fake exasperation.

For once, Juan was not smiling or joking around. "I just wanted to tell you that you did a good job. This was a tough drive. Another man might have lost more hands or more beeves but you didn't." Juan couldn't maintain his serious demeanor any longer. "I guess I could say I don't mind riding with you all that much."

Jared smiled. "Thanks, pard. Comin' from you, that's high praise. See you this evenin'."

Pueblo was a bustling little community nestled in the foothills of southern Colorado. The Arkansas River ran along one side of town. Jared had heard there were some fancy hotels and eating establishments on Union Street. As he rode in from the south, he saw two huge brick chimneys, which he guessed marked the site of the Colorado Coal and Steel Company headquarters.

Passing groups of citizens gathered on the sidewalks, he smiled to himself as he overheard their conversations. He knew the workforce in town wasn't large, so the mining company had recruited many workers from overseas. He heard Irish and Scottish accents as well as languages that he couldn't understand. He wondered what it would be like to pick up and go to a land where you not only knew no one, but didn't even speak the language. He decided he was content to remain where he was down south outside of Cimarron.

Using the brick chimneys to keep his bearings, he managed to wind his way a couple of streets over from the main thoroughfare and find the entrance to the Colorado Coal and Steel Company. It was surrounded by a fence with a gate house at the entrance. As he rode up, a man stepped out and asked him his business.

"I'm here to see Mr. Wheeler. I got a herd of cattle from down in New Mexico that I'm deliverin' to him. My hands are holdin'em just south of town and I need to arrange for delivery and payment."

The man grinned at him. "I don't know about Mr. Wheeler, but I'm glad to hear your news. We could sure use some fresh beefsteak around here." He looked Jared up and down. Pointing to a hitching post just inside the gate, he said, "Why don't you tie your horse over there and follow me. I'll take you to Mr. Wheeler's office."

"Much obliged, sir," Jared said.

He dismounted and led his horse over to the rail where he tied him. Then he turned to follow the man over to the entrance to a huge building. They walked in the door and Jared saw hallways going off in several different directions. He was glad the man was leading him to Wheeler's office, because he knew he would get lost in a matter of minutes in the maze of corridors. He had a good chuckle at his own expense as he considered that he had just traversed hundreds of miles through the wilderness with only the sun and stars to guide him, yet he feared getting lost inside a building.

The man led him around a corner and down a hallway, which opened up into a waiting area. There was a man behind a desk who turned out to be Mr. Wheeler's personal secretary. The guard explained Jared's business and the secretary nodded, rose and went through a door to another office. In a minute, he returned.

"Mr. Wheeler will see you now."

Jared thanked the guard for leading him through the maze to Wheeler's office and followed the secretary back with his hat in his hands. He looked around the office and was impressed with its size and lavishness. The desk appeared to be made out of mahogany and there was a moose head mounted on one wall. A small man wearing a suit and bow tie stood up behind the desk and walked around with his hand extended.

"Mr. Delaney, I presume?"

Jared reached out and shook his hand. "Yes sir, Jared Delaney from Cimarron. I've brought your cattle."

"Well, I'm glad of that. We can certainly use the beef." He seemed distracted, glancing back at his huge desk as if he had forgotten something. "Raymond Wheeler at your service, Mr. Delaney. I'm the man in charge here at the Colorado Coal and Steel Company."

"Pleased to meet you, sir. Your cattle are being held in a spot a few miles south of town. I just need to make arrangements for you to take possession of them and settle up with us financially, then we'll be headed on our way south."

"That's fine, Mr. Delaney. I can have one of my men bring a crew in the morning to look over what you've brought and make sure the numbers are right. Assuming they are, he'll be authorized to pay you and he'll drive the cattle to our company pens."

Wheeler continued to seem distracted. Jared asked, "Is something wrong, Mr. Wheeler?"

Wheeler took off his spectacles and rubbed his eyes. "I apologize, Mr. Delaney, it's been a busy day and I have a feeling I've forgotten something." He shook his head. "I'm sure whatever it is, it will come to me sooner or later. In the meantime, would you like a place to stay for the evening? I can recommend several reasonable boarding houses."

"Thanks, Mr. Wheeler but I had planned on returning to camp after we conduct our business. I intend to stay with the herd until we get her handed over to you proper tomorrow."

"I appreciate your thoroughness," Wheeler said. "I'll let my assistant, Evans, take you to meet my foreman, Bob Sullivan. He'll bring some help and will be handling the transaction with you tomorrow."

"Thanks, Mr. Wheeler," Jared said respectfully. "I think you'll be satisfied with the quality of the steers. I look forward to doin' business with you again in the future."

"Well, you certainly got here with the herd ahead of schedule, that's a plus," Wheeler said enthusiastically. "The people who work for me like their beefsteak. If they're satisfied, I imagine we'll be seeing more of each other." The men shook hands and Jared noticed that once again, Wheeler frowned as if something was on his mind. The moment passed, however, and Wheeler turned to go back into his lavish office.

Jared walked with Evans through another maze of corridors. Eventually, they came out a door to the outside where Jared saw stables, a corral and several large pens. There were some cattle in the pens, but clearly not enough to adequately feed the number of workers that must be employed at Colorado Coal and Steel. Jared took that as a sign that the supply was not keeping up with the demand, suggesting he might be able to develop an ongoing business relationship with Mr. Wheeler that could provide a steady income for the ranch for years to come.

Bob Sullivan was a big, strapping Irishman who greeted Jared with a hearty handshake. Jared filled him in on where he was holding the cattle and Sullivan was familiar with the place. He asked Jared how the drive had gone and Jared acknowledged that there had been some difficulties without going into detail. Not wanting to dwell on the hard times, he changed the subject by mentioning that he had two Irish brothers working as hands for him. Sullivan was immediately interested in that and when Jared mentioned the lads might be coming into Pueblo after drawing their pay, he brightened up.

"I'll speak with the lads in the mornin' and maybe I can stand'em to a pint . . . or two or three!"

Sullivan had an infectious laugh and Jared found himself liking the big Irishman. In the days before he became a family man, he would have been inclined to come back to town and join the boys for a night of drinking and carousing. His life had changed forever, though, and he was dead set on leaving for Cimarron as soon as the herd was passed on to Sullivan.

Sullivan told Jared he would head out before the sun was up the next morning and bring a crew of five hands to handle the cattle. He confirmed that he would bring the funds from Mr. Wheeler so that they could settle up and Jared could pay his hands. Satisfied that things were set for the next day, Jared shook hands with Sullivan and followed Evans, who led him back out to the front gate where his horse was tied. He thanked the guard for his assistance, and the guard promised to put in a good word for him if the beefsteak was to his liking. Jared rode away from the Colorado Coal and Steel Company feeling like he'd done a good day's work.

He arrived back at camp just before sundown to find that Juan and Miguel had gotten the herd gathered in the natural pen provided by the foothills. Stallings and Hargrove were holding the herd on the fourth side and Juan planned to rotate a two-man crew throughout the night. Miguel had gotten a fire going and was preparing a meal for the cowboys on their last night on the trail together. Everyone was in good spirits and they listened eagerly as he described his meetings with Wheeler and his foreman, Bob Sullivan.

"So he'll stand us for a pint, will he now," Patrick laughed. "That's a mighty fine offer if you're askin' me, isn't it, Sean?"

Sean nodded and smiled, saying nothing. Jared shook his head and chuckled as he contemplated the contrast between the two brothers, one gregarious and funny, the other quiet and serious. He counted himself lucky to have hired a group of hands that learned the ropes, got along with one another and handled the challenges of the trail as well as this one had. He knew cowboys had a way of moving on, but he hoped that if he got another contract with Wheeler for more cattle, he would be able to use some of the boys again.

The boys stayed up for quite awhile around the campfire, swapping tales, singing songs and listening to Joe Hargrove play his mouth harp. Jared and Juan took a turn holding the herd so the hands could enjoy their last night together before they all went their separate ways the next day. Around midnight, the O'Reilly brothers spelled them and Jared crawled into his bedroll, tired but happy.

The sun was up and the hands were drinking their coffee when Bob Sullivan and his five-man crew rode into camp. Sullivan dismounted and Jared walked over to greet him.

"Mornin' to you, Mr. Sullivan. Did you have any trouble findin' us?"

"No, Mr. Delaney, I didn't. As soon as you told me about the spot yesterday, I knew right where you meant. This is a good spot." He glanced over at the herd and said, "Let's have a look at these steers you've brought up the trail for us." He turned to one of his crew and said, "Bring your tally book, Norville."

The cattle were lethargic after their night's sleep, so it was not as great a chore to count them as it would have been had they been milling around. The count tallied up to an even three hundred and Sullivan expressed his satisfaction.

"You said you'd be bringin' us three hundred head, Mr. Delaney and it looks like that's what you did. As Mr. Wheeler's authorized representative for the Colorado Coal and Steel Company, I'll be givin' you your money now."

Sullivan handed Jared a canvas bag, and had a brief conversation with the O'Reilly brothers about their prospects for a night on the town as he waited. Jared counted through twice to make sure the amount was correct. He confirmed that the sum was exactly right and they walked over to the horses, talking as they went.

"I think Mr. Wheeler will be satisfied with what you've accomplished, Delaney," Sullivan said. "These steers look fat and healthy. Clearly, you gave'em time to graze and didn't push'em too hard up the trail like some outfits do. If he asks my opinion, I'll sure enough speak up on your behalf."

"Well, thank you, Mr. Sullivan, I appreciate that. It's been a pleasure doin' business with your outfit."

They shook hands and Sullivan put his foot in the stirrup. He stopped, stepped back down and turned around. "I almost forgot, Mr. Wheeler asked me to give you this telegram. He got it several days ago but didn't remember that he had it yesterday when he was meeting with you."

"You know," Jared said, "I could tell he had somethin' on his mind yesterday. It was like he was tryin' to remember somethin' but couldn't. I guess this was it."

"I expect you're right," Sullivan said. "Well, let's get this herd movin' along now."

Jared stuck the telegram in his pocket. "I'll have my boys lend you a hand in gettin' them movin'."

He hollered to the cowboys who spread out and began whooping and waving their hats. Fairly quickly, the cattle moved out of the three-sided canyon and Sullivan and his crew got them moving up the trail towards Pueblo. Jared gave a wave to Sullivan and rode back over to the wagon where he dismounted. He went over to where he had left the canvas bag and was about to begin counting out the wages for the cowboys when he remembered the telegram that Sullivan had brought him. He reached in his pocket, pulled it out and unfolded it.

Juan had walked over to help Jared count the pay. He was about to make a joke about running away to Mexico together with the money when he noticed that something was wrong.

"What's the matter, amigo? You look like you've seen a ghost."

Without a word, Jared handed Juan the telegram. Juan read it out loud. **Jared** *Stop* **Big trouble** *Stop* **Come right away** *Stop* **Nathan hurt, Eleanor in danger** *Stop*

"Juan, I don't know what this is all about but I've got to saddle up right now and beat it down the trail. I'll need to leave you in charge to take care of payin' the boys."

"Pardon me, amigo, but like hell you'll leave me in charge," Juan said heatedly. "If Eleanor is in trouble, Maria is, too. I'm going with you."

Jared rubbed the stubble of beard on his chin. "I can't argue with you about that, I reckon. What do we do?"

"We leave Miguel in charge. He's got to bring the wagon back anyway. He and Tomas can handle this." Juan looked at Miguel over by the wagon, then glanced at the cowboys who were scattered around the campsite. "You go tell Miguel what's happening, I'll round up the boys so we can tell them what we're doing before we leave."

Jared ran over to where Miguel stood and filled him in on the telegram. Miguel's initial reaction was that he would come too, but Jared prevailed on him to take care of the business at hand before heading south with the wagon. "Miguel, we need you to get these boys paid off and get the wagon back. Tomas can follow you with the remuda."

Jared looked over and saw that Juan had gathered the cowboys around him and was talking in an animated fashion. He jogged back over to them. "Boys," he said, "I don't know for sure what's happened but me and Juan have got to skeedaddle out of here pronto. I guess he told you that Miguel will settle up with you. You all know you can trust him. You're all good hands, it's been a pleasure workin' with you."

The cowboys began peppering him with questions and Jared raised his hands to silence them. "I can't answer your questions, boys. There's no time and I don't have the answers anyway. All I know is that there's trouble and my wife is in danger."

Jared turned and walked quickly towards his horse. Just as he started to mount up, he was aware of someone standing right behind him. He turned and saw Tom Stallings.

"Tommy, I don't have time to talk right now. Like I said, Miguel will take care of you."

"I didn't intend to talk, Mr. Jared," Stallings said. "I intended to ride along with you."

Jared was taken aback. "This ain't your fight, Tommy. I can't let you take the risk."

Stallings grinned at him. "Since this drive is done, I don't reckon I work for you anymore, Mr. Jared. You ain't my boss no more so you can't tell me what to do. Besides," he said in a more serious tone, "it kinda feels like my fight now. I think I'll mount up and ride along."

Jared started to protest, then thought better of it. He didn't know what trouble lay ahead but he knew Stallings had proven himself on this drive and it never hurt to have another hand by your side. "Suit yourself, then, but mount up now. We're movin' fast."

CHAPTER 18

The sun was just showing its face when Pancho Vega rode out to the Kilpatrick spread to see what he could find. He approached cautiously and snuck up on the house, but what he found was nothing. There were no signs of life and it didn't appear to him that anyone had been there for awhile. The horses had been turned out to pasture to the east of the ranch house and were grazing contentedly. He returned to Cimarron and reported this news to Curt Barwick.

"I don't know where they are," Vega said, "but they ain't at the ranch. The way the horses are turned out, it looks to me like they plan to be gone for awhile."

Barwick was silent for so long that Pancho thought maybe he hadn't heard or understood what he said. "Curt, did you hear me? I said . . ."

"Dammit, Pancho," Barwick shouted as

he slammed his fist on the table in the tavern where the two of them sat, "Would you shut up, I'm trying to think!"

Gentleman Curt Barwick may have been the only man Pancho Vega would allow to speak to him that way. He raised his hands as if in surrender and said, "All right, all right, I'll be quiet. You don't have to yell at me."

Barwick ignored him and continued to think. Finally, he spoke. "Hard as it is for me to believe, the evidence is pretty clear. Those women somehow got the best of Dick and made off with that old sheriff. They've got themselves a hidey hole somewhere and we've got to find it."

Cautiously, Vega asked, "How we gonna do that, Curt?"

Barwick showed a ghost of a smile but his eyes remained cold. "Simple, Pancho. We find out who knows them and we sweat it out of them. Comprende?"

After remaining unconscious all night and most of the next day, Nathan finally opened his eyes to find Christy sitting on a wooden stool next to the cot on which he rested. He wasn't sure where he was or how he'd gotten there, but he figured if Christy was there, things were all right. He smiled.

"You back among the living now, sheriff?" Christy tried to take a light-hearted tone although her eyes were brimming with tears. "You sure gave us a scare!"

Nathan attempted to speak but his words came out as a croak and he realized that his throat was as dry as the desert. Christy recognized the problem immediately and quickly bent over to grab the canteen she had set beside the cot. She'd been using the water to moisten a cloth with which she'd been wiping his brow to sooth his raging fever during the night. Nathan attempted to sit up but the pain in his head was far too intense. He sank back onto the cot.

"Nathan, honey, you open your mouth and I'll pour just a little bit of water into it. I won't pour too much cause I don't want you to choke." She gently stroked his stubbled cheek with her left hand then she opened the canteen. "Here, let's try it."

Nathan felt like a baby bird as he lay there helpless with his mouth open. True to her word, Christy poured in a trickle which was barely enough for him to moisten the inside of his mouth. He mouthed the word "more" and she poured in a slightly larger quantity. This time, he was able to swish it around in his mouth and then swallow, which soothed his throat a bit. They went through this routine a few more times until he finally felt like he could say a few words.

"Where are we and what happened?" He croaked.

"We're in a line shack in a hidden canyon up in the foothills northwest of town. It's an old place that Ned Kilpatrick used years ago. Nobody knows about it." Christy glanced away and then looked back. "I think we're safe for now but I don't know how long that'll last."

Nathan tried to think about what she'd said but his thoughts seemed fuzzy and jumbled. Finally, he said, "Barwick did this, didn't he?"

"He did," Christy said. "Him and those other two outlaws he had with him. You're hurt pretty bad, but you're awful lucky even to be alive."

"How did you get me away from'em?"

"That's a long story, hon. Me, Lizbeth, Eleanor and Maria hoodwinked one of'em, with a little help from an Irish girl from the tavern. When you're feelin' better, I'll tell you all about it but right now, you need to rest so you can get back on your feet."

Nathan started to argue with her but he realized that he was completely exhausted from this brief conversation. He knew she was right because he felt as weak as a newborn colt. Smiling at her once more, he closed his eyes and was almost immediately asleep again. Christy stayed beside him for a few more minutes, making sure his breathing was steady. Once she determined he was resting comfortably, she went outside the rundown cabin where Eleanor, Lizbeth and Maria were standing around talking.

"How's he doing?" Eleanor asked in a worried tone.

"He was awake for a couple of minutes," Christy said, "but he's back asleep now. He took a couple of sips of water. He's awful weak but I feel better now that he's talked to me. I reckon if he can come to once, he'll likely do it again."

"I hope you're right," Lizbeth said. "There's not much more we can do for him than keep him quiet and give him water when he wakes up. I doubt he'll be able to hold down any food until at least tomorrow, but I don't reckon he'll starve between now and then."

"The question is," Maria said emphatically, "what are **we** going to do. We can't stay up here forever and those pendejos might be able to track us, I don't know. I don't want to just sit here and wait for that to happen."

"There's a lot we don't know," Lizbeth

said as she gazed out over the valley from their secluded spot. "We don't know for sure that Mollie got the telegram to Ben Martinez, we don't know if Jared's gotten it yet. And we don't know when the men will be home."

"We can't wait for the men," Eleanor said.

The other women looked at her curiously. Finally, Lizbeth spoke. "Honey, you can't be thinkin' we can go up against those two gunslingers, can you?" She shook her head in amazement. "Those are two bad men. I don't know that Nathan coulda took 'em and he's as tough as they come."

Eleanor looked around at her friends. "We can't wait for the men," she repeated. "Like you said, Lizbeth, we don't know if they'll be here in time to help, and they may ride into the situation blind if they didn't get the telegram." Her eyes flashed. "I **refuse** to sit around helplessly and wait to be hunted down like some animal. I won't accept that!"

Lizbeth, Maria and Christy looked at one another. "So what do you think we should do?" Lizbeth asked.

"I say we fight back," Eleanor said grimly. "I say that we fight back hard, smart, and mean." She set her jaw firmly. "I say that we win at any cost, even if it means killing both of those scalawags."

All of a sudden, Maria started laughing. The other women looked at her as if she'd gone insane. "What in the Sam Hill is so all-fired funny, Maria?" Lizbeth asked.

It took Maria a moment to stop laughing long enough to where she could speak coherently. Finally, she said, "I'm just trying to remember if I've ever done anything to make Eleanor mad. She's scary! I wouldn't want her mad at me."

Slowly, the other women began to smile and then one by one, they burst into peals of laughter. They laughed for quite a while before finally calming down as the tension they'd been experiencing melted away like spring snow in the high country. Then they went inside and began to plot again.

It took Jared, Juan and Tom Stalling two and a half days to reach the north side of Raton pass. Jared wanted to ride on through the nights but Juan convinced him that they were pushing the horses as hard as they possibly could and needed to conserve some of their energy.

When they reached the pass, the sky was a vivid blue. Clearly, the foul weather they had experienced just days before had blown over. Realizing that nightfall would overtake them before they made it all the way through to Raton, they decided it was worth the risk so they pushed on. They made it through without problems, but they noticed their horses were just about done in.

"You know, if we want to keep up this pace, we've got to get new mounts, amigo," Juan said.

"Yep," Jared said. "I think I've got it figured out where we can get some, and maybe some extra firearms as well."

Juan waited for the rest of the story but Jared rode on in silence. Finally, he said with some exasperation, "Well, are you going to tell me or is it a secret?"

"Sorry," Jared said. "I got to thinkin' about what might be happenin' in Cimarron and it slipped my mind to explain it to you. I have a friend in Raton." Jared jerked his thumb in Tom Stallings direction and said, "He helped us out of the scrape that our young compadre over here got us into with those gamblers." Stallings looked sheepish as Juan stared over at him. "Oh, yeah, they were cattle rustlers, too, weren't they Tommy," Jared said pointedly.

"Hey, I'm sorry, Mr. Jared, but it turned out all right, didn't it? Besides," he said with a grin, "You did get to make a new friend."

"So who's the friend and how is he going to help us?" Juan asked.

"His name is Big Jim Rogers and he owns the Wild Mustang Saloon," Jared responded. "I reckon he'll have his own horses or else he'll know who can get us some in a hurry." Jared smiled at Juan. "He's the kind of a man who gets what he wants and gets things done. You'll see."

"I can't wait to meet this hombre," Juan said.

They rode on in silence for another twenty minutes and found themselves on the north edge of town. They rode down the middle of the main street until Jared saw the hand-painted sign for the Wild Mustang. He reined his horse in at the hitching post and Juan and Tom did the same. He motioned to them to follow him and they entered the establishment.

The place was as crowded as it had been the previous time he'd been there. He didn't see Big Jim's form towering above the patrons, but after looking around a bit, he did spy Ellie Rogers. She glanced his way and he waved to get her attention. For a minute, she didn't appear to recognize him, but then he saw her smile and hurry his way.

"Evenin', Mr. Delaney, it's good to see you again. You want a steak?"

Jared doffed his hat. "Evenin' back at you, Miss Ellie, a steak for me and my friends would be a welcome sight. But what I need to do real fast is to have a word with your daddy. Is he around?"

"He's back in the kitchen," the young lady said. "I'll go tell him you're here and get those steaks a'cookin' while I'm at it."

"Much obliged, m'am."

She walked away and Jared searched for an empty table. He finally spied one in the back and directed Juan and Tom to go claim it while he waited for Big Jim to come out. In a few minutes, he saw the towering figure of the saloonkeeper step out from behind the bar and head his way.

"Evenin', Mr. Delaney," Big Jim said in that high-pitched voice that didn't match his bulk. "You made it back sooner than I expected. How did your cattle drive go?"

"You can still call me Jared, Big Jim. The cattle drive had a few rough spots but we made it. That ain't what I need to talk with you about though. We got bigger trouble."

With a concerned look, Jim asked, "What is it and what do you need me to do?"

Jared felt a sense of relief that his instinct had been accurate and the big man was willing to assist them. "I don't know for sure what's happenin' down in Cimarron, but I got a telegram that my wife is in danger. We need to get there fast as we can and our horses are about done in. We've been ridin' em hard the last three days."

"I'll get you horses, Jared, that's not a problem. Do you need weapons?"

"Well, I was hopin' you could help us with both those things," Jared said. "We're armed but it never hurts to have a few more sidearms or an extra rifle or two, does it?"

"Better to be over-armed than under-armed, eh?" Big Jim laughed. "I can take care of you, nothin' to worry about."

Jared heard a noise and turned to see Ellie Rogers and another serving girl coming out of the kitchen with three plates with beefsteaks spilling over the sides along with three beers. He turned to Big Jim. "I can't tell you how much I appreciate your helpin' me out like this, Jim. If I can ever do anything for you, all you got to do is speak up and it'll get done."

"I know that, Jared," the big man said. "I could tell you was a straight shooter from the moment I first talked to you. Some people can tell about the weather and such, but me, I know people . . . and you're good people."

They shook hands and Jared tried not to wince when Big Jim gripped his hand. What he probably thought of as a firm handshake was nearly a bone crusher. When Big Jim let go, Jared said with a grin, "I hope I can use that hand to shoot with when I need to, Jim."

"Sorry, pardner, sometimes I don't know my strength." Jim smiled sheepishly. "Now why don't you head on over to join your compadres and get some of this food inside your belly. You'll be needin' *your* strength. I'll go check on those horses and weapons and get back to you before you're done eatin'. You'll be needin' a place to bed down for the night, I suppose?"

"Much as I hate to slow down at all, I reckon we do need a few hours sleep. We'll head out at dawn."

"I can put you up at the stable where I'll be securin' your horses if that's all right with you. It ain't a fancy hotel or nothin' but I figure you fellas been sleepin' out under the stars anyway. A nice bed of straw might be the lap of luxury for you."

"That'll do us just fine, Jim, thank you kindly."

Big Jim turned and headed for the door of his establishment. Jared quickly walked over to the table where Juan and Tom were busy chowing down on the beefsteaks.

"Thanks for waitin' for me, amigos," Jared said sarcastically.

Neither cowboy slowed down the rate at

which they were putting away the beefsteak but Juan waved a dismissive hand at Jared, who decided the smart thing to do would be to grab a plate and get busy eating. For the next ten minutes or so, there was no conversation at the table as they put away all the food they could hold in typical cowboy fashion. Eat as much as you can, when you can, because you're never sure when your next meal will be. When Jared had polished off all the food the other two had left on the table, he sat back in his chair.

"Big Jim is gettin' us mounts and he's comin' up with some weapons, too. He'll arrange for us to bunk at the stables so we can get an early start in the mornin'."

Stallings just nodded. Juan said, "This Big Jim is a fine fellow, amigo. He's the one who got you out of that mess on the way up here, que no?"

"He's the one," Jared said. "He's a good friend, all right . . . and I sure don't reckon I'd want him as an enemy." Jared yawned. "I expect we ought to turn in pretty quick. I want to get out of here at first light, if not a little before."

They pulled away from the table and walked over to the bar where Big Jim and his daughter, Ellie, were standing. Juan and Tom added their thanks to Jared's, and Big

Jim told them they were more than welcome. He asked Stallings if he'd been in any poker games lately, which caused him to blush, particularly when he heard Ellie giggle. When they tried to pay him for their meals, he refused, saying it was on the house.

"You're friend here has already promised that if I ever need anything, he'll come a'runnin'. I figure that if you're owin' me for a meal, you'll have to come a'runnin', too."

The big man laughed, and Tom Stallings spoke up for the first time. "Mister, you're lendin' a hand to someone that I respect a whole lot. If he's in your debt, I am, too. Thanks again."

Big Jim nodded to Stallings and turned to Jared. "These pards of yours are all right. Glad you got some good hands with you, it sounds like you might need'em when you make it back to Cimarron."

"I don't know what's waitin' for us there," Jared said, "but you may be right. Could we trouble you to direct us to the stables?"

"I'll do better than that," Jim said, "I'll walk you over myself. Teddy Cummings knows you're comin' and he should have picked you out some good horses for you by now."

"Again, Jim, we're much obliged."

Big Jim walked with them to the stables and introduced them to Teddy Cummings. They were surprised to discover that Cummings had taken their horses from where they had left them tied outside the Wild Mustang. He'd removed their saddles, brushed them down and spread some hay for them. He pointed out the stalls where their mounts for the next morning were and showed them that he'd slung each of their saddles over the boards so they'd be handy in the morning.

"Thanks more than I can say, Mr. Cummings," Jared said. He turned to Big Jim. "I don't know how you got all this set up so fast after we talked but it looks like I'm even more obliged than I realized." He stuck his hand out, risking another bone-crushing handshake. "For what it's worth, I'm your friend for life."

"I'll remember that, Jared. You never know when you might need a good friend. In the meantime, you boys oughta be hittin' the hay, don't you think?"

"You're right about that," Juan said. "I could ride all night but Tommy here, he's a young pup with no experience and Jared, he's getting too old. He just can't do what he used to do."

Big Jim laughed out loud at that. He looked like he was about to say something, but then he apparently decided there was little to add to Juan's evaluation of the situation. He just waved his hand at them and walked away, laughing as he headed back to his business establishment.

After a few hours sleep, they were saddled up and on the trail before daylight, riding in silence most of the way. They drove their horses hard and made the forty mile trip in good time. By early afternoon, they were a couple of miles north of the turnoff to the Kilpatrick ranch. Only then did Jared speak.

"I think we ought to split up. We don't know what's happenin' and we can gather more information if we go our separate ways. We'll rendezvous about an hour before sundown on the hill just north of town."

Juan considered this. "That makes sense. How do you want to do it?"

"I'll go to the ranch. You and Tommy head into town, you can split up when you get there." Jared paused and thought. "I reckon one of you ought to swing by the Colfax Tavern. If the trouble ain't happenin' there, they'll more'n likely know where it is happenin'."

"You got any ideas what this is about, amigo?" Juan squinted as he looked to the foothills to the east where the sun reflected off the pale rocks.

"I don't," Jared said. "Things have been quiet most of the time since we took care of Morgan O'Bannon and his crew." Jared rode along with a perplexed look for a ways. "I'd have to guess that some troublemaker's come to town, though. There ain't much that happens in town or on the ranch that Nathan or those women can't handle. I expect this is somethin' more than routine trouble."

They were approaching the point where Jared would turn to the southwest and take a trail that would lead him to the ranch. Stallings had been quiet all morning.

"You all right, Tommy?" Jared asked. "You don't have to do this if you don't want to. There'd be no hard feelin's. You showed yourself to be a good hand on this drive. You got nothin' more to prove."

"Nah," Stallings said with a slow drawl. "I expect I'll stick with you boys."

Jared looked at him for a long moment then he nodded. There was nothing left to say. In a few minutes, they reached the turnoff and reined in their horses. Jared reached into his saddlebags and pulled out a bandolier of rifle ammunition, which he slung across his chest. Juan and Stallings did the same.

Juan looked sideways at Jared. "You be careful, amigo, don't go getting yourself shot. If they kill you, I don't know who I'd poke fun at."

Jared smiled and shook his head. "You're a sentimental cuss, Suazo. I reckon that's why I like you. You boys be careful, too."

They separated with Jared riding southwest toward the ranch and Juan and Stallings riding due south into town.

CHAPTER 19

Maria Suazo slowed her horse to a walk as she picked her way through the brush on the west side of town. For the second time in two days, she was slipping in to see if any word had come from Jared and Juan. She'd snuck into the Mares Café the day before and spoken with Anita Mares and her son, Estevan. They'd heard nothing and were worried sick about Miguel. She told Estevan to check with Ben Martinez at the telegraph office each day so that if any messages came in, he could let her know the next day.

Tying her horse to a scrub oak out back of the café, Maria glided silently through the alley and slipped in the front door. There was no one in the dining room of the café, which struck her as odd, but it was mid-morning and she assumed they were in between the breakfast and noon meal rushes. Quickly, she entered the kitchen and was puzzled to see Anita Mares standing against the far wall with a stricken look on her face. Glancing down, she saw Estevan lying on the floor bleeding from a wound to the head. Maria couldn't tell from where she stood if he was unconscious or dead. Before she could ask any questions, she was seized roughly from behind. A huge, calloused hand covered her mouth and she felt the cold steel of a hunting knife at her throat.

"Glad you could join the party, senorita," Pancho Vega said with a low rumble. "Now we'll have us some fun."

The man's breath reeked of whiskey and was hot on her ear. Maria struggled very briefly, but stopped as soon as she felt the increased pressure of the hunting knife on her throat. She tried not to panic, knowing she would need a clear head to get out of this mess. She could feel the raw strength of the man who held her in this malevolent embrace, and she knew she could never overpower him. She could only hope to outwit him and pray that the others carried out their parts perfectly in this plan they had orchestrated.

Eleanor, Lizbeth and Christy left Nathan Averill at the line shack with enough food and water to last for several days and

337

headed into town. Lizbeth and Eleanor were horseback while Christy handled the buckboard. Nathan had been appalled at the plan they had developed to take on the two outlaws and begged them to reconsider. He had protested vehemently, making an attempt to get up and put on his clothes so that he could go with them. When he found himself too weak even to accomplish that, he gave up in resignation. Once he saw they would not be dissuaded, he told them where he kept the firearms in his office. He also told them they were the most hard-headed, opinionated and foolish women he'd ever met in his life. Then he wished them luck. They were going to need it.

Making no attempt at stealth, Christy drove the buckboard into town from the north while Lizbeth and Eleanor slipped around surreptitiously to the east side and snuck into the sheriff's office. The plot they were pinning their slim hopes on was that Christy would be able to lure one or both men to the office on some pretense. If they could catch them off guard, they could get the drop on them. With a lot of luck, they might be able to lock them in the cell immediately and then wait for help from someone with legal authority to step in for Nathan. They realized this was a long shot at best, with potentially deadly consequences for failure. But they were desperate and since they had no better plan, they settled in to Nathan's office. They took their shotguns, grabbed two spare pistols each and went to the far corners of the room so that both had clear shots at the door without endangering the other. Then they waited.

As Christy drove the buckboard on into town, she glanced down the main street where she saw a young cowboy dismounting and walking into the Colfax Tavern. Although it was early in the afternoon to be drinking, she knew from experience that this didn't stop many of the patrons of the tavern, so she gave it little thought. In a couple of minutes, she pulled the buckboard up to the hitching post outside the tavern. As she was setting the brake, she felt a sharp pain in her wounded left arm. She looked down at her sleeve and saw a patch of blood, which gradually grew wider. She climbed down and walked inside.

It took a moment for her eyes to adjust to the dark environs. Once she could see clearly, she saw the young cowboy standing at the bar in a conversation with the bartender, Tom Lacey. Irish Mollie was also behind the bar, and as the bartender walked away, Christy saw Mollie motion to the cowboy to lean over. When he did, she whispered something in his ear and the cowboy stiffened as he glanced over to a table across the tavern. Christy followed his glance and saw Gentleman Curt Barwick leaning back in a chair, propped up against the wall where he had an eagle's eye view of everything that was happening in the room. He had observed the entire interaction and had a smirk on his face.

Tom Stallings saw red. The young Irish barmaid had overheard his conversation with the bartender, who had told him he knew nothing of any trouble at the Kilpatrick ranch. When the bartender walked away, she had motioned him over and quickly whispered to him that the man across the tavern had tried to kill the sheriff and was gunning for Jared Delaney. Stallings owed his life to Jared Delaney and he'd be damned if he'd let some hired gun kill him. He walked over toward the man who sat smirking at him as if he knew what was happening and was in control of the situation.

"I hear you been makin' trouble for Mrs. Delaney and her friends," Stallings said in clipped tones. "That's gonna end right now."

Barwick stared at Stallings with an amused look on his face. He continued to lean back

340

in his chair and slowly reached over to get the shot glass full of whiskey that sat on the table. He downed the whiskey, set the glass back on the table, threw his head back and laughed.

"Is it, now? I'm going to ride out of town with my tail between my legs because some young, wet-behind-the-ears cowpuncher tells me to? Young man, I think you're very confused."

Stallings stared back at Barwick without expression. "I don't care if you ride out with your tail between your legs or not, mister, I just want you gone pronto. If you stay here, you and me are gonna have trouble."

Barwick laughed again, louder this time. "You're serious, aren't you? You really seem to think *you* could cause me trouble. That's rich!"

As Christy observed this interplay, her mind raced. She didn't recognize the young cowboy but she figured he must be one of Jared's hands. If he was here, that might mean Jared wasn't far away. In the meantime, however, she could see this was going downhill fast, and were she still a betting woman, she knew her money would be on Barwick if there was any gunplay. Quietly, she slipped out the door of the tavern and ran as fast as she could toward the sheriff's office. She didn't know where Jared was, but she knew where Lizbeth and Eleanor were supposed to be if they had followed their plan. Clearly, it was time to change the plan.

Jared stared down at the ranch house from the stand of aspens up on the hill. He'd been mounted there quietly observing for several minutes, and had seen no movement in or around the house. He could see that the horses were turned out to pasture and the wagon was gone from its usual spot by the barn. He decided he'd been cautious long enough. It was time to ride down and check things out first hand.

Hollering out for Eleanor and Lizbeth, he quickly dismounted and ran up to the porch. He slowed down briefly as he opened the door, but the room felt empty. It even smelled empty. The stove was cold and so were the lamps. Clearly, no one had been there for some time. What set his heart to pounding was what else wasn't there. There were no weapons present. Usually, there were two shotguns hanging on a rack on the wall and a Winchester rifle standing in the corner. They were gone. Wherever Eleanor and Lizbeth had gone, they had clearly felt the need to arm themselves.

Jared took stock of the situation. He saw no signs of a struggle, so he figured the women had left of their on volition, but he had no idea where they might have gone or why they left. He could think of nothing more to do at the ranch so he decided to light a shuck for town as fast as he could and catch up with Juan and Tom. Something was very wrong.

Juan left Tom Stallings at the entrance to the Colfax Tavern and trotted in the direction of the Mares Café. He needed an answer to the question of what had put Eleanor Delaney, Lizbeth Kilpatrick and his wife in danger, and he hoped Anita Mares could supply it or at least point him in the right direction. As he approached the door to the café, he realized that not a soul was out and about in town, which was completely out of the ordinary. Whatever was happening, the townspeople appeared to have gotten wind of it and obviously wanted no part.

Gun drawn, alert to unseen dangers, he cautiously opened the door and seeing no one, stepped inside. He looked around the dining area but there was no one in sight. Off in the distance, he thought he heard two gunshots coming from the north end of town. He started to turn and go investigate the shots but then he heard muffled noises from the kitchen and as he got closer, he recognized his wife's voice speaking in a tone that conveyed both anger and fear. He also heard a deeper voice speaking in a tone that was at the same time taunting and malicious. He needed no further evidence that the trouble was right here. Pistol in hand, he burst through the kitchen door.

What Juan saw horrified and enraged him. A huge Mexican man was straddling his wife, holding a knife in one hand and unbuttoning his trousers with the other. Maria was frantically swinging her fists as she attempted to defend her honor but it was clear that she was no match physically for the man.

"Alto!" Juan roared at the top of his voice. "Get up now or I'll shoot you, hombre!"

Pancho Vega was as agile as a mountain lion but he was at a disadvantage because his trousers were partly undone and had slid down his legs. He realized that he could not leap to his feet and draw his gun in time so he chose another route. He grabbed the woman he'd been terrorizing and rolled over against the wall so that she was between him and the raging cowboy who'd burst into the kitchen. With his back against the wall, he held his knife to the throat of the woman and smiled at the cowboy.

"Unless you want me to slit this pretty throat, you'd better put that pistola down right now, amigo."

Juan's mind raced as he sized up the situation. He looked in the eyes of the man who held his wife in a death grip and saw neither fear nor compassion. He shrugged and smiled back at Vega. "What makes you think I care if you slit her throat? All she does is cook my beans. I can find another woman to cook my beans." His smile widened as he thumbed the hammer back. "It looks to me like you brought a knife to a gun fight, senor."

Maria's eyes had widened in shock when Juan spoke but then a look of understanding came over her face. Pancho Vega's expression was vastly different from hers, though. He thought he'd taken the upper hand by using the woman as a shield, but now it appeared this vaquero cared little for her. He decided on a different plan of action and with one arm, he literally threw Maria across the room towards Juan. In the same motion, he dropped his knife, grabbed the front of his trousers with his left hand and leaping to his feet, went for his gun with his right hand.

Juan hesitated to make sure that Maria was out of the line of fire and this was nearly his undoing. Vega had his gun out of the holster and was swinging it in Juan's direction but he stumbled as he tried to gain his feet. This fraction of a second was all that Juan needed, and he blazed away with his Colt .45 Peacemaker, pouring all six rounds into the body of the villain.

Vega rolled over briefly and tried to lift his gun to fire. Drawing a second gun, Juan stood poised to leap behind a table for cover if he needed it, but as it turned out this action was unnecessary. Vega's eyes glazed over and he sank back in a heap. Juan watched anxiously for several moments, then he walked over carefully and checked the man for a pulse. Finding none, he turned and raced to Maria's side.

Maria had been stunned when she was flung across the room. She was just coming out of her fog when Juan reached her side and scooped her up in his arms. Hugging her frantically, he said, "Cara mia, are you all right?"

She hugged him back ferociously for several moments, then pulled back and looked at him. "The woman who cooks your beans? This is the best you could come up with?"

Christy was almost to the sheriff's office when she heard two shots from back at the Colfax Tavern. Fearing the worst, she doubled her speed and grabbed the door. Realizing at the last second that her friends were poised to shoot whoever came through that door, she stopped in her tracks.

"Eleanor, Lizbeth, it's me, Christy. We've got to change the plan. Don't shoot!"

Cautiously opening the door a crack, she said, "It's me, Christy. We need to talk . . . fast!"

Lizbeth said, "Come on in, we ain't gonna shoot you."

Christy came in the sheriff's office and tried to catch her breath. Eleanor came over and put her hand on Christy's shoulder.

"Take a minute to breathe," Eleanor said. "Whatever it is can wait a few seconds."

"No, it can't," Christy replied urgently. "I heard some shooting down at the tavern. It was Barwick and one of Jared's hands. He was just a kid and no match for Barwick. I'm afraid he's done for already but we need to go see about him."

When Eleanor heard that one of Jared's hands was in town, her heart soared because that meant her husband was likely close by. Just as rapidly as it soared, it sank as she realized that he might be in mortal danger as well, and the urgency of the situation struck home.

"We've got to get there fast," Eleanor said. "Jared and Juan may walk right into a trap."

Lizbeth found a gun belt, put it on and holstered her pistol. She took up her shotgun and said, "You two go down the alley and come in through the back. I'll go in the front." As Eleanor and Christy opened their mouths to protest, she interrupted. "We don't have time for this, just do as I say. Go now!"

Christy and Eleanor grabbed weapons and ran out the door. As they crossed the street and entered the narrow alleyway that ran behind the business establishments along Main Street, they heard multiple gunshots from the south end of town. Christy cast a questioning glance at Eleanor, who shook her head in confusion. She stood there for a moment thinking, and then whispered to continue on with the plan. They made their way down toward the back entrance of the Colfax Tavern. Lizbeth strode quickly down the boardwalk and crossing the street, entered the tavern with her shotgun leveled in case a welcoming party awaited her.

The tavern was deserted except for Mollie, who was kneeling over a young cowboy who lay bleeding on the floor. Lizbeth ran over to her side as Eleanor and Christy came in the back and peeked their heads around the corner of the hallway.

"Come quick," Lizbeth shouted. "This boy's hurt bad if he ain't already dead." She turned to Mollie and asked, "What happened, lass?"

Mollie's skin was the pale gray color of the weathered boards outside the tavern and she was taking shallow breaths. Eleanor came over quickly and pulled up a chair. Mollie melted into it.

"Easy, Mollie," she said gently. "Slow down and take long, deep breaths. You need to calm down so you can tell us what happened."

Mollie sat in the chair and began taking deep breaths. She kept her eyes on the young cowboy and the other women could read the anguish there. Finally, she was able to speak.

"It's my fault. It's all my fault." She got this much out and then began to cry.

Lizbeth reached over and grasping her by the shoulders, shook Mollie none too gently. "Calm yourself, girl, we don't have time for this." She took Mollie's chin in her hand

and directed her face up so that she was looking at her. "Tell us what happened."

With a shudder, Mollie managed to pull herself together. "This boy came in and talked to Tom at the bar, asking about the trouble Mrs. Delaney was having. Tom told him he knew nothing about it, the snake, and went on about his business." Mollie cast a venomous glance over her shoulder in the direction of the bar where Tom had been earlier, then she continued. "I told this boy it weren't true, that the outlaw Barwick was the one causin' the trouble."

She started to cry again and Lizbeth reached over and shook her once more. "Don't stop, Mollie, we need to know this."

Again, Mollie collected herself and continued. "Saints preserve us, I thought he would go get help but he didn't. He just walked over bold as could be and called out Mr. Barwick." She shook her head in amazement. "He told him to get out of town or he'd be sorry, is what he did."

Christy had bent over Tom Stallings while the others were talking, and found a bullet wound in the upper left corner of his chest. Apparently, Barwick had gone for a heart shot but his aim was off, if only by mere inches. The wound was still bleeding heavily but there were no bubbles in the blood, which made her think the shot had missed his lung. She quickly ran over behind the bar and came back with a clean rag that she held tightly to the wound. As she did, she bent over again and checked to see if any breath was coming out of the young cowboy's mouth and nose.

"I think he's still alive," she called out.

Eleanor said, "As soon as we hear the rest of this story, one of us needs to go get Doc Adams." She turned to Mollie and said, "Finish, girl, be quick."

"Barwick was laughin' at the boy, sayin' he couldn't be serious about callin' him out." In spite of her anguish, Mollie chuckled. "Sure and it was somethin' to see, miss. Quick like a cat, the boy kicked Barwick's chair right out from under him. He came crashin' to the floor and broke his bottle of whiskey, he did."

"We heard two shots," Eleanor said. "What happened after the boy kicked his chair out from under him?"

Mollie's eyes grew wide. "That Barwick fella moved twice as fast as the boy ever did. It was almost like he bounced off the floor and came up with his gun in his hand." Again, Mollie began to cry but she struggled on through her tears. "The boy got his gun out but Barwick fired first and hit him in the chest. As he was goin' down, he pulled the trigger and I heard Barwick holler like a stuck pig. He slumped against the wall for a moment, then he limped off through the back door without another word."

Lizbeth looked at Eleanor. "He's wounded and he's out there somewhere along with that big Mexican hombre." She turned to Mollie and said, "Listen to me, Mollie. You've got to put your feelin's aside right now and run as fast as you can to Doc Adam's office. Do you know where it is?"

"Yes, m'am, I do," Mollie said. "I've had to fetch him before when we had some dust ups here that resulted in busted heads."

"Well," Lizbeth said urgently, "Go find him and bring him back. You tell him I said we got a cowboy down and if he don't get here quick, he's gonna die. You understand?"

"Yes, miss, I do." Mollie got up and after glancing once more at the young cowboy, she walked quickly out the door of the Colfax Tavern.

Lizbeth looked at Christy, who was still tending to Stallings, and then over at Eleanor. "This'd be a durn good time for Jared and Juan to show up, don't you think?"

Jared pushed his horse as fast as he could,

but the mount was about done in from the hard ride they'd already made. He didn't know what fate he was rushing toward but he felt a strong sense of urgency and foreboding. Eleanor and her friends would never have telegraphed for help unless they were in dire straits. They were not the kind to make a mountain out of a prairie dog hill. It was especially disturbing that they apparently hadn't felt like Nathan could manage whatever the trouble might be. You'd be hard-pressed to find a tougher and more competent lawman in the West. Yet they'd felt the need to call out for assistance. He felt a chill travel up his spine and he knew it wasn't from the afternoon breeze that was rustling the leaves on the cottonwood trees along the trail.

Since Jared didn't know the exact nature of the danger he was riding into, he figured he'd better proceed cautiously once he got to the outskirts of town. He decided he would dismount at the livery stable at the north end of town and go on foot from there. He would stay on the west boardwalk, so that he would be partially hidden by the shadows until he knew who the enemy was and then he would show himself. He felt his fear for the safety of his wife gather like an approaching thunderstorm and struggled to push it down. Whatever lay in store, he knew he needed to be calm and collected in order to handle it. Everything depended on his being ready to take whatever action necessary when the time came. He'd lost his family when he was a young boy, unable to do anything to prevent it. This time, he was a grown man and he refused to let it happen. He spurred his horse into a fast lope and put the remaining mile to town behind him.

Barwick limped toward the south end of town where he knew Pancho Vega had gone to beat some information out of the woman who ran the café. His wounded leg was painful but he'd tied a bandanna around it, and that seemed to have stopped the bleeding. The bullet had passed through the muscle of his right thigh but luckily, it had missed the bone. Still, he was having some difficulty walking steadily. He cursed himself. He'd taken the young cowboy too lightly and had gotten careless. He hadn't anticipated that the boy would make the first move, kicking his chair out from under him. He'd beaten him to the draw, but having to get himself up off the floor had given the kid time to pull the trigger. He thought he'd made a killing shot to the heart but he wasn't sure. If not, he knew the cowboy was badly wounded at the least, and he doubted he'd be much trouble in the immediate future. His main concern now was to find Pancho and finish this thing off.

Damn those women anyway! They were making more of a stand than he'd ever expected but they had to know it was a lost cause. No one challenged Gentleman Curt Barwick and lived to tell about it. He felt the rage well up inside and had to stop to take a couple of deep breaths to get himself under control. His eyes narrowed as he anticipated dealing with them. If he'd had any reservations about killing the women before, they were gone. They would pay dearly.

Barwick was still a block north of the Mares Café when he heard six pistol shots in rapid succession. He backed up onto the sidewalk and took cover behind a rain barrel as he waited for Pancho to come out. He wasn't sure who Vega had shot, or why, but he figured it was someone who needed killing. As he waited, his leg throbbed and he wondered if the bullet had passed on through or was lodged in the muscle. He could make do for now, but he knew he would need a doctor pretty soon.

After waiting for several minutes, he began to wonder if something hadn't gone wrong.

He thought it likely that if Pancho had killed someone in the café, he would get out of there and come find him so Barwick could plan their next move. Pancho was good at killing people but not much for thinking independently. After several more minutes passed, he knew the situation might be spinning out of control. He couldn't wait any longer for Vega. He needed to go find the women and put an end to this.

Jared dismounted quickly at the livery stable and drew his Winchester .44 out of the scabbard. He had his Colt pistol in the holster at his side and a snub-nosed Peacemaker tucked into his gunbelt in the back. Glancing up at the sky, he gave a word of thanks for his new friend, Big Jim Rogers. He'd supplied all the weapons they could possibly need. Now all Jared had to do was use them with deadly efficiency and make no mistakes.

Jared was running across the street when he heard the familiar sound of a Colt .45 firing six times. He knew that spelled trouble, but he still didn't know what he was getting into. He made his way to the west side of the street and waited in the shadows to see what developed.

He waited for what seemed like hours, but

was in reality only minutes. With the sun slipping down toward the horizon, the temperature was dropping. In spite of this, he found himself sweating. Then in the distance a little south of the Colfax Tavern, he saw a man walking in his direction. The man appeared to be limping. He also was wearing a gunbelt and even from a distance where Jared stood, it looked like a gunfighter rig. Jared abandoned any efforts at stealth, breaking and running down the middle of the street. To his horror, he saw Eleanor and Lizbeth walk out of the tavern. They were each carrying a shotgun and when they saw the man, they brought the weapons up to their shoulders but didn't fire. Jared jacked a bullet into the chamber of his Winchester carbine and redoubled his efforts to cover the ground that lay between him and the danger confronting the love of his life.

Gentleman Curt Barwick was almost to the Colfax Tavern when he heard a noise. He turned and saw the two women walk out the door of the tavern. They were both armed with shotguns, but he knew he could draw and shoot them both in their tracks before either could pull the trigger. After all, he was a shootist and they were just a couple of ranch women . . . nothing to worry about.

He looked left and right quickly to see if the Mexican woman who'd gotten the drop on him before was anywhere to be seen. He didn't want any unpleasant surprises like that this time around. When he saw no sign of her, he faced the women who stood on the board sidewalk.

"Good afternoon to you, ladies," he said in a mocking tone. "You've been up to a great deal of mischief, haven't you?"

Lizbeth lowered her gun from her shoulder a few inches. "Mister, I ain't interested in talkin' with you. I'll give you one chance to turn around, go find a horse and ride out of town. If you don't do it right away, I'll shoot you down where you stand."

Barwick gazed contemptuously from one woman to the other. "I'm afraid it isn't going to go that way, Mrs. Kilpatrick. When I first came to town, this was just business but you've gone and made it personal." He smiled. "Now I'm looking forward to killing you both. I'll take my time so you'll understand before you die what a horrible mistake you made in thinking you could get the best of Gentleman Curt Barwick."

Out of the corner of her mouth, Lizbeth whispered to Eleanor. "Get back in the tavern, Eleanor! You got to protect the baby.

If he shoots me, you blaze away from behind the door."

Eleanor ignored Lizbeth's admonition. Instead, she spoke to Barwick. "We've seen your kind here before, Mr. Barwick. They were no more gentlemen than you are. We're still here." She smiled at him. "Do you know where they are?"

"No, Mrs. Delaney, pray tell, where are they?"

"They're six feet under, that's where they are," Eleanor said defiantly. "And that's where you'll be if you don't do what the lady told you."

Time seemed to stand still. Jared felt as if he were running in mud even though the street was dry. The man appeared to be talking to Eleanor and Lizbeth, but Jared could tell from the way he was standing that he was prepared in a heartbeat to begin shooting. He was torn between stopping where he was to attempt a shot at the man, or closing the distance some more to give himself a better shot. He held his rifle in front of him so that he could stop in an instant and shoulder it if he felt like he needed to fire as he continued racing forward.

"That's bold talk coming from a delicate flower like yourself, Mrs. Delaney." Barwick smiled back but there was nothing friendly in it. "After I kill Mrs. Kilpatrick, I'm going to make good on my promise to make you beg. You give that some thought, missy, before you decide to pull the trigger."

Lizbeth saw motion from the south end of the street and when she looked closer, she could make out the figures of Juan and Maria Suazo striding purposefully in their direction. Apparently, they had just walked out of the Mares Café and were coming to investigate the shots at the tavern. She realized that she needed to give them a bit of time to narrow the distance, so she continued the dialogue with Barwick.

"Let me think this through, Mr. Barwick," she said in a halting voice. "I'm not sure if I'm ready to die for that land." Eleanor shot a sharp, questioning look in her direction but Lizbeth remained focused on Barwick. "Can we trade the ranch for our lives?"

Barwick chuckled. "I'm glad to see that you're finally thinking straight, Mrs. Kilpatrick, but I'm afraid you're a little late. I would have made that deal before, but now you've gone and made me angry." His eyes narrowed. "There'll be no negotiating."

Jared was afraid that the man would begin shooting at any second, and he thought frantically of a way to cause a distraction to give himself time to get close enough to make a sure shot. He knew he'd only get one chance. He put on an extra burst of speed and at the same time, shouted at the top of his lungs.

Barwick heard a shout from the north and turning his head, saw a cowboy running his direction carrying a Winchester rifle. The man was still about fifty yards away, which was no problem for a rifle but quite a distance to make an accurate shot with a pistol. He knew he was in trouble and he had to do something fast. He fanned two shots in the direction of Lizbeth and Eleanor, then turned toward the rapidly approaching cowboy. As he stepped forward to assume a shooting stance, he put all of his weight on his wounded right leg, and for just an instant, it buckled.

Jared was still about fifty yards away when he saw the man draw his pistol and fire two shots in the direction of the women. He thought he saw one of them go down but he couldn't tell which one. He realized that there was no more time and he slid to a halt, throwing the carbine up to his shoulder. As he took aim, he saw two figures on the street just past the man and he realized that if he missed, he ran the risk of hitting one of them. He felt panic rise up through his gut and the thought flashed through his mind that he was about to lose everything he'd fought so hard to obtain. There was a time in his life when he would have faltered . . . but that time had passed. He took a deep breath, let out half of it and squeezed the trigger.

Juan had given Maria his carbine and was carrying his reloaded pistol. He saw the gunman in a standoff with Lizbeth and Eleanor, and knew they had to get there fast or it would be too late. All of a sudden, he heard a shout and looked to the north end of the street where he saw a figure racing in their direction. He hoped it was Jared but he had no time to ask questions. He saw the man draw and fire two shots towards Lizbeth and Eleanor. At that point, he knew he had no other choice and he drew down on the lone gunman. As he was pulling the trigger, he heard a deafening roar to his right and realized that Maria had fired the carbine. Almost immediately, he heard the crack of another Winchester from the other side of the man, followed by the blast of a shotgun and the pop of a small caliber pistol. After that, he lost count of the gunshots. He saw the gunman's body jump around as if he were doing a little jig, then the man crumpled to the dust in the street.

The silence hung as heavy as the gunsmoke. They stood like statues, waiting for something to happen. Then with a sob, Eleanor ran to Lizbeth's side where she'd fallen, joined almost immediately by Christy who had been standing just inside the tavern doors. From where he'd taken his killing shot, Jared broke into a run. When he arrived, he found the situation grim.

"Don't move, Lizbeth," Eleanor said in a husky voice. "Mollie will be back with Doc Adams before you know it."

"Too late," Lizbeth said with a shudder. "I won't make it." She turned her head to look at Jared and smiled. "Glad you made it back in time, cowboy."

Jared felt as if he'd been punched in the stomach. "God, Lizbeth, I don't know why I ever went on that cursed drive. If I'd been here, things would've been different."

Lizbeth coughed and then groaned from the pain. Jared saw a trickle of blood appear at the corner of her mouth. As Eleanor took her hand, Lizbeth said, "Nonsense, Jared. You did what had to be done to give your ranch a future." Her voice was weak but there was resolve in it as well.

"It's not *my* ranch, Lizbeth, it's our ranch," Jared said with equal fervor.

"No, sir. My time has passed. I'm goin' to see my Ned." A peaceful smile appeared on her lips. "It's up to you, Eleanor and the baby to carry on."

Jared frowned in confusion and looked at Eleanor for clarification. "What does she mean . . . me, you and the baby?"

Eleanor reached out and grasped Jared's hand. "I would never have wanted this to be the way you got the news but it's true. We're going to have a child."

Jared had been crouching but when Eleanor made her statement, he sat back on the sidewalk in amazement. He started to speak but then shut his mouth because he could think of nothing to say. He opened his mouth a couple more times but nothing came out.

Lizbeth was getting weaker and when she started to speak again, Eleanor had to lean over to hear the words that came out in a raspy whisper. Jared couldn't make out what was said but he saw Eleanor smile even as tears ran down her cheeks like a spring rain in the mountains. Then he saw Lizbeth return the smile and close her eyes. He didn't dare move, hoping against hope that she was just resting and would wake up as feisty as ever . . . but he knew she wouldn't.

Eleanor looked at Jared and said, "She's gone."

"I know," he said. He wiped his eyes with

his sleeve. "What did she say at the end?"

With a sad smile, Eleanor said, "She said if it's a girl, name it Elizabeth. If it's a boy, she wants it to be Edward. She said that was Ned's given name."

They sat in stunned silence for several moments, then Jared pulled himself to his feet and reached over to give Eleanor a hand up. She rose and he pulled her into a fierce embrace, which they held without speaking. Juan and Maria had slowly walked over and Christy stood a few feet away on the boardwalk in front of the tavern. No one seemed to know what to do or say. They heard voices and when they looked around, they saw Doc Adams approaching at a trot, accompanied by Mollie. He ran up to where they were standing and knelt down to tend to Lizbeth.

"I'm afraid she's gone, Doc," Jared said.

Doc Adams checked her pulse but found nothing. He stood up and turned around with a somber look on his face.

"Doc, we got a wounded cowboy inside the tavern," Christy said urgently. "He was still breathin' a little while ago. You might be able to do somethin' for him."

The doctor and Mollie followed Christy inside quickly. Jared started to follow but Doc Adams turned and said, "I don't need a bunch of folks lookin' over my shoulder, Jared. You stay out of here and I'll send Miss Johnson to tell you how he is as soon as I know."

Jared looked around helplessly for a second, then he nodded. "We'll be down at the café when you got somethin' to tell us." He turned to walk away, then turned back around. "You take good care of that boy, Doc, and save him if you can. If anyone has earned a right to live, it's Tommy Stallings."

Jared walked back over to where Eleanor stood and quietly took her hand in his. Juan and Maria just looked at the two of them. Finally, Jared said, "I reckon we ought to find a quiet place to sit down and have y'all explain everything that's been goin' on. I got a feelin' we missed a lot."

CHAPTER 20

They walked down the street to the Mares
Café and when they entered, they found an
agitated Anita and a groggy Estevan in the
main dining room. Pancho Vega had hit
Estevan in the head with the hilt of his knife
and he had been unconscious for more than
half an hour. His eyes were glazed over and
he was unsure of what had happened. Anita
had gotten a wet rag for him and was helping him hold it on the cut on the side of his
head.

As they walked through the door, Anita
Mares jumped up. "Where is my Miguel?"

"He's bringin' the wagon, Anita." Seeing
the alarm in her eyes, Jared said in as calm
a tone as he could manage, "He was fine
when we left him. I know he's worried about
you. I reckon he'll push the team to get here
as fast as he can." Jared added, "He ought
to be here tomorrow by sundown."

While Juan took a look at Estevan's head

wound, Maria motioned Jared to join her at the door that led to the kitchen. "That cabron, Vega, is lying on the floor in there. He's dead . . . Juan killed him." Her eyes blazed with an intensity that Jared found a little frightening. "I wish I had been the one to pull the trigger."

"Did he hurt you?"

"Not my body but he hurt my pride," Maria said. "If Juan hadn't come when he did, I don't know what I would have done." Maria shuddered. "He was too strong, Jared. There was nothing I could do. I fought as hard as I could but there was nothing . . ." Maria's voice trailed off.

Jared knew from bitter experience that some wounds are deep on the inside. Just because you can't see them doesn't mean they don't hurt as bad as the ones on the outside. He also knew there wasn't a great deal someone else could say to make the pain go away. It took time for the wounds to heal. In the meantime, he figured what would help Maria most would be to have a meaningful task to do.

"Maria, I think Doc Adams ought to take a look at Estevan's head. Would you mind goin' back to the tavern to let him know we need him down here just as fast as he gets done fixin' up Tommy Stallings." Jared realized he didn't know whether Stallings would be all right or not. He was just hoping for the best. "I'd appreciate a report on Tommy when you come back, if you don't mind. That boy made a hand on our drive and I come to like him a pretty good bit."

Maria cast a sideways look at him. "You think I'd be better off keeping busy and not thinking about what happened, is that right, Senor Jared?" Maria chuckled. "I think you're probably right. Sometimes a person can think too much, que no?"

Maria turned and walked out the door of the café. Jared hollered over to Juan to join him by the kitchen. When Juan came over, Jared explained where Maria had gone.

"While she's up fetchin' Doc, I think maybe you and me ought to get that body out of the kitchen, don't you think?" Jared saw comprehension dawn in Juan's eyes.

"Si, we'll take him out back and find a place to bury him. We'll get the other one, too." Juan's eyes narrowed. "I think the cemetery is too good for those hombres. I would leave them for the buzzards, but we'd have to look at them. I think two graves with no markings is just what they deserve."

Jared and Juan set about the unpleasant task of hauling Pancho Vega's huge body out of the kitchen and up onto the mesa just behind and west of the café. Initially, they tried to pick him up at either end but they found him to be too heavy. They wound up each taking a boot and dragging him out the back entrance to the café. Although Vega was long past feeling any pain, out of the corner of his eye, Jared noticed Juan's grim smile every time the outlaw's head bumped on a rock.

Once they got Vega in position, they quickly went back to Main Street and gathered up Gentleman Curt Barwick's lifeless body. Although he'd been a good-size man, he seemed as light as a feather compared to the enormous Pancho Vega. They laid Barwick out next to Vega and returned to the café where they found two shovels in the shed out back of the kitchen. They returned to finish their grisly job and by sundown, they had both men buried in unmarked graves.

As they dug, they rehashed the shootout in front of the Colfax Tavern. Jared hadn't been able to tell how many shots had been fired and was surprised to hear that Christy had taken a shot with her short gun from the door of the tavern. He felt a small sense of satisfaction in knowing that he had given her the gun for just such an occasion when she needed to defend herself.

Before they buried Barwick, they examined his body and found what appeared to be four bullet holes in his chest and stomach along with a load of buckshot in his left hip. With all the rounds fired, it was hard to say who had made the killing shot but it appeared likely that they all had hit their target at least once. Jared and Juan decided to bury this information with Barwick and if asked, they would claim not to have examined him. Carrying the weight of taking a human life was not something they would wish on Eleanor, Maria and Christy, even if the two outlaws had richly deserved their fate. Once the men were in the ground, Jared and Juan took the shovels back to the shed and went up the street to the Colfax Tavern to find the others and begin to pick up the pieces of their lives.

Over the next several days, they went about tying up the loose ends. The women took turns explaining to Jared, Juan, Miguel and Tomas, who had made it back to town by late afternoon the next day, what had transpired while they were gone. When Maria told about their tricking Dick Cravens and shooting him when he attacked them with his knife, Juan looked at Jared with wide eyes. Jared just shrugged his shoulders . . . so much for protecting them from the knowledge of having taken a human life.

The citizens of the town reappeared. But with the exceptions of Reverend Richardson and Father Antonio, they all seemed inclined to pretend that nothing much had happened. It turned out that the two men of God had gone to the telegraph office as the gun fight was about to start and persuaded Ben Martinez to send a telegram to the county seat, telling the sheriff there that they had a desperate emergency in Cimarron and asking for help. The last word was that help was on the way, but it would take two days to get there. As help goes, it wasn't much, but at least they had tried to do something, which was more than anyone else in town had done.

Jared and Eleanor had gone out to the line shack the morning after the gun battle and found Nathan pacing the small cabin, mad as a hornet. He calmed down a bit once he saw that Eleanor was all right, but when they shared the sad news about Lizbeth Kilpatrick, he just shook his head and sat down on the cot.

"This is my fault," he said, looking from Jared to Eleanor. "If I had done my job, Lizbeth would still be alive and the rest of you wouldn't have been put through this mess. I think maybe I'm too old to handle this job anymore."

"Nonsense, Nathan. They had you outnumbered and they ambushed you to boot," Eleanor said. "I think we all have regrets about the choices we made . . . after all, you told us to come into town where you could look after us and we ignored your advice."

"She's right," Jared added. "If I could do it all over again, I'd have never left on that cattle drive so I could have been here to help." Jared looked down at the floor. "But the fact is, I can't do it over again, nor can any of us. If we could, Lizbeth would still be here with us. That's hard to swallow but it's the truth." He looked back up at his friend. "I guess we try to learn somethin' from it and get on with life."

"I think that's what Lizbeth would want us to do," Eleanor said. She looked at Nathan imploringly. "Can't you just hear her telling us to stop feeling sorry for ourselves and get to work?"

Nathan remained unconvinced. "You may be right, but I still have to wonder if I can do my job anymore. I got a feelin' them boys in the Santa Fe Ring ain't goin' away anytime soon and there's always more outlaws they can hire to come try to steal us blind."

"Well, Sheriff Averill," Jared said emphatically, "until someone else comes along who can do your job better than you, I ain't interested in seeing you retire."

Nathan looked at Jared for a long moment. "I think you could do it, Jared, if you were of a mind to."

Jared looked at Eleanor who returned his questioning gaze with a poker face of her own, giving him no clue as to what she thought about this idea. He looked back at Nathan. "Nathan, we've talked about this before. I don't see that anything has changed to make me more inclined to consider it. If anything, I might be less inclined now."

Nathan nodded. "I know, but as a favor to me, would you just think on it a few days before you give me an answer?"

Jared considered the request. "Since you're the one askin', Nathan, I'll do it but I sure don't see myself changin' my mind."

"Just think on it," Nathan said. "That's all I ask."

Tom Stallings had remained unconscious for two days, but when he came to, his color had improved and his wound appeared to be on the mend. The doctor insisted that he remain bedridden for at least three weeks and after initially protesting, he seemed to realize that he was might lucky to be alive and it would be best to follow the doctor's advice. The fact that Mollie was a constant presence at his bedside was probably helpful in his coming to terms with the conditions of his recovery.

Jared and Juan came by to visit every day and Jared offered Stallings a job on the ranch once he mended. As they were walking away from St. James Hotel, where one of the rooms was serving as Doc Adams' infirmary, Juan looked at Jared and cleared his throat.

"So . . . how many hands do you think you need at the ranch? Counting me and Stallings, that makes two. We never needed more than one before. Que paso, amigo?"

"Well," Jared said, "I think we can still get by with one hand. That'll be Tommy."

Juan stopped in his tracks and looked at his friend with suspicion and alarm. "So where does that leave me?"

With a mischievous glint in his eye, Jared said, "I just thought you'd be too busy to be a hand, what with all your new duties as my partner."

Juan's mouth dropped open and he was unable to speak for a moment. When he finally collected his wits, he said, "What do you mean, 'partner'?"

Jared laughed at his friend's discomfort. "I mean you'd be half owner of the ranch, amigo. That's what a partner is."

Juan started walking slowly down the boardwalk again. "You can do this?"

Jared nodded. "Lizbeth told me the ranch was mine so I figure I can pretty much do what I want to with it."

Juan laughed. "As long as Eleanor agrees, right?"

Jared laughed with him. "I reckon that goes without sayin', although you just said it." Jared poked his friend playfully on the arm. "I already talked with her about it and she thinks it's a great idea."

"What will I do as partner?" Juan asked.

Jared became serious. "I think we got us a market for our beeves up in Pueblo but we'll have to build the herd and we'll have to drive some more head up that way again on a regular basis. It means someone will have to be in charge of the ranch and someone will have to be the trail boss." Jared stopped walking again. "Are you interested?"

Juan nodded slowly. "Si. It's something I never dared to dream about before. At least I never said it out loud." Juan began to grin. "Hey, you never know, maybe one of these days, you might be working for me. I might hire you as a cowboy." His grin grew wider. "Of course, I would have to train you some more so you could do the job right, que no?"

Jared grinned back. "I'll take that as a yes." He chuckled. "Of course, you ain't asked Maria's permission yet. I reckon you'll need to do that."

Juan laughed out loud. "I think that goes without saying.

Superficially, things began to return to normal over the next several weeks. At the same time, however, they seemed different in a number of ways. Many of the townspeople avoided Jared when he came to town, looking down when they passed him on the street. He figured they were ashamed of their cowardly behavior and were afraid he was going to call them on it. He didn't intend to do so, but he wasn't interested in listening to or making any excuses for them either. He knew who to count on when trouble came calling.

Jared was worried about Nathan. When the deputy from Taos came over several days after the gun battle, Nathan had seemed almost disinterested. He told him he hadn't been able to handle the trouble, and when the action took place, he was stuck out in a line shack with a busted head, miles from town. After questioning all the parties involved in the altercation, the deputy declared that the world was a better place without the likes of Gentleman Curt Barwick, Pancho Vega and Dick Cravens.

As for the involvement of the Santa Fe Ring, however, he claimed to have never heard of such an organization. When they had tried to explain the roles played by Tom Catron and Bill Chapman, the deputy declared that since they were both upstanding members of the New Mexico Territorial Legislature, they were above reproach. He refused to hear anymore of their "slurs" and as he left, he told them that he would try to overlook their slanderous behavior.

Nathan had remained silent during this interchange and when the deputy left, he had just shrugged. He told Jared that things had always worked that way in New Mexico as far as he knew and they weren't likely to change. When Jared asked him what they were to do about the threat that still existed from the Santa Fe Ring, he just said that they all needed to watch each other's backs.

Although Nathan seemed to have recovered from his concussion with no lingering physical effects, Christy hadn't fared so well with her knife wound. Her arm had become infected and she had been in bed with a fever for over a week. At one point, Doc Adams was afraid that he might have to amputate her arm, but she wouldn't hear of it and begged him to wait. Luckily, he was able to bring the infection under control and gradually, she had begun to feel better. Her emotional state was a different matter entirely.

Nathan had visited with her on a couple of occasions while she was recovering but he hadn't stayed long and had been rather distant. Christy had been hurt and confused, and had asked Eleanor if she had done something wrong. Eleanor had to confess that she had no idea because she had never seen Nathan act this way before. Later, Eleanor asked Jared to talk to Nathan to see if he could get to the bottom of what was bothering him. Although he would rather have taken a whipping than pried into a pard's business, he reluctantly agreed when Eleanor insisted.

Jared knocked on the sheriff's office door and heard Nathan say, "Come on in, it's open."

When Nathan saw who it was, he asked, "Since when did you start knockin'?"

Jared cleared his throat and pulled up a chair to Nathan's desk. "Nathan, I wouldn't even bring this up but Eleanor asked me to do it for her sake."

Nathan looked at him for a long moment, then said, "All right, if it's important to Eleanor, let's hear what you got to say."

"It ain't even what I got to say, it's what I got to ask. I mean, I understand you're wonderin' if you can still do your job and all. I get that, even if I don't agree that you're over the hill." Jared stopped, wrinkled his brow and looked around. "What's got Eleanor confused is the way you're treatin' Christy."

Nathan sat up straight in his chair. "I've been nothin' but a gentleman to that woman," he said defensively. He paused, then sat back with a look of resignation on his face. "Yeah, I know, I been treatin' her like a stranger." He shook his head. "I don't know what she expects from me, Jared. I darn near got her killed. She'll be a lot better off if she puts as much distance between us as she can."

"I know this is none of my business, Nathan, but don't you think maybe she ought to have a say in that decision?"

"I don't know, maybe so. I ain't much good at this romance thing." Nathan frowned and then sighed. "I been single all my life and I'm used to makin' tough decisions about folks' lives. I just don't know if

I'm cut out to have a partner. You know what they say about teachin' old dogs new tricks." With a wistful grin, he said, "I'm sure 'nuff an old dog."

"You may be right about all that, Nathan, I don't know. But it just don't seem right for you to decide this without includin' Christy in the discussion." Jared got up to leave. "She's got more guts and more class than just about anybody in this town, never mind what she used to do for a livin'. It wouldn't be fair for her not to have a say."

Nathan rose and extended his hand. "I know you don't like to pry in people's business but I guess just this once, I don't mind that you did. I'll think about what you said." Jared nodded and as he turned to go, Nathan said, "You know, you've grown up a lot in the few years I've known you. Used to be, I was the one givin' you advice." Nathan smiled. "I'm proud of you."

CHAPTER 21

The setting sun cast a rosy glow on the foothills to the east as Jared and Eleanor sat on the porch in their rocking chairs. Eleanor had made a meal for them and Jared had helped out with the dishes so they had time to enjoy the last rays of sunlight.

They were quiet for a time, taking in the artistry of the hillside. Finally, Eleanor spoke. "I miss Lizbeth. I don't know if I'll ever get over the hurt."

"I know. It's hard to believe her and Ned are both gone. I don't reckon things will ever seem quite right." Jared shook his head. "I wish there was somethin' else I could say, but I don't know what it is."

"There's nothing more to be said," Eleanor said quietly. "Sometimes that's just the way it is."

They sat silently, breathing in the fresh evening air. Finally, Eleanor said, "Thanks for talking to Nathan. I let Christy know that you did. I guess we'll just have to see what happens."

"I don't know what he'll do," Jared said. "I've never known him to be uncertain before so I don't know what to expect. I think he'll talk to Christy, though." Jared looked off toward the hills. "He's been alone a long time, Eleanor. I just don't know if he can change."

"Maybe not. I'll be sad if he can't, though." Eleanor wiped a tear from the corner of her eye. "He's the closest thing to a father I've got, Jared, and Christy is my best friend. They both deserve to be happy."

"That they do," Jared agreed. "But you know as well as I do that people don't always get what they deserve, for better or for worse."

Eleanor nodded. "True. That's why we're both worried about what those rascals with the Santa Fe Ring are going to try next."

Jared smiled at his wife. "How do you know what's in my mind before I say it out loud?"

Eleanor reached over and took her husband's hand. "Because I know you, Jared Delaney." She smiled back at him. "I know you're worried about our baby and what kind of future he . . . or she . . . is going to have. You're wondering if you should consider signing on as deputy sheriff so you can take over for Nathan when the time is right."

Jared chuckled. "You're a scary woman, Eleanor Delaney. Next time I'm annoyed with you, I'm gonna have to be careful what I'm thinkin'."

Eleanor pretended to be hurt. "Why Jared, I didn't know you ever got annoyed with me."

They both had a good laugh. "Well, you're right, I been thinkin' about Nathan's proposal. Somebody's got to do somethin' one of these days cause Nathan's right. There'll come a time he'll be too old to do the job."

Eleanor squeezed his hand. "You're right, somebody has to do it, but does it have to be you?" She frowned and looked away. "Anyway, where were all the 'good people' of Cimarron when we needed them? I don't think you owe *them* anything."

Jared was quiet for a moment before answering. "You may be right, Eleanor. Maybe no one will step up until they have to and we've sure enough done our part and then some." He squeezed her hand back. "We've got a chance to make somethin' out of this ranch and we've got a family to think about. I want our child to grow up lookin' out at these hills, knowin' that there's good honest work he . . . or she . . . can do to live off this land."

Eleanor's heart soared as she listened to her husband voice the same thoughts she'd been thinking. "That's what I want, too, Jared."

"Then, Eleanor my love, that's what we'll do." Jared grinned his big Texas grin. "We'll look out for our family and friends. We'll fight to protect what we got if we have to . . . we've done it before. But I want to spend most of my time raisin' kids, growin' the herd, takin' care of the land and sittin' on the porch with you." He sat back in his rocker and looked out at the sunset. "I can't see anything that would make me change my mind."

ABOUT THE AUTHOR

Jim Jones lives in Corrales, New Mexico with his wife and three dogs. His first novel, *Rustler's Moon*, was a New Mexico Book Awards finalist in two categories. Best Historical Fiction Novel and Best First Book. He is also an award-winning singer/ songwriter of Western music. He is a proud member of the Western Writers of America.